A Fresh Start

A Fresh Start

and Other Stories

JAMES C. BOTTOMLEY

WOLF HOUSE PRESS

DEL MAR | CALIFORNIA

A Fresh Start and Other Stories

Copyright © 2024 by Wolf House Press. All Rights Reserved.

For information about this title or to order other books and/or electronic media, contact the publisher:

Wolf House Press
2010 Jimmy Durante Blvd., Ste 205,
Del Mar, CA 92014
info@wolfhouse-press.com

ISBNs:
979-8-9903050-0-7 (hardcover)
979-8-9903050-1-4 (eBook)

Printed in the United States of America

Cover and Interior design: Bill Greaves, Concept West

To Suzy Bowen, Kristin Oster, Courtney Fuqua,
and Jeffrey Bottomley

Foreword

Stone walls do not a prison make,
Nor iron bars a cage.

–Richard Lovelace, *"To Althea, From Prison"*

The seventeenth-century poet who wrote those famous words undoubtedly downplayed the drawbacks of incarceration. However, his larger point—that a prisoner's freedom to think and create can thrive even behind bars—is validated through this collection of short stories by James Bottomley, a Stanford-educated former attorney who has spent most of the twenty-first century in California prisons.

Early in his imprisonment, Bottomley found the prospect of more than a few years behind bars unimaginable. In desperate letters to family and friends, he described the physical discomfort, frightening companions, bad food, intrusive noises, and tedium of being in jail. He twice attempted suicide, hoping to spare himself an ordeal he was certain would be too overwhelming to endure.

The misery of prison life was compounded by Bottomley's guilt at the violent act that landed him there, facing a forty-to-life prison sentence at the age of fifty-one. He chronicled his difficult adjustment to incarceration in the 2016 memoir, *Free Fall From Grace*, which also explored the events leading up to his crime. The book inspired an episode of a true-crime television series.

In the years since he took a friend's advice and wrote his own story, Bottomley has continued to write, deploying his innate attention to detail to produce dozens of fiction pieces ranging from short stories to novels. While this pastime has not removed the prison bars, it has given him a measure of freedom to inhabit faraway places in his mind. His vivid settings in such titles as "A Really Fun Day" and "A Father's Tale" demonstrate his ability to evoke environments far different from those of his daily life.

With *A Fresh Start*, Bottomley explores human nature, relationships, and our capacity to improve ourselves, change course, and begin anew. Its pages feature characters struggling to triumph over rivals, free themselves from toxic situations, and reframe their understanding of their own past values and experiences. This is not to say that these stories are uniformly uplifting. Many feature flawed people making flawed decisions, mistreating those they are closest to, and only sometimes finding the will and the strength to become better human beings.

Most of us will never experience physical captivity, as Bottomley has. But, like the people who populate *A Fresh Start*, we are all imprisoned by ingrained ways of thinking and encountering the world, from cultural norms to family dynamics to our personal biochemistries. Our actions are often influenced by more than our conscious choices or stated beliefs, and the decisions we make today frequently narrow the range of possibilities for tomorrow.

As he writes in his preface, Bottomley has also confronted this metaphorical type of imprisonment. In particular, he has wrestled with his mental health and its role in his crime. Such soul-searching is also on display in some of Bottomley's fictional characters, for whom change is both terribly urgent and extremely difficult to achieve. Perhaps the surprising idea in *A Fresh Start* isn't that many of us fail to evolve beyond the constraints of our past and present circumstances but that any of us manage it at all.

Christina Murray, editor
September 2023

Table of Contents

Preface

The stories in this collection were all written in prison between 2015 and 2022. I've been imprisoned since 2000 for a serious crime, but I hope to be released soon. Although my prison experiences have influenced my writing, I have written only two stories which relate directly to life in prison, neither of which has been included here.

Instead, I have relied on my imagination in writing these stories, many of which are derived tangentially from my own background. My time in prison has been rather stifling and monotonous, so I have used my memory to retrieve events from the fifty-one years of my life prior to my crime. Many of my writings are focused on relationships and draw on my background as a child, student, husband, lawyer, father, and mentor.

I grew up in La Jolla, California, and received an excellent education at La Jolla Junior and Senior High Schools, Stanford University, and Hastings College of the Law. In 1974 I received a JD from Hastings and passed the California Bar Exam. I became a practicing attorney and remained such until the day of my life-crime. I worked for two law firms before establishing my solo law practice in 1981.

My ex-wife, Suzy, and I raised three amazing children.

Before my incarceration, I enjoyed such activities and hobbies as surfing, golf, backpacking, coaching youth sports, and reading.

Despite the material advantages of an upper middle-class background, I have spent my whole life feeling that I had a dark cloud over me. From a little boy trying—and failing—to please his parents and teachers to an adolescent experiencing the mood swings that decades later would be diagnosed as bipolar disorder, I have suffered from depression, low self-esteem, obsessions, compulsions, sleep disruption, and manic periods. I now manage this disorder with several medications that help moderate the symptoms, but they are still painful. I believe this disorder played a significant role in precipitating my life-crime.

My creative writing has been a major factor in helping me cope with bipolar disorder. When I feel depression coming on, I can write or rewrite and my mood is elevated. When I feel manic, writing helps me calm down and find a peaceful place. Writing also has improved my self-esteem.

My writing instructor, Zoe Mullery, has been an enormous positive force in my life. I have treasured her instructions in weekly seminars which require each student to write a short story and read it to the group, which then shares criticism and accolades.

I would not have been able to write these stories without the support and love of my three children, Jeff, Courtney, and Kristin. I give my profound gratitude to my editor, Christina Murray, for her outstanding work and keeping me on the straight and narrow, and to my dear friend, James D. Jameson, for making this project possible.

I have written all my stories in my cell, at the prison library, or on the prison yard. I write some drafts in longhand on yellow legal pads and then type them on my mini word processor or send them to a friend outside of prison to type for me. Other stories are composed directly on the word processor.

I have loved every minute of writing the approximately seventy-five short stories I have undertaken. Novels, novellas, essays, and poems are daunting challenges to me, but short stories seem to come easily. I simply allow my imagination to come up with storylines, and then I fill in the beginning, descriptions, characterization, dialogue, denouement, and closing. I edit and rewrite the stories several times until I arrive at a satisfactory final draft. I try to include one or more moral lessons in my stories, but that is not a requirement.

I enjoyed writing each of these stories, but none, I believe, more than "A Really Fun Day." I have always wanted to swim with reef sharks and go down in a cage to observe great white sharks. I have seen sharks nearby while surfing at my local beaches in San Diego County and on Kauai, Hawaii, while traveling, but I have not experienced anything that I could call an "encounter." I also have read several books about sharks, including *The Devil's Teeth*, Susan Casey's book about her experiences among the great whites on the Farallon Islands off San Francisco. These islands are the destination for my contentious couple in "A Really Fun Day."

The story "Fair's Fair" takes place on the opposite side of the continent. It also involves a contentious couple who cross-country ski to a mountain in Vermont, then try to climb it in a life-threatening snowstorm.

"The Stranger" is a story about three adolescents who enjoy regular games of pool in a bar while their parents think they are studying at the library. One night, a rough, older stranger invades their game and then their lives.

"A COVID Christmas" is my stab at magical realism. When the deadly disease strikes a town northeast of Reno, two brave helicopter pilots challenge the elements to try to rescue the inhabitants. They encounter the most unlikely of circumstances during their mission. This story was informed by my own horrific battle with COVID in 2020.

"A Short Short Story" is really a spoof about a writing instructor demanding of her students that they keep their stories brief and even briefer.

"The Secret" is the story of a young couple caught up in a faltering relationship. Amid an argument about their future, the male character threatens to reveal their "secret" to his lover's parents, with potentially catastrophic consequences for her life.

"The Smiles We Left Behind" is a personal favorite. An elderly couple spend their twilight years bickering about inconsequential matters, suppressing their discontents with each other and the direction their lives have taken, until their youngest child's latest relationship brings the pain and disappointment of a long-ago indiscretion to the surface. Now they must either resolve their differences or allow a final rupture in their marriage and possibly their family. I conceived this story while listening to a Barbra Streisand song from one of my favorite movies, *The Way We Were*. It is in part about the dangers and pleasures of reminiscing about the past.

"The Women's Track Club" is a story that I wrote after watching a track meet on television. I made the main character a woman because female athletes and their accomplishments are too often overlooked. In sports, I almost always root for the underdog, and Little Katie is certainly that as she takes on the accomplished bully at her new running club.

"The Confessional" features an alcoholic priest trying to balance the demands of this world and the next as he decides how to handle the time-sensitive information he hears during a parishioner's confession.

"The Man Who Didn't Exist" was inspired by my own deflating experiences at the DMV office and my reading of works by the master of confusion, Franz Kafka, such as "The Trial" and "The Castle." The protagonist in this story suffers delays, frustration, confusion, and humiliation while trying to accomplish a routine, bureaucratic task.

"A Father's Tale" could almost be labeled "memoir," because it reflects some of the circumstances and events that my own father experienced on a destroyer during the Battle of Okinawa in World

War II. This story within a story is told from the perspective of a war veteran's young son hearing his usually taciturn father talk about that battle for the first time. Like the character in this story, my father kept a piece of the kamikaze plane that crashed into his ship and killed his shipmates. Despite this concrete evidence, Dad told us about that fateful day almost with an air of lingering doubt that it had really happened.

"A Fresh Start" is about a woman who seeks to break out of the lonely, exploited rut of her life, with its dead-end job, unappreciative boyfriend, and spiraling cost of living.

I chose to name this collection for its final story because the process of writing fiction has opened up new vistas for me and allowed me to approach the future with a fresh perspective. After decades of living under that dark cloud, I am thrilled to finally see the light shining through.

James C. Bottomley
San Quentin State Prison
August 2023

A Really Fun Day

Melinda had always wanted to do this. She leaned over the railing of the cabin cruiser called "Too Much Fun," her long, blond hair flying in the breeze, her sparkling eyes watching the boat's progress through the choppy water approaching the Golden Gate Bridge.

Thomas, her longtime boyfriend, stood apart and asked, "Mel, what are you doing?"

"Don't bug me!" she snapped. "I'm trying to see one."

He knew right away what she was looking for. "We're not even close."

"C'mon, Thomas, don't be your usual downer. You want nothing more than to stare at a screen all day. Today is supposed to be a really fun day." She observed his blank expression and asked, "How long have we been looking forward to this day?"

The captain's deep voice roared on the loudspeaker, "Hey, lady, you're not gonna jump, are you?"

Thomas reacted first, shaking his head at the metallic voice.

Melinda pulled her head up, stared in the direction of the cabin, and yelled, in Melinda's way: "No fuckin' way, Cap. Why would I want to do that?"

She laughed loudly at how preposterous the notion of suicide was.

Thomas educed a sheepish expression and uttered a weak, "Yeah!"

The boat was big enough to carry the captain, three young deck hands, and twelve passengers, mostly youthful couples clinging to each other with wan smiles and nervous chatter.

Melinda was thankful that, despite the inexorable rolling of the swell from the Pacific Ocean, Thomas hadn't vomited from seasickness yet. She checked out the other passengers, and they all seemed to be holding steady without any green faces.

That's all I need is Thomas embarrassing us by puking out his guts over the rail, she mused. *Even worse would be to see one of these tourists decked out in her $300 navy blue parka puking her breakfast all over the deck. I can't stand the retching sounds that emanate from the stalls in the ladies' restrooms of upscale nightclubs.*

Mel had been around water most of her life. She had been the coxswain of the three-time national champion women's crew team at Stanford. That's where she met Thomas, a nerdy computer programmer who never ventured more than knee-depth into the water when they went to the beach.

She worried about him around water, suspicious that he was secretly afraid of it.

When they had discussed this trip, though, he assured her he'd be fine. Yet, she knew it'd be a giant step for him into the unknown, which was another thing that frightened him.

It was still early, and a dense, gray layer of the fog typical for San Francisco Bay settled around them. Their boat cruised through it, but it rendered the visibility of the bay and the islands a challenge. Melinda could barely make out the cabin twenty feet away. The massive Golden Gate Bridge simply disappeared.

"I can't see anything, Mel," Thomas commented with a trace of apprehension in his voice. "Didn't you promise that this would be a sightseeing trip too?"

He tried to laugh, but it sounded shallow and forced, like someone afraid of the dark exploring in a pitch-black cavern.

She responded, "Are you sure you're okay? I bet it's just a temporary thing. You know what they say, 'a patch of fog.'"

She stared at him curiously, like he was odd, a soldier in the ranks out of uniform.

"Why are you complaining to me?" she asked. "What do you think I can do about the fog—wave a magic wand to change the weather?"

She scoffed and slugged him playfully on his arm. It didn't hurt, but he took it as a putdown. She quickly turned back toward the water even though she couldn't see it.

Thomas didn't just shrug off the dig. "Hey Mel, what was that for?"

"'Cuz you're being a jerk! You know it was just a playful tap, so don't be a baby. Fog or not, view or not, just relax and enjoy the boat ride. When we get there, the fog won't matter. The exciting sights will be underwater."

"Okay, I'll cool it, but I keep worrying . . ."

She turned and stared at him stiffly as if to say, "Don't you dare say what I think you're going to say."

He spurted it out anyway as sensibly as he could, "I think we're getting in over our heads, especially with this crazy fog."

She angrily barked, "Shut up, Thomas! Just shut up! Don't talk to me."

Thomas was hurt by what she said, but as usual he turned on himself with a castigation for violating one of his girlfriend's cardinal rules: She required a showing of optimism by herself and those around her. She demanded nothing less. He was aware that he wasn't conforming, and he asked himself why.

As if she was reading his mind, she bluntly told him: "You're scared, aren't you?" Then she said sarcastically: "Petrified that the bogeyman's gonna get you? Oh, Thomas baby, Mama Mellie will protect you! Don't worry, Sweety-Poo, you'll be safe with me."

Her teasing was humiliating, and he was glad that no one else on board could hear their bickering.

As long as Thomas had known her, Melinda's personality had wavered between sweet/welcoming and abrasive/derogatory. She worked at a prominent marketing firm in San Francisco, which was perfectly suited for her. She had a fluent ability to sweet-talk her clients, but she was cunning enough to ruthlessly dismiss those who wouldn't go along with her agenda. Today that seemed to be him.

Thomas finally caught sight of the bridge. It appeared like an enormous ghost rising from the fog. As they motored under it, Melinda tried to get her bearings by checking out the cliffs on the Marin side of the bay. It didn't work. They were still enveloped in fog. The cliff edges infrequently jutted out of the fog and were quickly swallowed again.

When the cliff summits momentarily appeared, they reminded Thomas of the dorsal fins of a gigantic shark. He shuddered at the idea and gazed back at his pretty girlfriend.

For a few minutes everything disappeared—the bridge, cliffs, cabin, all the other passengers, and even the water just below the rail.

Thomas feared that he and Melinda might disappear as a couple too. He felt like he was sitting alone in the front row of a dingy theater, trying to watch a shoddy film of their lives where the actors were all shrouded in shadow—the kind of movie where it's impossible to figure out what is happening, but the future appears dim.

They certainly didn't have the passion in their relationship that, say, Romeo and Juliet had. He remembered Mel snickering about that story when he had invited her to attend a performance at a nearby community college. When Juliet awakened to discover Romeo dead beside her, then stabbed herself in grief, Mel had laughed aloud, causing other theatergoers to turn and look at them.

"What a croc!" she had muttered afterward. "What's the point of killing herself? It's not going to bring him back."

"They were so in love they would do anything for each other," Thomas had argued, sheepish but not ready to share her cynicism.

Now, shrouded in fog and unable to see clearly, he felt like he was floating, with no bearings to help him move forward or return home. It was a disorienting feeling that was incapacitating at a time when he needed strength. In a world without his five senses, he was forced to focus inwardly, and what he found was fear—not only for his own safety but more for hers. *If I lose her, I lose everything*, he told himself. *I may as well lay down and die.*

The engagement ring in the tiny black jewelry box was burning a hole in his pocket. He intended to get down on one knee and give her the ring when the boat passed underneath the Golden Gate on the return trip. He felt this plan was suitably romantic, a departure from his customary formality that he hoped would sweep her off her feet.

As he caught a whiff of a strong stench, Thomas realized he had been wrong about the absence of sensory signs. Intense and primal, it was the scent of the bay. The odor was a mixture of brine, kelp, and the carcasses of creatures who had once roamed freely in their vast realm. The smell of the sea had enchanted and terrorized sailors for thousands of years as they climbed aboard their vessels and glided off into the unknown. To Thomas, it stank of sudden and irreparable death.

His hearing was diverted to a pinpoint source—the regular blast of the foghorn. The closer he listened, the more it overpowered him, carrying him far from the boat—and from the bay—to the lonely ocean. The foghorn sounded like it was coming from all directions.

Before he was completely blown away by his fantasies, he extended his hand to Mel.

She surprised him by taking it.

"Are you alright? You look like you've just seen a ghost."

He said, "I'm surprised you can see me."

"Yeah, it's gloomy out here," she agreed. "This fog is heavy even for the bay."

Thomas was still rattled. "Do you think it's gonna lift?"

Her Marketing Department smile lit up her face. "Oh yeah! I keep telling you . . . this is gonna be a really fun day!"

The fog did begin to lift slightly, and Thomas could now see the deck. He began to do what seasick-prone people are warned about—stare at the deck or the water. On the surface of the deck, he espied a dead bumblebee and bent over to examine it. While Melinda observed him with utter disinterest, he reached down and picked up the bumblebee delicately between his thumb and forefinger and brought it closer to examine.

What's this idiot doing now? Melinda reflected. *Serves me right for picking a Stanford man as my boyfriend. I could have anyone.*

"What are you doing, Thomas, playing with that stupid bee?" she said aloud. "You don't know anything about bees."

Without taking his eyes off the insect he responded, "For your information, Mel, I'm trying to figure out how it died."

"What difference does that make, Einstein?"

"I'm trying to determine whether the bumblebee's death is an omen for what we're about to do."

"Typical Thomas!" she scoffed. "Let you alone for a few seconds and you weird out on me. What you're doing is really dumb! It's childish. I'm embarrassed to be seen with you, and I want you to stop RIGHT NOW!"

He recognized she really meant it and started to offer one of his typical lame excuses, "Well . . ."

"Well, nothing! You're spoiling all the fun . . . Thomas! If you were afraid to go on this trip, why didn't you tell me? There are plenty of guys at my office who'd be *thrilled* to go with me."

Even if she was teasing, he didn't appreciate how that sounded, particularly her emphasis on the word "thrilled."

"I'll tell you the truth, Mel. This trip isn't any fun. I can't see a damn thing, and I shudder to think what's waiting for us underwater at the far end. The only reason I came out here was my hope to talk you out of it."

"Bullshit, Thomas! You play around with those buttons and screens all day, but you couldn't talk your way out of a wet paper sack." She imparted a hard look at him. "I imagined some low behavior from you, but this takes the cake. You don't care anything about what I want. You're only concerned about yourself and your anxieties. I might have known you'd try to ruin things for me. I don't know, Thomas. I'll think over 'Us' when I'm not so angry."

He winced at her threat. This was not an auspicious start to the day of their hoped-for engagement, but he couldn't stifle his misgivings.

"Ask yourself, Mel, how can any sane person go unprotected into a flimsy metal cage and drop into freezing water that is infested with the most dangerous creatures on the planet? You think that's fun?"

"That's exactly what I signed up for, and so did you. And that's what I'm gonna do this morning. You said you were gonna do it too. Now I don't know. Maybe you're gonna chicken out. Bluck, bluck, bluck." She made the chicken noises in his face to annoy him or possibly to spur him on.

"Maybe you're right," he replied, "although I wish you wouldn't use the 'c' word. I'm being sage . . . Let me ask you a practical question: What happens when an eighteen-foot-long monster shows up inches from you, its rows of sharp white teeth ready to snatch you out of the supposedly impenetrable cage? Its appetite is voracious and will have been whetted into a frenzy by all the chumming they do. Do you think that it wants to do synchronized swimming with you? I'll let you in on a little secret about cage diving that I saw on TV's Shark Week."

He probed her eyes for any sign of curiosity before continuing.

"The shark repeatedly rams the metal bars in the same place, trying to create a large-enough indentation for it to stick its head in and pull out the diver."

Like the best storytellers, he looked at her and paused for a reaction. She was now showing interest but no fear.

"Why do you think it wants to do that?" he defiantly asked. He again scrutinized her mood. It was clear from her conspicuous signs of impatience that his shark story was having a contrary impact to its intended effect.

She again flashed her angry glare at him as if to say, "How dare you try to scare me with such a ridiculous story?"

However, he noticed something else in her eyes and wondered, *Has a trace of fear finally crept into her consciousness?*

"The simple truth, Mel, is that the shark wants to devour you," he continued. "That isn't fun and games. It's not your crew of rowers digging for the finish line. This shark cage stuff is seriously dangerous. You better think about that before they lower the cage into the water with only you facing the great white."

Suddenly—and contrary to his intention—Melinda relaxed. Her eyes softened toward Thomas because she was impressed by his eloquent entreaty. She figured an element of loving someone is caring about that person's safety. She was sure that he loved her.

No matter how hard her shell was on the outside, she still possessed a young girl's sweetness on the inside. She had asked herself many times whether she truly wanted to spend a lifetime with this computer nerd she had hung with since their freshman year. She couldn't deny it. The answer was always "yes."

Sometimes she felt like her love for Thomas was like loving a favorite pet. No matter how naughty your dog was, you would scold it but still follow that up with a hug and a kiss on the head. Right now, though, after his treason against their shark plan, she felt she was still in the scolding stage and couldn't relent.

It'd be a sign of weakness for me not to condemn him, she reflected, *and there's nothing I hate more than being weak.*

So, she said, "I don't want to hear any more of this talk about all the negative things that can happen by going down in the cage. If you're afraid, do what you have to do. I'll do what I have to do, and it won't affect 'Us' . . . I don't think. Fair enough?"

"Before you dismiss me completely, let me tell you what I actually saw on Shark Week," he replied. "A woman was in a shark cage somewhere off the coast of South Africa. There was a massive great white shark pounding with its snout on the bars of the cage. The camera clearly showed that she was in a panic, wildly flailing her fists at the shark, which was, of course, oblivious to the blows. The deck hands should have hoisted her back onto the boat, but they must have been on their coffee break.

"The hole between the bars kept getting wider and wider. She had no way to communicate to the people on the deck. As she became more frantic, it incited the shark to greater excitement as it banged on the bars. Once the hole was big enough to accommodate the shark's head, it made desperate attempts to snatch the woman in its teeth.

"She was able to dodge the first few lunges, and there was actually some hope she might survive. I know this is hard to believe, but it was on film. I saw it. The rows of teeth hit home on the woman's torso. A red cloud rose through the bars, obscuring the camera's view. When it partially cleared, the camera showed the interior of the cage, and there was no one there. The woman and the shark had disappeared.

"If you want to take a chance of that happening to you, then you're mighty brave, Mel, and I admire you for that."

There was silence until Melinda exclaimed as steadily as she could manage: "You're making this up to scare me from going into the cage. It's nothing more than your version of a fish tale."

"No, Honey, I swear I'm not making it up. It's true, according to the TV narrator."

"Why didn't you tell me about this shark story sooner—you know, before we paid all that money to go on this excursion?" she asked.

"I don't know. I should have, but I had forgotten about it. I saw it one night when you were out doing something. It didn't seem that important at the time. I guess I didn't think you were serious about goin' underwater with great white sharks."

She scrutinized him. She was experienced at that. Finally, she blurted, "You're exaggerating, Thomas. You do that a lot. You're doing it now to control me and get your way, trying to spoil a really fun day."

She gazed out to sea under the clearing fog, trying to collect her thoughts.

He thought her profile looked beautiful. She had a pouty look that she liked to flaunt.

Soon, she turned to him, her jaw locked, her blue eyes narrow and focused on his. She said in an icy tone that he didn't recognize: "I'm not gonna fall for your games. Lying is part of our business. Bottom line, Thomas, I know you're lying. You believe you have a good motive, but you're pissing me off. Your meager attempt to snow me is not working. We'll talk about it at home tonight. In the meantime, I'm gonna dive with a great white shark; I'm gonna be the first in the cage; and I'm gonna have fun!"

As if to emphasize her point, the boat came to a sudden stop. The lurch forward sent Thomas sprawling. Melinda caught him in her arms and absently hugged him. He offered a weak, "Thanks."

She straightened him out and replied, "No problem."

The moment was not lost on either of them, and Thomas mouthed the words: "I love you."

She smiled and said out loud, "I love you too, Honey."

The engine was still running, but there was no more forward movement. Mel observed one of the deck hands toss out the anchor.

"I guess we're here," she said with a trace of nervousness that only Thomas could notice. He was hoping that she'd back out at the last moment, but she seemed resolved to proceed. He figured he had dodged one bullet trying to warn her, so why chance a second bout of her anger?

Melinda was a bit disoriented due to the continuing presence of the fog. She knew the Farallon Islands were out there somewhere, but she didn't see them when she scanned the horizon. Suddenly their jagged peaks appeared, poking through the gray shroud like apparitions emerging from the miasma of a mystic swamp. The sight sent a cold chill down her backbone.

Again, Thomas noticed the slightest hesitation in his girl's resolve, but she recovered quickly and calmly asked, "Do you see the islands?"

"Yup, and I couldn't help noticing that they're the shape of shark fins."

She looked more closely and saw that he was right. Her heart felt like it was sinking into her stomach. She had a sudden urge to run to the railing, but she stopped herself and thought, *What would that do to my image as the brave girl willing to take on any challenge?*

She knew there was no backing down now . . . she was in the game for keeps, and she might as well steel herself to the task. The heebie-jeebies that had been stalking her for weeks were stuffed into a dark place inside her. Keeping them there wasn't going to be easy. Her nerves felt like a swarm of insects crawling under her skin, ready to pop out through her pores at any second.

To Thomas, she pretended that the "stumble" she took when the boat came within view of the shark fin cliffs was due to the sudden pitch of the boat.

To herself, Melinda admitted that she was scared. She suspected it was a different kind of fear than she had felt during the moments before the starting gun was fired at a big meet. This was a more primal fear where her life was at stake. After hearing Thomas's Shark Week story, she couldn't free her mind of an image of herself dressed in diver's regalia being dragged out of a hole in the bars in the jaws of a ravenous shark.

She murmured under her breath: "God, what a horrible way to go!"

"What's that, Honey?" he asked solicitously.

"Oh nothing. I'm just gearing up to go down in the cage." She thought, *How could I ever admit that he's right? That this is a crazy thing to do? NEVER! No matter how scary it'll be, I'm going down to meet the shark!*

Thomas, who had been holding the dead bumblebee all this time, tossed it over the rail to give it a proper burial at sea. He read Mel's tenacity as final and hoped he wouldn't have to do the same for her. Along with the bee, he hoped to rid them of a bad omen.

As an afterthought, he leaned over the rail and gazed down at the surface of the water to the spot where he suspected the bee had landed. He couldn't see it in the rolling, murky sea. It was as though the water had swallowed the insect, and Thomas had the discomfiting thought that the sea did that to all creatures bold enough to enter it.

He looked back at the island, still partially shrouded by gray mist and surrounded by murky water crashing on the rocks. Now it was his turn to shudder with an overwhelming sense of foreboding. At that moment, he made his final decision not to go down in the cage.

His huge sense of relief was tempered by the hideous thought that Melinda was still going to descend. An image of her in the cage being hoisted over the rail made him dizzy, and his stomach twisted in knots. He leaned back over the rail, feeling like he would heave, but his morning bagel and coffee wouldn't come up.

"Are you okay?" Melinda inquired with real concern.

"Yeah, I'll make it, but Mel, I've decided I'm not going into that cage."

He braced for her disapproval, but her response was surprisingly cheery.

"That's okay, sweetie. It's your decision," she said. "It's probably a wise one if your concern is making you uncomfortable. Look at it this way—you paid a lot of money for a long boat ride."

"But what about you?" he tried again. "Will you reconsider?"

"I'm going down," she insisted. "Wouldn't miss it for the world. I'm going to try to be the first."

Just then, a lethargic deckhand dragged a table onto the deck. It would act as a temporary station for the dive signups and to pass out the equipment.

Melinda pivoted and made a dash toward the table. Several other passengers saw her movement and also scrambled for a priority spot. Thomas overheard one mutter, "That little bitch!"

The other two deckhands, wielding buckets spilling over with red froth, began chumming the surface of the water with a pungent mixture of blood, fish guts, and whole fish.

With their shark encounter imminent, the passengers' anticipation created a carnival atmosphere on the deck, and Thomas wanted no part of it. He disengaged to the stern, intending to stay there until all this craziness was over.

He could see Melinda at the front of the crowd elbowing others back to maintain her position. Then he saw her bend over the table and sign a form—probably some sort of liability release. Next, she was given a black wetsuit, a pair of dark blue divers' fins, a face mask, booties, and gloves. Thomas presumed these last items were to keep her extremities warm for the fifteen or twenty minutes she would be waiting in the cage for a shark to show.

As Melinda was donning her gear and one of the deckhands assisted with her oxygen tank, she overheard a short, middle-aged woman with unkempt mousy brown hair asking the captain something like: "Will we really see any great whites?"

Melinda could clearly hear the captain's response. "I'll tell ya', ma'am, it can get very exciting out here. About a month ago, three great whites were ramming the cage at the same time. It was a coordinated commando assault. The cage held together, though, and no harm was done."

He leaned in close before continuing in a pretend whisper that was loud enough to carry across the deck.

"When the diver was hoisted back on deck, her face was white as a sheet. That paleness wasn't from the cold, guaranteed. The poor woman's entire body was shakin' like a leaf in a gale-force wind."

As he told this story about the "poor woman," the captain's already-red face lit up like a bank of stadium lights, and his smile was so vibrant it appeared that he was closing a big sale. "Yeah, I was afraid she was gonna have the Big One."

"The Big One?" the tourist asked, confused.

"You know, a heart attack."

Mousy hair reflected about that for a moment and asked, "Is going down in the cage dangerous?"

The captain didn't hesitate, "Not as dangerous as going down without it! Harhar."

Mousy hair was aghast, and as soon as the captain was out of earshot, she told the deckhand at the table that she was canceling her dive. Her chronic lower back had unexpectedly flared up, she explained primly when he asked why.

Melinda couldn't help but snicker, but her own fear factor had jumped off the chart. What scared her more than the sharks was the captain's callous disregard for the diver's safety. The crawling bugs had returned, and they were under her wetsuit. She wanted to scratch them out of existence. She also wanted to scream. She couldn't do either, and it was driving her nuts!

As they called for the first diver over the loudspeaker, Melinda had that same queasy feeling that Thomas had fought and lost. She reflected, *I'm glad I didn't eat that bagel.*

She looked at the starboard rail and thought, *Is it too late to make a break for it?* Then, *Don't be silly . . . where's Thomas? Why isn't he here? Maybe he's mad at me.*

As the deckhand was giving her last-second instructions, she spotted Thomas hanging over the stern railing. *What in the hell is he doing?* she fumed. *I'm about to descend into the scariest experience of my life, and my boyfriend is off contemplating his navel!*

"Ma'am, are you going to get into the cage? You'll forfeit your turn if you don't get in now."

She climbed in and waited impatiently for the on-deck crane to begin hoisting. She took a last look back at Thomas, who was looking at her but not smiling. She couldn't figure why at that very moment an overwhelming sense of passion and love for him gripped her. She could feel it in her brain all the way down to her loins—especially there!

She had an impulse to call out to him: "Let's get married!" She knew he wanted to, and now she did too. She knew she'd been the one holding up their nuptials. *No longer . . . I'm ready! I'm so ready!* she told herself.

Just before splashing into the frigid water, she saw him. It was as if her loving thoughts had beckoned him to join the small crowd of well-wishers, many with both thumbs up or waving T-shirts in the air like fans at a soccer game after a goal was scored.

Melinda didn't look triumphant. She looked at the group and the smiling captain with trepidation and the feeling that soldiers must have just before they hear the signal to charge.

The captain shouted, "Are you okay?"

He glanced at his watch and then his line-up sheet, "Er, Melinda?"

She looked straight into Thomas's eyes and gave him two thumbs up and a tepid smile.

The captain yelled to a deckhand: "Okay, lower her."

When the cage plunged into the water, Melinda received a shock greater than the jolt caused by the starter's pistol at the Big Game meet. Although she expected the ocean's extreme chill, it still irritated her.

The crowd on deck didn't stop cheering until the cage disappeared into the murk. The last trace Thomas saw of her was the top of that beloved head covered with luscious blond hair.

Then the cage and its precious cargo were swallowed up by the swirling water.

He gritted his teeth, knowing that this was going to be the most agonizing twenty minutes of his life. He overheard a teenage girl say, "There goes the first. Brave girl." Thomas concurred but would have added, "Crazy girl."

He saw the captain trying to smile while wiping off his perpetual worried expression. Thomas suspected he was pleading to some unknown god, *No shark accidents, please! They're bad for business.*

Thomas wondered, *Is he hoping the opposite, for the explosive publicity that a shark mauling a tourist would generate—the kind of notoriety that would put him on the worldwide shark excursion map?*

Thomas spat on the deck in an angry display against the cynical role the shark tourism industry plays in the wake of a loss of life.

All sight of the cage had vanished as it continued on its undersea voyage. Thomas could no longer see the bars through the seemingly black water, but the bubbles from the tank bursting at the surface were a welcome sight—and his only connection with his lover.

Even the creaky sound of the crane ceased. She must have hit bottom.

For Melinda, the sound had changed to a repetitious gurgle as gravity sucked the cage down. She wondered whether her final destination would be the ocean floor or hanging in midwater, where the sharks could attack her from all angles and rip her to shreds.

That question was answered seconds later when the cage stopped with a jolt, bouncing her off her fins and across the floor into the bars.

She stood up, dazed, and looked around, but she couldn't see much. She realized that if she was going to view sharks, they'd have to swim awfully close to the cage. *What was that old and overused phrase? "Up close and personal."*

She reflected on her situation—alone, isolated from all help, and trapped behind bars in a totally alien environment. She asked herself: *Is this how a prisoner feels? Bars all around, confined space, menace lurking? Do I feel free of the world above or caught in the world below?*

At that moment, she saw an obscure object moving toward her. As it approached out of the shadows formed by the gloomy water, she recognized it as a massive shark—her prey. Exactly what she had come to view.

She assumed it was a great white. *What other shark could be that big?*

The first blow against the cage was ferocious. It slammed Melinda hard to the floor, and she failed to rise again.

The shark seemed to have performed this role before. With one crushing blow after another, its attack was relentless and primarily focused in one spot. The bars began to separate right away, and the hole grew with every blow.

This was frighteningly similar to the attack that Thomas had told her about. She closed her eyes so she wouldn't have to witness the brutal finality of it. Feel it, yes, the rows of sharp teeth ripping into her flesh, thrashing at the veins in her neck, the excruciating pain until she felt nothing at all.

Yet, she reasoned, *with my eyes closed, I'll be at a disadvantage.*

She was a smart girl from Stanford with potential in marketing, many social friends, and a loving boyfriend. She had a bright future ahead that she hoped would include a family.

Never in a million years had she envisioned that her final seconds would be in the jaws of a shark crunching her bones and sinking its teeth into her skull in its ancient quest for survival. She was no different than the shark's regular prey—a harbor seal or perhaps a husky sea lion. With that thought, she finally started to cry.

But she also made a gritty decision: *The body that the shark pulls out of this cage will already be dead, drowned from a lack of air.* She unhooked the regulator from her oxygen tank, and bubbles flowed frantically upward into the void.

The bubbles rose rapidly to the surface and popped as if Neptune was enjoying a glass of fine champagne in celebration of another new denizen to his ocean domain. One of the deckhands saw the bubbles breaking the surface and yelled to the captain, pointing to the disaster.

The captain didn't hesitate: "Pull it up NOW!"

The hands scrambled to the hoist, and Thomas heard its whirling noise.

His first thought was, *Isn't it early to bring her up?*

He ran to the rail to join the excited, milling crowd. He searched for answers from the captain, but he couldn't be found. One thought circled like a hamster wheel in his head: *Oh my God, no! Help her!*

The cage broke the surface suddenly like a runaway car crashing into an outdoor café. It was empty.

As the cage was lifted toward the deck, a torrent of rivulets flowed down the bars and dropped into their source. Thomas could see an enormous hole on one side of the cage, easily wide enough for a girl of Melinda's petite size to be pulled through.

Certain now of what had happened to Mel, he ran to the dive locker and pulled out the equipment he needed. Thomas knew exactly what he must do.

In the meantime, nobody was doing anything to save Melinda. As Thomas straddled the rail, the teenage passenger pointed him out to the captain, who yelled in his direction: "Hey, buddy, what do you think you're doing?"

Thomas stared at him blankly and didn't waver. He flipped over the side, making a splash that all those on the boat could hear.

No one had yet noticed a small figure with long blond hair, wearing a wetsuit, fins, and a face mask, swimming on the surface toward the boat. Her tank was missing, and she was exhausted, but Melinda was otherwise sound-of-body.

Soon another passenger spotted her climbing over the rail onto the stern of the boat. It happened to be the same rail that Thomas had lingered over for a while when he was sulking about Melinda's stubbornness over going into the cage.

She staggered across the deck searching for Thomas, anticipating an enthusiastic reunion and celebration of her close survival. Failing to find him, she approached the captain, who looked like he was seeing a ghost.

He looked at his line-up sheet and asked, "Melinda McCary?"

"That's me. Where's my boyfriend, Thomas?"

Her anxiety was evident in her shrill voice and tense expression.

"We were sure that a shark had broken through the cage and pulled you out," the captain explained. "No one could survive that ordeal. But here you are! We all saw the damage to the cage, so how did you save yourself?"

"The shark was incredibly big," she answered, her voice faltering at the recent memory. "He kept ramming the cage, making the hole wider and wider. I figured he was gonna get me for sure if I stayed in the cage. Eventually, the hole was big enough for me to slip out. He was so busy smashing up the cage that he didn't notice me swimming out the hole and away. I didn't have air, so I had to swim fast, but I made it to the boat. I guess it was pure luck. Now, please tell me where my fiancé is."

The captain's expression was a mixture of pure horror and curiosity. He explained, "The young man saw the empty cage and went over the side to search for you."

Her eyes immediately filled with tears, and she cried out, "Oh my God! Oh Thomas! That monster is still down there. My baby doesn't stand a chance."

Her look conveyed pure violence at the captain. "How could you let him get off the boat? Without a cage, it was suicide."

Her head drooped, and she could barely hold it together. The captain's expression held steady.

She pleaded, "Can't you send divers down to bring him back?"

"No way. The cage is too damaged to go back in the water, and like you said, it is suicide to go down without one. I can't risk sending any free divers down."

"But to save Thomas?"

"Face facts, lady. You saw the shark. He's snatched your boyfriend or fiancé by now. But he's your guy, so if you want to put on a tank and go down again, be my guest."

Melinda heard what the captain was proposing and looked away. Her eyes were red, and tears were flowing down her face.

She gazed into the Pacific and then back at the Golden Gate. It was now perfectly clear in all its majesty, glowing like golden treasure in the morning sun.

She wouldn't look at the captain when she answered, but her words were firm, "No, I won't go down again. I'm not Juliet."

Fair's Fair

When I was twenty-four, I nearly lost my life and gained it on the same winter day.

My name is Jeremy Parkins, and I was a graduate student at Vermont State University in Montpelier, Vermont, when I had my first adventure in the wilderness. My companion was Lisa Carter, a very attractive, vivacious, undergraduate senior at the same school.

Lisa was pretty and brainy, and she had that kind of smile that drew smiles and greetings from everyone she encountered, whether they knew her or not. From the first time I spotted her on campus, I had romantic designs on her. Though I doubted she harbored a reciprocal feeling for me, I was quite happy that she invited me to join her on this fling.

The day of our excursion started out beautiful—crisp, cold air and a blue sky (somewhat rare in Vermont in the winter). We had spent the night at the Lodge at Deerfield Springs so we could leave early in the morning. Our target was Paulson's Peak, a protuberance in the middle of Vermont's vast forest which rises to a height of one-thousand feet. It is located about twenty-five miles from the lodge.

Our plan was to ski to the base of the peak and enjoy a picnic there before climbing to the top. I had never done any mountain climbing or rock ascents, so I was apprehensive about our mission. Lisa, on the other hand, was a strong backcountry skier, an experienced and able climber, and a veteran of similar one-day trips. After descending, we planned to ski back to the lodge, celebrate and spend another night together. In warmer seasons, we might have planned to stay overnight at the base of the peak, but we expected cold and windy weather and figured that it would be uncomfortable, even painful, to stay overnight in the wilderness. So, we decided not to pack a tent, sleeping bags, or a stove.

I looked forward to our adventure because I had heard somewhere that a romance could flourish on an escapade, especially when we were the only two parties on the trip. I figured that the intimacy of being together two full days might trigger a speck of desire on her part. Perhaps it was my wishful thinking, but I sensed there were favorable signs from Lisa that she and I might commence a rewarding affair.

Lisa was a part-time employee at Kap's Ski Shop in Deerfield Creek, where we would be outfitted for our adventure. She was as popular at Kap's as she was on campus and was the object of attraction for dozens of guys. The amount of male attention that Lisa got caused me to wonder why on earth she selected me for the Paulson's Peak endeavor. However, since I was thrilled to join her, I didn't worry too much about why.

Lisa was blessed with unbridled confidence, and one didn't need to be one of the Three Wise Men to know why. In addition to her brilliant smile and perky ways, she had a trim, tan body, which she had shown off in early September, basking in a tiny bikini while lying on a beach towel on the Commons lawn. She had bleached blond hair, which she sometimes wore up in a bun and sometimes let flow down her back.

As we became friends, Lisa informed me that she hailed from the pristine beaches of Southern California. She related that she had dozens of beachboy and surfer boyfriends out there too. She confided that she loved keeping them guessing. However, winter was ski-time, and the windchill and storms were fierce, as we were about to find out.

In contrast to Lisa's romantic experience, I had had only one serious relationship in high school and the years following graduation. Her name was Julie Johnson. We both lived in an affluent suburb of San Diego. During Julie's and my senior year in high school, she applied to and was accepted by UC Berkeley in Northern California. She urged me to follow suit, but (making the worst decision of my life) I went to Vermont State instead. Our long-distance relationship didn't work, so when Julie found a new boyfriend, she pulled the plug on us. I went down the drain with the dirty water, and I was devastated. I declared to friends and family that there would be "no more girlfriends."

That's about the same time Lisa and I connected. She reminded me of Julie.

Before we left the ski shop with our gear, the owner, Kap, cautioned us against the trip. "The storm approaching us is supposed to be the biggest and nastiest of the year," he said. "It's predicted that it will wallop us with the most snowfall, the highest winds, and the coldest temperatures. I urge you two—for your safety and maybe your lives—to consider rescheduling your expedition to another weekend."

Lisa listened politely and even nodded a few times. When Kap was finished, though, Lisa turned to me and abruptly snapped, "C'mon, Jeremy! We have a lot of ground . . . er, snow, to cover!"

We put on our skis and unloaded our backpacks from her SUV in Kap's parking lot. Between the two bags, we were carrying our picnic lunch; a pair of binoculars; a water filter, matches, and a mirror for emergencies; some ski wax; and the crampons we would wear for the climb. We each had a water bottle as well.

A clear blue sky emerged through the pine trees. The sun's rays touched our faces and backs but had no warming effect. Vermont's icy cold air saw to that.

Lisa glanced again at the lovely blue sky and announced (wrongly, it turned out) that "The trip will be easy and the climb up and down Paulson's Peak will be a piece of cake." Based on her solemn prediction, that's exactly what I expected.

The only dark cloud that blew in our direction was the local weather report, which naturally had come on the TV while Lisa was catching some extra "Z"s. The curly-haired young weather girl announced, "Breaking News: The National Weather Service has predicted a severe storm will hit New England later today, with its center near Montpelier, Vermont. Residents of the area around Deerfield Springs, in particular, are cautioned to stay indoors and burn wood instead of using gas furnaces. The most precise prediction we have is of the storm beginning in late afternoon."

I figured, based on Lisa's confident assessment, that we would be back in the bar at the Lodge drinking hot toddies by the time the first snowflakes touched down.

We left Kap's in a hurry, heading in the direction of the evergreens. Fortunately, a trail wound its way through them. We schussed through the pure white show with only a thin layer of icy crust. The only sound I could hear was the surface snow crunched by our skis. Lisa led, and I followed in her tracks.

I was concerned that twenty-five miles seemed like a long way to ski, but with our new advanced skis, we only fooled around a little and had a good time. At a water break, Lisa regarded the sweat beads pouring off my forehead and flowing down my cheeks. Grinning, she boasted that she hadn't begun to sweat.

I decided this was a good time to make my move, so I put my arm around her and tried to kiss her lips.

Her sunny smile turned to a grimace, and she uttered, "What in the hell are you doing, Jeremy, you sweaty dog?" She flashed a cutting look at me.

I responded with (faked) shock: "What?" My expression was of exasperation rather than embarrassment. "I thought we were becoming more than just friends!"

"Honestly, Jeremy, how did you possibly get that impression?"

"Duh—because we slept in each other's arms all night?"

"C'mon, buddy, I was drunk. . . . Anyway, big boy, you know as well as I do, we didn't do anything."

"Yeah, but . . ."

"Don't you 'but' me! You're my friend but not my boyfriend. Don't push it, okay?"

"But Lisa—what about my feelings for you?"

"Fine, just keep them to yourself. Your status as 'friend only' is not going to change."

We plowed forward in silence. The trail narrowed, and pine branches crowded us on both sides. It felt like we were skiing through a storm drain, although I've never done that.

Our skis made a pleasant sound forging through the snow. That sound, along with the rhythmic motion of the skis, nearly hypnotized me. Twice I had to stop myself from being lulled to sleep. I kept myself awake with a sweet daydream about Lisa but got so absorbed in my fantasy that I almost skied off the trail.

Lisa turned around and chastised me: "Watch where you're going! Quit being so careless, Jeremy!" If she only knew. I almost shouted back at her that it was her fault.

We skied around a bend, and the upper half of the spire came into view. Tension seemed to detonate in my stomach and travel to my brain, where it registered as fear. *We're going to climb that? It's straight up and down!* Lisa, on the other hand, appeared excited.

The clear weather we had set out with was gone now. Ominous dark clouds swirled toward the summit and completely blacked out the blue sky and our view. By the time we reached the base, large white flakes were landing on our parkas and obscuring our vision.

The flakes stuck wherever the ground was bare. Patches of white appeared around the peak, and our nylon snowsuits were rapidly turning from blue to white.

Lisa showed no signs of fatigue. She wasn't even breathing heavily. To the contrary, I was breathing deeply and trying to catch my breath. My lungs felt like they were half of their size when we started out. My lips were quivering and, I imagined, as blue as the sky had been earlier. My knees shaking, I thought I might collapse on top of my skis.

Lisa had a miffed expression. I glanced at her nervously and she glared at me. She didn't need to say it—"You wimp!" was in her eyes.

Although we were somewhat protected by the trees encircling the base, the wind had reached a gnarly stage and was bending the upper branches over so much, it appeared they would snap off. Fresh snow, from the sky and blown up from the ground, blew sideways into our faces.

Our hands and heads were protected, but neither of us had thought to bring face masks. Maybe I was getting paranoid, but I felt the early signs of frostbite. I mused to Lisa: "My face will look awfully funny without a nose." Actually, I was even more concerned about the winter curse of hypothermia.

I admired Lisa, however, because she did not appear to be spooked about anything. I wanted to embrace her for warmth if nothing else but backed off when she looked like she was going to spit at me. To my nose joke, she replied sharply: "Why are you staring at me? Quit daydreaming and get your crampons on!"

"Hey Lisa, why don't we climb another day when we have better weather? Let's picnic and go back."

"It's too cold for a picnic, dummy. C'mon, let's get moving. That will warm us up." She paused and obviously read reluctance in my expression. She rattled me with the sarcasm of her question: "Jeremy, are you going to wimp out on me? The weather might be bad for lollygagging around, but it's perfect for climbing. You'll see."

She didn't convince me. I flat out didn't believe her, and I felt insulted by her calling me a wimp. I never thought it'd come to that, but Lisa's strong personality was beginning to bug me. I wondered, *Why does she assert herself as a ruthless tyrant? We are supposed to be having fun as a pair of equals. Is she pulling a 'fem thing' to show me up?*

I paused to contemplate a sensible response that wouldn't piss her off. I said, "Be reasonable, Lisa, we could get hurt in the crappy weather!"

"Okay. That's fine with me. You wait here, and I'll climb the bugger. I'll see you when I return."

I reflected, guardedly, *This is a bad idea. If she is going up, then so can I!* I told her tersely: "No way, Lisa. I'm climbing too!"

"Fine. Now get your crampons on." I couldn't help but notice the frostiness in her tone. It seemed she was as tired of me as I was of her.

"Hang on—I can only put them on so fast."

"Need I remind you that we only have so much light left? You wouldn't want to climb down from the peak in the dark."

The lower segment of the peak climb wasn't difficult. We walked up a narrow, rocky trail which gradually inclined to a point that required actual climbing. Lisa was stoked and uttered, "Finally!" She could see that the slope was very steep above us.

Now the snow was falling in heavy bursts, no longer the flurries of a while ago. Another unpleasant factor was the wind. We were somewhat exposed in the clearing and would be more so on the upper half of the climb. Gusts were driving loose snow from the terrain and blowing the churning flakes into our faces. As a result, my cheeks were stinging.

We reached a place where the soil ended, the gradient steepened, and we faced a slippery slab of granite, which appeared like the surface of an ice-skating rink tilted toward the sky. There would be no mercy in this section of the climb. I thought, *There's no way I'm gonna make it up that wall!* It appeared to me to be vertical, without any hand or footholds.

Lisa confidently hadn't brought any rope or pitons. She had declared at Kap's: "We won't need them!" However, now she gazed upward, rolled her eyes, and sighed.

I figured that even this climbing vet was stumped. I said, "We have no rope."

She replied, "Sometimes a rope is a disadvantage. If one partner falls, it takes the other partner down too."

I admired her logic, as well as her graceful movements and grim determination as we inched up the wall. However, she realized I was in trouble, so she looked around and said, "Let's traverse to the left side. It might be easier over there."

Sure enough, the left side was easier to climb, and we made good progress. We got into a groove, and I discovered small ledges and cracks in the rock's surface large enough to insert a hand or a foot into. Lisa seemed to be having fun, and she turned her head around and smiled. That small, spontaneous gesture lifted my spirits and fortified me for the challenges above.

I discovered an unknown characteristic about myself—a bit late, I concluded. I had a mild case of vertigo. I was afraid to look down, unlike Lisa, who constantly did so to gauge our progress. I also struggled to prevent the swirling wind and pelting snowflakes that felt like hard nuggets from plummeting me off the rock into oblivion. While Lisa showed no signs of fear during the climb, I was petrified. It was a miracle that I could continue moving, rather than being paralyzed—a statue on the rock, like a miniature version of Mt. Rushmore. Fortunately, this peak was only a thousand feet high.

I looked up at the patches of fresh snow on the slab. Thankfully, we didn't have far to go to the summit. I was underneath Lisa, following her lead, using the same foot- and handholds she used. I couldn't help noticing, even through her snowsuit, her knock-out figure, her strength pulling herself up by meager handholds, and her windswept hair, which exposed the fine features of her face. At first glance, she was an ideal companion to share the cold wilderness or a warm bed.

Yet, despite my vivid imagination, she had never taken a serious look at me. Of course, I felt taken advantage of, but what did I expect? She was one of the most popular girls on our campus. My friends told me: "You're privileged to go into the wilderness with such a fox!" And so she was—and she knew it.

Above me, I saw her gaze at the sky and glower, the clearest indication yet that she was anxious regarding the remainder of the climb. Gaining momentary relief, we stepped onto a snowy ledge about six feet wide. It signified a false summit about sixty feet below the actual summit. We scrambled over that last distance on a narrow ice bridge. Finally, we were standing proudly on Paulson's Peak Summit, which I felt was a substantial achievement, especially in those abysmal conditions.

As soon as we began trekking across the ice bridge, we were blasted by a whistling wind so strong that I was seriously worrying about getting blown right off the pinnacle. It blew even harder on the top. To me, it felt as if the wind were trying to protect the summit from intruders. I was aware that if I were blown off, I would have a thousand-foot tumble and freefall down the spire.

Another hazard on the summit was the windchill, which had to be almost thirty degrees below zero. We had dressed for cold conditions, but not that cold. My body shook and my teeth chattered.

Lisa glanced at me and made a face that held a combination of pity and irritability. She looked like she could camp out up there, but I knew that we couldn't last for more than a few minutes. I reflected with trepidation that we had only completed half of the climb and that the second half—down the peak—was more treacherous than going up!

The sky seemed a darker shade of gray than earlier, and the snowflakes were no longer drifting down like in the movies but were pounding us relentlessly. It was impossible to tell how soon it would be totally dark or how much filtered light we still had. Any estimate was questionable. It could be daytime by our watches but dark as night in the sky. Of course, we lacked a tent and bags, so staying anywhere in the wilderness that night was out of the question unless we desired to freeze to death. I wasn't quite sure how Lisa felt about our predicament, but I suspected it was dire.

I took a chance and tried a victory hug with Lisa before we departed from the summit. I intended it to be nothing more than a sentimental gesture. She deftly maneuvered away from my outstretched arms and snapped, "C'mon, Jeremy. Quit screwing around! We have some risky climbing ahead, and obviously, we don't have much time to get down."

We couldn't enjoy the view, so after a few minutes, she announced, "Let's go!" As we took our first step over the edge, she said almost tenderly: "Take care going down, Jeremy; it can get tricky. We don't want to lose you."

No kidding. These were the nicest words she had spoken to me the whole trip.

I carefully selected my handholds and footholds, seeking ledges and cracks. Lisa was right. The descent was more dangerous! The holds were harder to find, even though they should have been familiar from the earlier climb.

Lisa was silent during the entire descent. I assumed either she was concentrating on her climbing or she was disgusted with me for unknown reasons.

Communication helped me to keep my mind off the possibilities of injury or death, so occasionally I tried to jumpstart a conversation about the weather or our school. She didn't respond other than looking up at me with a frosty, contorted expression.

Despite our precarious situation, I couldn't believe how beautiful the wilderness below us was, the background flecked with white, freshly fallen flakes. I tried to share my awe with Lisa, but her countenance was as stony as the wall we were climbing down.

As we approached the boundary between the rock and the snow-spotted dirt slope, we were lashed by particularly powerful gusts and snow blowing sideways again. The slope below us was still steep and now had patches of snow and ice. With the scary ice, this section of the descent appeared to be an accident waiting to happen.

In fact, the slope didn't have long to wait for a human disaster. For once, Lisa thought conservatively and, by dropping to her torso and army crawling over the icy surface, she was able to make it down safely.

By contrast, I tried to stay upright over the same route, slid on an icy patch and lost my balance. I fell sideways and tumbled down the remainder of the rock surface and partway down the dirt slope until I crashed into some bushes, scratching the hell out of my face but arresting my slide. Fortunately, I stopped a few yards short of a cliff that would have dropped me into a cold, fast-flowing stream.

I tried to stand up but couldn't.

Breaking out of her taciturnity, Lisa was shouting my name and pleading for me to come out. Of course, I couldn't move, but Lisa found me, nearly frozen and tangled in the branches. Her first utterance was, "Jeremy, are you alright?" She actually seemed to care about my condition. She came close enough that I could feel her warm, gentle breath on my cheek.

I whispered, "It's my right leg. There's something wrong with my right leg. I can't move it. I can't move at all!"

The wind had picked up, and snow was already covering me.

"We can't just leave you here; you'll die," Lisa said. "I'd never forgive myself."

She found a solid stick long enough for me to use as a cane. Then, with an astonishing display of strength, Lisa half-carried and half-supported me down the last segment of the slope. She got me down as far under some low-hanging tree branches as possible while still sitting upright, making at least a semblance of shelter.

When she tried to fit my feet into my ski bindings, my swollen right foot wouldn't go in. Her attempts caused me so much pain that she gave up. I had lost all control of my right leg, so skiing the twenty-five miles back to the lodge was impossible.

Lisa regarded my motionless body with a mixture of disappointment and blame. It was difficult to tell whether the blame was directed to herself or at me, but it was obvious to me that she resented me for being "a failure."

From my standpoint, I didn't believe my injury was anyone's fault. It was just something that happened, and there was no sense in pointing fingers. These kinds of accidents happen naturally when someone faces challenges.

When I mentioned my take on the accident to Lisa, though, her skeptical reply revealed her true feeling about the accident and me: "You should have been more careful."

Kneeling next to me in several inches of fresh snow—as pure white as a swan sliding across the placid water of a lake—Lisa suddenly stood up and turned her back to me.

"I'm going back now," she announced in a tone as cold as the storm around us. "I'll really hustle so the rescue crew can get here. I'll be with them. So, I'll see you then."

As she put on her skis, I called out, "How long will I be out here? I'm frozen already!"

Her reply didn't sound very reassuring, "They'll be driving snowmobiles, so it should be no more than three hours. Don't worry. I'll snuggle with you to keep you warm until we get to the clinic."

After her assurances and allusion to the prospect of togetherness, she quickly peeled off her smile, slung her backpack containing all our uneaten picnic food over her shoulder, pointed her skis south toward Deerfield Springs, and used her ski poles to schuss away through the pines.

I watched the back of her navy-blue ski suit until it seemed to disappear under cover of the forest. She was gone, but I counted on seeing her again soon.

I was alone in the premature darkness and the penetrating cold, wishing too late that I had asked her to leave me something to eat. I was almost out of water because I drank so much on the climb, but I decided I could eat snow if I got thirsty.

I stomped my boots in a futile effort to keep my feet warm. My right ankle hurt like hell until it finally went numb. Eventually, I laid down in the snow and rolled into a ball.

The cold penetrated my nylon ski parka, woolen sweater, and undershirt. My body felt as stiff as I imagined a dead body felt. I wondered when my rigor mortis was going to begin. My teeth were chattering so loud it sounded like a skeleton was being shaken.

After a while, my ears gave out and I couldn't hear anything. I figured that was a clear indication that I was dying. I imagined my face looked like I had shoved it into a freezer for a few hours. I worried that I would look like shit for Lisa when she arrived.

There was a bit of filtered sunlight, but it was soon swallowed up by the approaching dusk. With complete darkness, the temperature was likely to fall into the negative tens or worse. The snowfall had not let up. In fact, it was snowing as fiercely as it had all day.

The fresh snow continued to pile up around my stationary body. I knew it would cover me soon. I had once seen a survival show on TV where I learned that a cover of snow would help to maintain a higher body temperature and could save an accident victim's life. I understood now why they called it a "blanket of snow."

I checked the time while I could still move my arm: 5:15 p.m. I figured I had to fight the cold for another three hours. Could I do that, or would I yield to the gentle lure of the forever sleep? Building a fire was impossible, as Lisa hadn't left any matches.

I realized that I might go crazy before I died if I didn't have something to take my mind off my plight. My body felt cold and stiff, like how I imagined a cadaver in a medical examiner's steel drawer might be.

My head wasn't fully buried yet. My vision was still functioning, so I figured I could count the squirrels, chipmunks and other creatures who scurried across the clearing and through the trees. When I tried counting them, it was so dark that I couldn't tell the squirrels from the chipmunks, so I knew I counted some at least twice. Then night fell and I couldn't see them at all.

I fell asleep for a while, and when I woke up I felt the weight of snow on my face. I thought about a *National Geographic* TV special I had seen about different burial techniques around the world and in different eras. I imagined what it would have been like to be a dead Egyptian pharaoh buried in his own personal pyramid.

The mound I was under reminded me of the ancient burial mounds found by modern scientists and explorers in open regions such as Mongolia. Usually, burial mounds were reserved for fallen warriors. *Is that what I am? I doubt it.*

Anyway, as frozen as I felt, the snow mound was insulating me from the bitter cold. I thought, *This mound is probably saving my life.* However, the downside of being inside the mound was that I blended with the terrain, and it would be nearly impossible to find me or my corpse. I remembered that Lisa would be along, though, and would surely recall where I was lying.

The hours went by like troops on the move. I assumed that 6:00 p.m. was my benchmark. I couldn't see my watch, but I guessed that it was already past that.

My status hadn't changed in hours, and I was sure Lisa had been gone longer than the estimate she had made to return "with the cavalry." Yet, I didn't hold any hostile thoughts against her. I rationalized that she must have taken a wrong turn and gotten lost. The rescue mission was delayed accordingly, but I knew she was coming back for me. In fact, the longer she was away, the more passionate my daydreams about us became.

I formed a pocket in the snow above me in order to breathe, but each breath was a painful challenge. The parts of my body which weren't already numb hurt like hell. My injured ankle felt like it was in a vise which a hidden force was cranking tighter and tighter.

I began moaning, which served no purpose, but I had no control over it. I figured my pain and involuntary reaction to it were signs of the last stage before death. I was resigned to that outcome any moment. Some of the highlights of my life flashed spasmodically through my mind. There weren't many, so I "saw" some of them two or three times.

I tried to speculate about an afterlife but concluded, *What's the point? I'll either have one or I won't.*

My daydreams faded to dark shadows as I lost consciousness.

I only know about the next sequence of events because the ski patrol officer, Kimmy, later told me what happened. She had been covering her usual search and rescue area, which included Paulson's Peak.

It was a typical mundane patrol, and she didn't expect to find anything out of place. Given the dire weather reports for the day, most people seemed to have stayed indoors out of the elements. Nevertheless, her protocol required her to search for lost hikers and cross-country skiers around the base of the peak. If she determined that a full team were necessary, she was to call in.

"Your situation was a no-brainer," she explained bluntly. "You were nearly a corpse."

Her first clue that someone was out there, possibly injured and needing her help, was a pair of skis she saw leaning upright against a tree. Her curiosity aroused, she approached the tree and nearly tripped over my backpack, now completely buried in snow.

She soon found the suspicious-looking mound I was under and began to dig, almost slicing the shovel blade into my body, which she didn't know for live or dead.

When Kimmy started to uncover and pull me out of the deep snow, I shrieked in pain, confirming her suspicion of an injury.

My eyes fluttered open, and she asked, "Can you hear me? Can you talk?"

There was a long pause and then I whispered, "My ankle was injured coming down from the peak. My companion went to get help."

Kimmy was flabbergasted that anyone would try to climb Paulson's Peak in storm conditions, she told me afterward, but in the moment she remained calm and professional.

For me, awareness returned with sounds of "thud, crunch, thud crunch" from somewhere outside my cocoon of snow. Was I dreaming?

As I felt myself being uncovered, I quickly realized what was happening. I was being saved! I was being given a second opportunity for life.

I vowed to be more careful during my "second life" and not take on dangerous conditions to "challenge myself" unless I had the confidence to achieve them.

The shovel carefully broke through the snow. When my head was uncovered, my first sight was a flashlight's bright beam in my eyes. I didn't mind. It was like the proverbial "light at the end of the tunnel," or could it be the "light from Heaven" that a few people report after they've supposedly died and been restored?

Either way, I was ecstatic to see it. I wasn't far off the mark in assuming that I might have come close to Heaven, because the beam of light shifted to a presence I can only describe now as a blond angel dressed in a bright red ski parka with a white cross on her back. I wasn't befuddled enough to miss that she was young, pretty, and conveyed an anxious expression of grim determination to extract me from the mound. She shoveled fervently, tossing the snow away and making conscientious efforts not to stick me with the shovel.

After she finally pulled me out and I lay awkwardly in the soft snow, I was able to focus on only one subject. I murmured to the blond 'angel,' "My partner, Lisa, guided you to where I am? Is she okay?"

"Who's your partner?"

"Hold it." I was trying to maintain my consciousness and I was worried about my ankle and hypothermia. "Lisa Carter. We skied from Kap's to here, climbed Paulson's Peak, but I had an accident on the way down during the worst part of the storm. Lisa said she was going to ski back to the ski patrol to get help."

She said, "I don't think so. As far as I know, our ski patrol hasn't had any calls about lost or injured climbers."

My entire body shivered with shock and disbelief.

She added, "I've called for a full paramedic team and they're on the way."

She called into Ski Patrol Headquarters again now that she had some information from me. There were three or four of them on speaker, and when she was finished, the senior member asked her, "Kimmy, can you handle this until the paramedic crew gets there?"

"Sure, no problem."

She turned to me and said, "What's your name?"

"Jeremy Parkins."

"Okay, Jeremy, you've been exposed to life-threatening cold. I'm going to do whatever I can to warm you, to prevent hypothermia. The procedure I'm going to use isn't ski patrol protocol, but it should work."

Her sweet smile was already beginning to warm me. She said, "Open your jacket. I'm going to let your body draw heat from mine."

She unzipped her own jacket and laid down on top of me. I spent the next hour in the pleasant embrace of this lovely stranger, from whom my body seemed to suck life-sustaining warmth.

At one point she asked me, "How are you doing?"

I brazenly responded, "What do you think?"

Then, in a businesslike tone, she said, "Oh, good—it's working."

I was beginning to feel like a package of thawed hamburger.

Our heads popped up when we heard the snowmobiles, and she quickly slipped off my body. My fingers fumbled to rezip my ski jacket.

An older man wearing a red parka identical to hers dismounted from his snowmobile. He jogged through the heavy layer of fresh snow to where I was lying with Kimmy standing dutifully next to me. I could hear his boots crunching the top layer of crust.

In a deep voice, he said, "Mr. Parkins, I presume?"

Kimmy responded for me, "That's right, sir. Been through an ordeal."

"I'm Lt. Swenson," he said to me. "I take it Kimmy took good care of you after she found you?"

I glanced at Kimmy and replied, "You could say so. I'm convinced that she saved my life. Without her assistance, I would have frozen to death."

He gave Kimmy a brief nod, as if to say, "I don't care how you did it. Good job!"

Swenson added, "Now we have to get you to the clinic while there's a slack period in the storm. We'll pull you on a toboggan-like stretcher. Leo, our paramedic, will check you out, so don't try to stand yet."

Leo examined my ankle for any broken bones and asked me: "How did this happen?"

I explained the fall in as much detail as I could recall. He said, "I don't believe it's broken, but we won't know for sure until X-rays are taken. It's at least a severe sprain. If that's all you suffered, you are one lucky SOB."

He nodded toward his colleague. "Lucky, too, that she came along and knew life-saving techniques."

Kimmy, who was still standing next to me, dropped to her knees and squeezed my hand. After they loaded me onto the stretcher, I noticed they were a seat short—Kimmy was the odd one out.

I smiled despite my pain and asked her: "Aren't you coming with us?"

"Nope. Gotta finish my patrol. Maybe we'll see each other later at the lodge bar."

"See ya—and thanks again."

As an aside, Lt. Swenson said to Kimmy: "Looks like you made a new friend."

Kimmy shrugged her shoulders and skied off through the woods.

Before the engines were flicked on, I casually asked Swenson: "You must have been contacted by my climbing partner, huh?"

"What's your partner's name?"

"Lisa Carter."

He scratched his red ski cap and replied, "That name doesn't ring a bell." He turned to the rest of the crew, "Does the name Lisa Carter sound familiar?"

They all shook their heads. Swenson said, "I'll call in to headquarters and ask if they've heard from her." He spoke into his hand-held and then turned to me and shook his head.

"No member of the public contacted anyone in our ski patrol about your predicament. It was pure luck—or maybe back country instinct—that Kimmy found you when she did. Another hour and you could have been a dead man, disguised as a popsicle."

That image horrified me, but I could think of nothing else all the way back. Fortunately, the roar of the snowmobiles spared me from any more of Swenson's "humor."

My body was partially numb, but my brain was functioning, and I was so angry at Lisa, who appeared to have abandoned me, that I felt like my head would explode. Unless she hadn't made it back herself? I felt a fleeting moment of concern but quickly dismissed that idea. Lisa was too experienced and confident an outdoorswoman for that. I asked myself: *Why did that friggin' bitch leave me stranded in the freezing cold to die? Did my life mean so little to her? What did I do to her? How could she promise to help, then leave me to a slow, lonely death?*

They carried me into the clinic, where X-rays revealed a severe sprain but no broken bones. The nurse on duty fitted me with crutches and released me into the clear, freezing air at 1:00 a.m.

Exhausted, I felt like lying down in a soft bed of powder, but I fought that notion, kept on trudging, and made it to my relatively warmer but empty room.

I phoned the night clerk. He had no clue where Lisa was. He cracked, "She must have disappeared on ya'." His implication was clear.

I was exhausted and planned to crawl into bed—the one I had shared with Lisa—when I heard a knock at the door. "Lisa?"

It was Kimmy. Naturally, I invited her to come in. She somehow looked fresh after a grueling eight-hour shift in the storm. She was quiet but very sweet, inquiring about my injury and the strange disappearance of my climbing partner.

"How did you find me?"

"In a tiny outpost like Deerfield Springs, it was no problem."

"I'm glad you did."

She smiled. I noticed she was still wearing her ski patrol outfit, so she had probably come straight to the lodge.

"Would you like a drink? Too late to go out for one, but I can fix a rum and Coke right here."

"I'm sorry, Jeremy, I've got to get back to the office. My crew has possession of me for now. They'll be worried if I'm back too late. They call me the 'baby' of the team. My days off are Tuesday and Wednesday. Call me then."

We started to shake hands, settled on an awkward hug, and she was off.

I wasn't aware until later that Lisa was standing in the shadows watching us. I never discovered her reason for being there, but I assumed she had wanted to make amends, possibly to assuage her guilt. Or maybe she just wanted to collect her luggage before heading back to campus.

I was fully awake with excitement after seeing Kimmy, but my ankle was killing me. I decided to get some ice to help with the pain. That required a trip to the first floor to use the ice machine. I hobbled downstairs, filled my bucket and limped briskly back toward my room, using the handrail as an improvised crutch. Rounding a corner on the staircase, I bumped hard into Lisa, who looked hale and hearty but wore a funny half-smile.

I barked in my nastiest tone: "What in hell are you doing here?"

My ice bucket tumbled to the ground and so did Lisa. Conk! Her head hit the concrete landing with force.

She didn't open her eyes or get up, so I added, "I thought you'd be long gone by now, peacefully sleeping in your warm bed at the college!"

When I thought about how she had promised to come back for me, then left me stranded alone in the deadly cold, I felt like smacking her, but that seemed unfair to do to an unconscious girl lying flat on her back.

When she came to and tried to sit up, her expression conveyed shock and fear. Then she laid back, and her eyes closed.

I put my ear to her mouth and couldn't detect any breath. There wasn't any pulse. Her hand was clutching at her chest. Her left arm was limp as a rag. I was unable to carry her, and I suspected she might not have enough time if I relied on 911. I reflected, *Leaving her would be the perfect revenge.*

Then, something signaled in my brain: a sense of compassion or a need to obey the universal urge to help someone in trouble. At that moment, I knew I couldn't leave her to die, so I dropped to my knees and commenced compression CPR. My ankle hurt with a searing pain, but I shifted to mouth-to-mouth resuscitation.

I had a brain flash of the irony. I was essentially kissing her, which she hadn't allowed me to do earlier in the trip. Severe medical necessity had finally brought us together. Lisa was dying before my eyes, and yet, I felt an odd sense of satisfaction about the reversal.

I continued blowing into her mouth. When I surfaced for air, I yelled, "C'mon, Lisa—live, Lisa, live!"

Something deep inside her was triggered. Her life force stirred, then awoke. Her eyelids rose.

I couldn't believe that I had kissed her back to life—her rejected Prince Charming—and I was happy. The image of her maliciously abandoning me to die had been repugnant; yet now I hovered over her, willing her back to life.

I learned something about myself in those early morning hours. I can't explain what it was, but I knew a fundamental attitude in me changed. Lisa was a beautiful young girl with a cold, unsympathetic heart. I had been in bed, clutching her, just one night ago. My immature self had only one goal: to kiss her everywhere and have passionate sex with her. Almost any girl would have been sufficient.

When Swenson informed me that Lisa had not done anything to save me, I was so furious I felt like slapping her. This early morning, I had my chance—yet *I* saved *her*. Who can figure?

Another lodge guest popped his head out of his door, and I asked him to call 911.

I instructed Lisa to stay down until relief arrived. Her eyes focused on who had saved her, and she managed another half-smile.

The rescue squad was slow, so I thought about carrying her to my car, but I couldn't put any weight on my ankle. We had to wait.

Finally, the county emergency squad arrived and took over care of a still-groggy Lisa. I furnished her vital information to one of them. They allowed me to ride in the ambulance, and I held her hand the entire way. She was able to mumble something, and I brought my ear close to her mouth: "Thanks for saving me. I love you, Jeremy."

I waited for them to check her in, then walked out of the clinic into the freshness of Vermont's air. I never looked back.

I tried hard to figure a rational reason—just one—for Lisa's abandoning me in the frigid conditions that the snowstorm had brought to Paulson's Peak. She knew that I couldn't ski or hobble back to Deerfield Springs, and she clearly hadn't been lost or injured herself.

I was left to speculate on some illogical and potentially dangerous explanations. The first was that she had bumped into some other friends and decided to have a drink or two at the Lodge. Once the alcohol was in her, she simply ignored my plight. A second possibility—and even a scarier one—was that she rationalized leaving me because I would die eventually anyway.

I never sought Lisa out to demand an explanation. I didn't want to hear whatever excuse she would make. None would be satisfactory to justify abandoning an injured skier in the snowy wilderness. Whatever story she came up with would be a lie to somehow make her look good, but as far as I was concerned, she had displayed her colors, and they smelled nasty.

I later discovered that the clinic doctor had transferred Lisa to a hospital for further monitoring. Before she was released, Lisa left seven or so messages on my cellphone. Some were a desire to meet with me. In others, she pleaded pathetically for me to accept her gratitude for saving her. "I wouldn't have made it without you!" She cooed in some messages that she wanted to pick up where we had left off in the lodge bed. "I'll make it worth your while."

Lisa continued to call me after she returned to campus, but I never returned her calls. I erased all of her voicemails, hoping each time that with one push of the button she would be out of my life forever. I also avoided her on campus. Occasionally, one of her girlfriends blindsided me to tell me that "Lisa wants to get together with you, if you know what I mean." She usually winked or rolled her eyes. I always walked away.

I was relieved a few months later when I learned through the grapevine that Lisa had transferred to a university in Florida. She never once apologized for leaving me in the wild to die.

I learned from this experience that there are choices associated with all conduct and that some choices cannot be forgiven, excused, or even explained. It is what it is. I learned this valuable lesson the hard way.

There was another axiom that I had mulled over but eventually concluded was such an obvious part of human conduct: If we are to get along and survive, then when a person is presented with a duty, he must just do it as efficiently and completely as possible. . . .

. . . And when someone is presented with an opportunity, he must seize it and not look back. Successful fulfillment of opportunities is the key to happiness. An opening fortunately had come my way and, uncharacteristically for my life until then, I seized it.

Kimmy and I seemed to click. So I returned to Deerfield Springs to see her. There's not much to do in Deerfield Springs at night, but we went on many "dates" anyway. That's a euphemism for "drinking at the Lodge bar and listening to music on an ancient jukebox."

Eventually, we became intimate and talked of marriage. I dedicated my heart and the rest of my life to Kimmy, and she did so with me. When our children came along, our lives were complete.

The Stranger

I tried to give the detective a good account of what happened tonight:

"My name is Mark Sorenson. Luke, John, and I were playing our regular Tuesday night game of pool at the tavern attached to the Sleepy Eyes Inn. It's called Ray's Tavern, ingeniously named after the owner, Ray.

"We began these pool games to avoid homework that we probably wouldn't have done anyway. We each lied to our parents, saying that we were members of a study group which met on Tuesday and Thursday nights at the library. We chose pool because . . . well, none of us could recall why. Probably because pool was fun, and the bar-room atmosphere made us feel grown-up and somewhat delinquent. We are high school seniors, but unless we can major in pool for our last semester, we'll have to take summer school to graduate."

While standing in the street in front of the bar, I explained to the cop: "I don't know how it happened. Everything seemed to happen so fast."

This explanation was contradicted by the steady dripping of blood from a nasty gash on my forehead which I tried to stop with my shirt.

I continued, "Me and my friends were playing 8-ball—you know, taking turns. It was Luke's turn to play John. We were yucking it up like we always do. Making a bit too much noise. Ray, the owner, is also the bartender. He allows us to play here as long as we don't try to sneak any booze. Also, we aren't allowed to go into the bar area except to use the head. We bring in our own soda and snacks, which nobody seems to mind. We were just whilin' away another school night . . . you know, just goofin' around . . . when a stranger entered the bar.

"The place was almost empty, but I could tell that no one had ever seen this guy before. He strode directly toward the bar and gruffly told Ray to pour him a double Scotch straight up with a Bud chaser.

"The stranger was only about five-foot six inches but had huge biceps and looked like a modern version of Popeye. You know, built like a fire hydrant. He had tattoos of dragons, snakes, and logos all over his visible skin and on every inch of his head, which was as bald as a cue ball, including his face. He smelled like metal, which might have been from the chain he wore over his shoulder. He had mean, black eyes which followed movement like a hawk searching for prey. His complexion was a dull shade of red. He looked angry, like a guy with a grudge. All in all, he looked like someone to steer clear of . . . a guy who'd be delighted to see a fight break out in the bar."

The detective asked, "What do you mean by that?"

"I took one look at the guy and wanted to get the heck out o' Dodge."

"What did the other boys say about him? Did they express any concern?"

"Not really. Guys our age never want to admit we're scared about anything. Their silence didn't tell me nothing about this guy. I said to them, 'Let's get out of here.' They both gave me a funny look, and John asked me why. I motioned my head toward the stranger and whispered, 'I don't like the looks of the new company,' figuring they'd go along with me. They didn't. They didn't want to leave yet 'cuz they had a good game of 8-ball goin'."

"Okay, your friends wouldn't go with you. What happened next?"

"I assumed the stranger spotted us at the pool table. He ordered his second combo from Ray and moseyed over to our table. He stood over it to watch us play, not saying anything at first. I'm not quite sure why he cared about what we were doing. He had to be at least twenty years older than us."

The cop said, "I've already talked with Ray about this. From what the guy said to him, Ray figured this stranger wanted to show you kids a thing or two. He apparently said something like, 'They don't know shit about nothing.' Ray said this stranger had the look and attitude like he had just gotten out of prison and had something to prove."

"That's the feeling I had. Anyway, he apparently was familiar with 8-ball 'cuz he smiled a few times when Luke or John chose their shots. I was surprised to see him smile even if it was just on the surface. It seemed to be out of character. I actually began to think that this wasn't such a bad dude after all. Boy was I wrong!

"Luke had a good run and sank the 8-ball. When I didn't step forward to begin the next game, Luke broke the silence by saying, 'That was our last game. Right, guys?' The stranger slapped a quarter on the rail and growled, 'No you ain't. I got winners,' pointing to Luke. He began tossing balls from the pockets onto the table and ordered Luke to 'rack 'em up. My break.'"

The detective gripped his notebook tighter, his eyes narrowed, and he moved closer to me, as if I had some secret to share with him. As I told him about the stranger's coarse behavior, he seemed to scowl and asked, "What happened after that?"

"I could tell that Luke wasn't into it. I figured that he wanted to lose the game on purpose to appease this guy."

"Let me guess, the stranger was pretty bad and lost the game right away."

"Not just right away! He lost it on the break. Can you believe it? He sank the cue ball on the break! Luke began to walk away, but the stranger smirked and said, 'Don't forget your quarter.'

"Suddenly the stranger fished another quarter out of his pocket and walked around the table to deposit it onto the felt. Without a word, he racked them himself. He turned to Luke and ordered him to 'Break.'

"Luke didn't move, as if the stranger's voice had frozen him in place.

"The stranger glared at him and barked, 'If you're not gonna break, I will.' Then he said in a slightly gentler tone, 'This here fella is goin' give me a chance to win back my quarter, aren't ya', boy?'

"Luke bobbed his head up and down but still didn't say anything.

"'Okay,' said the stranger enthusiastically, 'Here's what it'll be . . . dollar a game?'

"Luke didn't respond, so I stuck my neck out and said, 'We don't gamble. It's against our principles.' This wasn't true, but I lied to get out of this scene.

"The stranger's stare was like a poison dart straight at my brain. He raised a cue stick as if to hit me but pointed at me instead. He appeared to be calculating a way to deal with us dumb kids. It was like if he couldn't beat us in pool, he'd dominate us in other ways. I didn't want anything to do with him. He said, 'You can gamble tonight. It's an exception. I promise not to tell your parents.' He snickered. 'And don't worry about ol' Ray. He's a buddy of mine. We go way back.' This was a lie.

"Then he turned to Luke and said sharply, 'Let's go, kid. You do have a dollar, don't you?' Luke nodded again like he was afraid to say anything.

"The stranger snapped again, 'My break.' He took careful aim at the tightly packed balls and slammed the cue ball into them with great force. However, his furious thrust was his downfall. The balls scattered in all directions. Two stripes went into pockets, but the cue ball again disappeared into the side pocket.

"I cried out, 'Game!'

"The stranger grimaced at me like I caused him to lose.

"I urgently said to the guys, 'C'mon, let's go!'"

The detective nodded his approval.

I continued, "The stranger's face turned bright red, and he spit out his words. 'Just a goddamn minute! Those games were flukes, not tests of skill. It was my bad luck.' Reracking, he pointed at Luke and uttered, 'Your break.'

"Ray popped up out of nowhere with a tray and handed the stranger another drink and us each a soda pop. 'On the house,' he said, then asked, 'Is everything okay here?'

"Nobody said anything. Finally, the stranger replied, 'Yeah, sure.'

"Ray looked at our blank faces and said, 'Just watch the felt. I had it resurfaced last week, okay?'

"The stranger exploded, 'Shudup, Ray. Go do what you do best.' Ray snorted and walked back to the bar.

"'Let's go, kid. These balls aren't gonna break themselves.'

"Luke also scattered the balls, but none went in. The stranger looked over the table and smiled greedily. 'What do we have here? You're making it easy for me to run the table.' He sank one solid and his 'run' was cut short. He badly missed the next shot and cursed. Then, he blamed his miss on John supposedly moving in the background.

"Suddenly, luck became his enemy. He whined, 'If I didn't have bad luck, I'd have no luck at all.'

"Luke made his first three shots on stripes but then missed a simple one. The stranger observed what was going on, and before he took his next shot, he snapped, 'You missed that easy one. What are you trying to do, game me?'

"Luke is a small guy. In that moment he shrank about two sizes. He looked like an eighth grader. It appeared that he was on the verge of crying. The stranger must have felt sorry for him because he casually said, 'I guess it's my shot.'

"He made two but again missed badly and bounced his stick off Ray's new felt and then tried to break it over his knee. It bent but wouldn't snap. That was a relief because he undoubtedly would have told Ray that one of us broke it. He uttered, 'I can't believe I missed that one. I'm just givin' you the game gift-wrapped on a platter.'

"Luke looked confused, like he didn't know what to do next. I saw that his legs were quivering. It was his turn, but he was frozen in place.

"I said, 'It's your shot, buddy.' I thought for sure he was gonna miss it, but he glanced at me and then ran the table.

"He had a tough shot on the 8-ball and missed it. The stranger let out a loud 'Ha.'

"He, too, went on a nice run but missed the shot on his final solid. He grumbled, 'Hell's bells.' I couldn't help smiling but tried not to let him see it.

"Then Luke made an easy shot on the 8-ball. Game over.

"The stranger quickly slapped four more quarters on the table. He had so many of them I figured he had knocked off a vending machine or something.

"It was obvious that Luke didn't want any more of the stranger or his quarters. He mumbled, 'I gotta get home. Big test tomorrow.' He scooted out of the bar and probably breathed a sigh of relief.

"The stranger stared at the retreating Luke and shouted derisively when Luke stopped briefly to wave back at us, 'If you're leaving, then get the fuck out of here!' Then, for good measure he added the word, 'punk.' He looked at John, 'You're next.'

"It struck me that this guy was attempting to flex his muscles in order to boost his ego. We see that kind of thing all the time in school. He certainly wasn't playing for the money. He never considered that he'd lose to Luke. When he did, I figured that it was vital to him to beat one of us, and John looked like the easiest mark.

"Suddenly the stranger said in a somber but bitter tone, 'You guys remind me of my kid. He'd be about your age. I haven't seen him in over seven years 'cuz I've been in prison. I think he was glad when they put me away. I used to make him play all sorts of games with me, but he'd beat me in every one of them. I got sick of losing like that. Let me tell you, I got to hate that kid . . . and his mother too.'

"He then racked the balls again. Without asking John, he thrust the cue ball at the others with so much force that I thought that the white ball was going to fly off the table. It settled down in the corner near one of the pockets. None of the other balls went into a pocket, so then John could pick either stripes or solids.

"John didn't pick up a cue stick yet. The stranger regarded him with disdain. 'What's the matter, kid?' He sneered. ''Fraid I'll tear you apart . . . on the table that is?'

"John responded, 'I'm not that good. Let Mark play.' The stranger pointed his finger at John, who shot at but missed a solid.

"Then the stranger shot at a stripe at the other corner, but it rimmed out.

"By now John had zipped up his jacket and picked up his back-pack. The stranger stared at John and growled, 'I said you were next. Now pick a stick and shoot!'

"The implication was if John didn't shoot, the stranger would shoot out of turn or do something worse. John was quaking but nailed a solid on the money. He went on to win two close games and one relatively easy one.

"The stranger was fuming but reached deep into his pocket and set twelve quarters on the rail. John ran to the bar's only bathroom. I figured he was so nervous he might pee in his pants.

"I was determined not to play any games against this wacko. It was time to go. I refused to look at him until John returned. I pretended to ignore him when he signaled to me that I was next.

"When John anxiously returned to the table, the stranger announced loud enough for Ray and the one remaining bar patron to hear, 'I'm sick of you . . . Johnny Boy. This other kid is up.' He flicked his head at me. I could tell that the heat inside him had been turned up a couple of notches, and it looked like he was ready to pounce.

"The stranger bitterly remarked, 'I can't stand scared punks like you two. You have no clue how things work. Let me tell you that in prison boys like you . . . barely eighteen . . . are the lowest of the low. You're taken as a girlfriend by a guy like me, and all you can do is whine and complain about it. I command respect in prison and that's what I'm gonna get from you.'

"I let him win the first game, so he could restore some of his self-respect. I also hoped it would cool him down.

"Then, I decided, 'What the hell?' and ran the table, including the 8-ball. This was a reversal of the direction I had planned, and I feared that he would blow up. I couldn't help myself. I wanted to show him that I could hold my own in pool. I roasted him again in the next two games, with him only sinking two balls in each game.

"Then I quietly signaled to John to get ready to make a run for it. The stranger was bound to figure that I threw the first game and he'd be pissed off. I could tell that he was again ready to explode. He refused to pay the two dollars he owed, claiming that I 'cheated.' When I protested, he flung his stick at me.

"The sharp end bounced off my stomach. The blow buckled me over. I groaned to John, 'Let's go. Run!'

"We took no more than a couple of steps, when the stranger—in a rage—ripped another cue stick off the rack on the wall, wound up like a major leaguer with a Louisville Slugger, and swung it at me. I ducked and it barely scratched my forehead, but the stick hit John on the side of his head with a hideous thud. The stranger didn't seem to be concerned. He strutted out of the bar with a broad smile."

I told the officer I didn't know which direction the stranger went or whether he was driving a vehicle. I reflected on the final scene at the bar and told the officer: "John slumped to the floor and laid there unconscious. Ray called 911, and the paramedics rushed him to the hospital."

The word I got afterward was that John had a concussion. He eventually woke up with a sore head and went home. John was fortunate. It could have been a lot worse for all three of us. Now I know why my parents have always warned me not to talk with strangers.

The officer commented how lucky we were. He plugged some information into his hand-held tablet and came up with an identity. The stranger's name is Butch Synder, and he's a parole violator. The officer proclaimed that as soon as they caught him, he'd be checking into prison again.

I called Luke later and told him what happened after he left. He said he was still in shock and, even watching TV, he couldn't get his mind off the stranger. "He scared the shit outta me."

"Yeah. Me too. But what an experience. I just hope I don't have to go through anything like that again."

"I hear you, Mark. I'm gonna quit pool for a while."

"Not me. I'll be back at Ray's next Tuesday."

"You're a lot braver than me."

"No, just broker."

A COVID Christmas

The COVID-19 virus spread like the flu during the Great Pandemic of 1918. The San Francisco Bay Area and other metropolitan areas were hit hard.

Victims suddenly came down with flu-like symptoms: a raspy cough, vomiting, diarrhea, and a deep congestion of the lungs. Many people could not even rise from their beds. Thousands of cases were reported, seemingly at the same time. The ER and ICU beds in all the hospitals were full. Patients were lining the hallways and waiting rooms on cots, and even these were almost full.

The virus was already causing over two hundred deaths a day in California alone. Residents hid out in their homes, which was called "sheltering in place." If they ventured into public—to go to work, for example—they were required by the government to wear masks. An informal rule required them to stay at least six feet apart from other people.

General panic, even among social and hospital workers, continued to widen. No one was immune. Even the president and first lady were infected. Cops, firefighters, doctors, and judges came down with the dreaded disease, and many were dying.

At first, some fortunate rural areas escaped COVID-19. Experts believed that the infection rate in those places was so low because the residents lived far apart. Thus, they avoided infecting one another. One rancher named Clarence Cook exclaimed, "Hell, my nearest neighbors live five miles away. I only see them once or twice a year, and that's usually from a distance."

Most experts calculated that, as a result of the circumstances in which they lived, rural folks would avoid the worst of the pandemic. In the case of Sagebrush, Nevada, they were wrong.

Since the outbreak started, Cindy Stewart had been working double shifts as an entry-level 9-1-1 dispatcher in Reno, Nevada. She was working on Christmas Day, 2020, when she was surprised to receive a call from the tiny, high-desert town of Sagebrush, about fifty miles northeast of Reno. She looked it up quickly. Sagebrush had a population of ninety-six.

The caller was Norma Jean Wickerstam, age ninety-seven (although Cindy didn't know that yet). Barely audible, Mrs. Wickerstam murmured, "The whole town almost has come down with this crazy virus—What's it called? Oh, yeah, 'COVID." People are dying out here, and no one knows what to do."

Despite her advanced age and the lethal circumstances, Mrs. Wickerstam did not sound panicky. Yet.

Cindy asked, "Where are the sick people, ma'am?"

"About half of them are here in town. They're holed up in The Oasis, the town cafe. The rest of them are too sick to leave their homes. Our trailer park has a whole bunch of sick ones. The rest of them are scattered all over."

This situation sounded grave to Cindy. She was new and not used to coping with such a big crisis involving the lives of so many people. She realized that she needed an assessment from someone in authority other than this old lady. She also realized that she needed to confer with her supervisor.

She said, "Ma'am, can you hang on for a minute? I have to check with my supervisor as to how we can best help you." She was surprised that she was, for the most part, maintaining her cool.

"Uh, I guess so . . ."

"Okay, I'll be right back."

The young dispatcher grabbed her notebook and ran down the hallway to Mr. North's office. He was a large man who sported a protruding belly that stretched his button-down shirt. He always chomped on a cigar, even though it was against County rules to smoke. Christmas music was being piped into his office.

Cindy appeared to be nervous and in a panic. Mr. North sternly demanded, "Cindy, why did you leave your station? You know that can't be done except in emergencies." This comment seemed to be characteristic.

She gasped excitedly, "This is an emergency! I have a woman on the line with an actual emergency. She wants us to decide what to do. An entire town is at risk with COVID in various stages. Some of them might have already died. Others are bedridden. Others are functioning, but barely."

Mr. North said in his most soothing tone: "Why, you know, Cindy, everyone who calls us refers to their situation as an emergency."

"Sir, this is a big one! It involves life or death for a lot of people. The lady on the other end of the line is elderly, but she seems to have all her wits. She's waiting for us to do what we can to help them."

"Okay, spit it out, but make it quick! What's the problem?"

"Nearly the entire town of Sagebrush has come down with COVID."

"Sagebrush!" he said impatiently. "Where the hell is that?"

"I don't know, sir. I haven't had time to look on the map."

"I suppose it's somewhere near Reno. If they were down south, they'd have called Vegas."

"Makes sense, sir."

"Okay, Cindy, here's what we're gonna do. Tell the caller that help is on the way. I'll get the choppers going."

"Are we going to take the whole town back to Reno?"

"Every person who's sick. But tell her there'll be no free rides. If a person is not sick, he or she doesn't get on the chopper. Now go!"

"Yes, sir" Cindy replied. "It's weird, huh?"

"What is?"

"It's Christmas Day—hear the music?"

She ran back down the corridor, gasping from the tension and from moving so fast. She wheezed into her phone: "Still there, ma'am?"

Norma Jean cracked, "Where do you expect a ninety-seven-year-old woman would be . . . the MGM Grand Hotel?"

Ignoring the sarcasm in light of the serious nature of her call, Cindy blurted, "My supervisor wanted me to tell you that the helicopters will soon be on the way to Sagebrush, so please round up all the COVID sick people and bring them to the cafe. Only the infected persons can ride to Reno."

Norma Jean said defensively, "Which is almost the entire town."

"Right."

Norma Jean inquired, "What about those in the outlying areas who are too sick to be moved?"

Cindy wasn't prepared to cope with that problem so she had to wing it. "The able bodied members of your community will have to go out and get 'em and bring 'em into town. Our choppers are very large and aren't set up to do that. Okay, ma'am, are you clear on what's going to happen?"

"Yeah, honey. What do you think I am—a little kid?"

"Good luck, then. 'Bye."

In the meantime, North was calling North Star Rescue, the helicopter outfit used by the county. It was the most reliable service in the Reno-Carson area. He identified himself and asked to speak with Johnny Jumper.

"You've got him," Johnny answered.

The twenty-seven-year-old lead supervisor was a college grad. He had received his pilot's license while at the University of Nevada, and then his helicopter specialty in order to get a job within the air rescue business. He had been with North Star for five years, and he loved helping people in distress.

"This is North from County Emergency Services. I know it's Christmas and all, but can you handle an urgent assignment that requires two of your largest choppers?"

"I know who you are, Frank. We can handle the job. Our medical chopper is out on a mission, but we've got two big ones here on the ground. What's up?"

"We just got a call from an old lady in Sagebrush, wherever the hell that is. She said that practically the entire town of ninety-six people has COVID or is coming down with it. They need an urgent lift to Reno General. The rub is, I don't know what percentage of the town is seriously ill and whether some are too sick to be moved."

"Listen, Frank, I got a pretty good idea where Sagebrush is. I passed near it when my group drove out I-80 to go dove hunting a couple of months ago. I'll check on the USGS map here . . . There it is! Sagebrush is a no-stoplight speck of a town in the high desert, forty-five miles northeast of Reno. It's in the middle of nowhere. The population probably doesn't change much. It's around a hundred unless some of those poor folks have already died. This job definitely will require two birds and several runs if necessary."

"Okay, Johnny, fire 'em up. Go get those folks. I'll alert the hospital that you're bringin' in a bunch of older folks and that it's not to gamble at the casinos."

"Will do. On our way."

Johnny checked with the coordinator and quickly conducted some preflight procedures. Larry Patera, their most experienced pilot, volunteered to fly the second bird.

Larry was a U.S. veteran of the Iraq war and had flown rescue copters back in those days. He had been hired about a year earlier and was an invaluable member of the team. Both pilots were also trained paramedics.

Johnny said, "We need to maintain radio contact between us at all times."

He was worried about whether they'd find Sagebrush, even with the coordinates, and whether they'd be able to land safely. Heavy rain and some unusually dense fog had rolled into the Reno area. The airfield was engulfed by the creeping crud.

He called the National Weather Service on its hotline and reached a recording of Christmas carols. A message interrupted the music, stating that the FAA had grounded all aircraft due to inclement weather. The fog and rain were expected to last throughout Christmas Day. The high desert was socked in, and the fog was not expected to lift until tomorrow.

Johnny asked Larry's opinion as to whether they should fly to Sagebrush.

"I'll tell you, J.J., it looks bad. Sane pilots would not fly in this stuff. Looking out, I have some bad vibes—looks like zero visibility, the worst I've ever seen. If we make it to Sagebrush, coming back could risk many lives. I don't know, J.J.—it's your call."

"I'm like you. There's no way I'd fly in this stuff, except in the present circumstances. I feel that it's only gonna get worse, but we've got to consider all those sick and dying folks. We're the only ones who can reach them in time. It's our job, no matter what the conditions are. I'm for taking a chance, but I wouldn't blame you for remaining here on the ground. It's your call—stay here if you want to."

Larry stared at his partner and friend, took a deep breath, and calmly exclaimed, "We're wasting time. Let's go!"

They rushed to the exit door leading to the airstrip. They couldn't even make out the huge choppers sitting on their pads. The pilots sliced through the fog like a hole opened up and then promptly closed behind them. The air was as still as Johnny had ever felt. All he said was, "Whew!" as they reached the birds.

From his pilot's seat, Johnny signaled that it was time for lift-off. The sound of the choppers being ignited simultaneously was deafening. They lifted off, and Johnny led. They flew high to try to get above the fog but couldn't. The sky was socked in, seemingly to the peaks west of Reno. It was claustrophobic, but Johnny knew he had to stay calm. They turned east and maintained their formation.

Larry questioned himself: *What the hell are we doing? Flying through this muck is not good for our health. I feel like it's more dangerous than flying in Iraq under heavy enemy fire. One slight miscalculation and one or both of us will go down without enough altitude to escape by parachute. Instant death! On Christmas, no less!*

He radioed Johnny: "We've tried to get there. Don't you think it's time to turn around?"

Johnny didn't hesitate. "We've got to bring those folks in. If we fail them, how many will die?"

"But if we continue, we'll probably crash—and how will that help them?"

The moisture was turning to condensation on their windshields. Things were going from bad to worse. They were literally flying blind and entirely with their instruments.

Larry tried sticking his head out the side window. That trick had once saved him while driving on Highway 99 through Fresno.

He was about to turn back to base on his own when he heard Johnny's voice crackle on the radio. At first, he figured that his partner had also decided to turn back.

Johnny's voice was clearly saying, "It's so strange, and I may be dreaming. You know, like being in a state of confusion—but I see a bird. It's all white and flying directly in front of me. It appears to be headed in the direction of Sagebrush."

Larry thought about that for a moment and almost laughed. *Yep, he's definitely hallucinating!* He radioed back: "Yeah, your mind must be playing tricks on you!"

"Believe me, Larry," Johnny answered. "I think this bird is a dove, and he's leading us to Sagebrush!"

At that point, Larry figured it'd be rude to clog up the airwaves making fun of Johnny, but he also felt he ought to set him straight. The pressure was too much, and Johnny sounded like he was under the influence of some narcotic. He decided to take a low-key approach.

"What makes you say that?"

"I don't know, exactly. It's just the way it appeared like magic out of nowhere."

Larry was stumped—*How could Johnny determine what a bird's intention was?* But he'd rather not contest what Johnny was saying—just let it all go and chalk it up to Johnny's enthusiasm.

Yet, hallucinating like this could be dangerous for both of them. He asked, "So what's the plan?"

Without hesitation, Johnny replied, "We follow the dove."

Larry was afraid of that. He was exasperated and suddenly very tired. It was like all the adrenaline in his tank ran dry. He felt like Johnny's obstinacy might get them killed. Nothing was making sense. *A bird leading them? Preposterous!*

He recalled the old days with his ex-wife back in their small apartment. No matter what he said to her, he found himself trapped in an endless irrational argument. Reason had fled that apartment for a calmer environment.

This thing about the bird guiding them seemed just as crazy. Johnny might as well claim to be seeing a jolly fat man in a red suit climbing out of a chimney. Was the bird like Rudolph's red nose, leading the sleigh to safety?

He heard Johnny say, "Larry, hear me out. I wouldn't blame you if you turned around and flew back. There's no reason for you to risk your life further. Don't put your ass on the line in reliance on what might be a fictional bird."

There was a long pause like the silence before a coffin was lowered into the grave. Larry finally asked, "Is the dove still there?"

"Yep—it's amazing. She's staying only a few feet in front of me. I've never seen anything like it. If she were any farther out from me, I wouldn't be able to see her."

"Then you can count on me. I'm going with you."

There was no chatter for a while. Larry was doing his best to follow Johnny's copter.

Johnny was doing his best to follow the bird, whose whiteness blended in with the fog. It was undoubtedly navigating by some inner guidance system and flew a steady course.

Larry contemplated the difficulty of landing these big copters if they ever reached Sagebrush. The dove might get them there, but it couldn't land the choppers for them. The odds of making a successful blind landing were slim.

But maybe Johnny wasn't as daft as he sounded. He was already working on the landing problem. He informed Larry that he had called the new dispatcher and told Cindy to begin working on the challenge.

Cindy listened to Johnny describe the dilemma and thought it through. There were obviously no searchlights or floodlights in Sagebrush, but she had an idea.

She called the cafe and spoke to Mrs. Wickersham. Cindy explained to the excitable woman that the helicopters were on the way, but they needed a guiding light to land safely. She told the old lady her plan.

Mrs. Wickersham responded, "Don't worry, honey, I'm on it."

She enlisted George Sayler, the owner of the cafe, and bartender Philly White, and together they half-carried and half-dragged the cafe's fully decorated Christmas tree to the open field adjacent to the cafe. Fortunately, none of the three had any COVID symptoms yet. They rounded up all the extension cords they could get and were able to bring electricity to the tree.

Mrs. Wickersham—a five-foot-two dynamo despite her age—was a woman on a mission. She declared, "That's not enough light! We need more." She thereupon raided all the nearby houses for strings of colored lights. They strung them up and Mrs. Wickersham clapped her hands and joyfully stated, "That's more like it!"

By then, the townsfolk had begun congregating in the light rain outside the cafe. This wasn't good for their health, so George and Philly started serving hot coffee and sweets to all takers. The sickest ones were not interested; some were paralyzed by a fear of dying.

They finally heard the chopper blades. Philly later remarked that the huddled survivors looked like grunts waiting for extraction from a heavy firefight.

On the radio, Larry pointed out to Johnny that the fog and rain were surprisingly heavy, even though this was usually dry high desert. They knew they must be approaching Sagebrush—the instruments told them that—but Johnny wasn't sure where or when they should commence their descent.

Suddenly, the dove made a spectacular nosedive. Johnny felt he had no choice but to follow her.

Larry could just make out Johnny's chopper banking into a sharp turn and descending—presumably toward either Sagebrush or sure death. On the radio, he heard Johnny call, "Dive! Dive!"

Larry couldn't quit on him now. He followed Johnny's course and held his breath.

The dove flew downward through the rain and fog. Her mission was nearly complete.

Making his reckless descent, all Johnny could see was an impenetrable gray wall. He sensed that he was flying in a puzzling void. There was a complete lack of sight, feelings, thoughts, and objects to touch. Even the copters' engines seemed far away. It was all a vast nothing—still as death.

He was bewildered and needed the comfort of a human voice. "Hey, Larry, we're in trouble. I can't see the ground."

Tell me about it, Larry thought. *Reality is finally catching up with us. It's been a good effort.*

Johnny continued, "Any ideas? We can fly up, but that will mean we'll have to abandon our mission and return to base. That course of action will strand many desperately ill people. No other help will be available to the . . ."

"Down, boss! Go down. That's the only alternative I can live with!"

Johnny strained his eyes and detected a faint glow of colored lights—all the colors of the rainbow. He steered his big bird through the fog directly at the lights. As he approached, he imagined them as decorative lights on a giant Christmas tree, an apparition floating in the fog. He asked himself: *Could this be real, or is this a figment of my overactive imagination?* Were the lights a product of wishful thinking, a delusion? Why would a Christmas tree be outside on the snow?

Despite these doubts, his intuition told him to trust the dove. She had led them this far. "That's it," he radioed Larry. "We're going in!"

The Christmas tree lights, with the dove in the foreground, were a magical sight for the pilots as they came into view. Johnny could just make out the dove landing on the top of the tree where the angel usually perched.

In the next few seconds, Johnny's experience with the dove and the Christmas lights—no matter the final outcome—was transcendent. He could hear Christmas bells and see angels circling around the tree. A choir was singing, "Oh, Come, All Ye Faithful."

He felt goose bumps over his entire body. It was a physical sensation he hadn't encountered since he was a boy. He hoped the power of that sensation would pull him through to a successful landing.

He believed that the white dove and the Christmas tree lights were guiding them, but whether they were supernatural messengers, he couldn't fathom. Johnny wasn't a complicated person; he got busy landing his chopper.

Larry heard his radio crackle and asked, "Johnny, are you alright? I thought for a sec I had lost you."

"I'm fine. Getting ready to land near that lit-up Christmas tree. Did you see its lights?"

"Just faintly."

"I'm taking them as a sign."

"You mean some kind of Christmas miracle?"

"Something like that. Either way, I know my dove-hunting days are over."

"We needed guidance, to be sure."

"Amen, Larry. Let's land these birds!"

They were both relieved as the choppers set down, one after the other. They shut off the engines, and the blades gradually rotated to a stop. The dove watched from her lofty perch until her faithful followers had landed safely, and then she flew away.

A restrained cheer from the small crowd on the ground broke the silence. Larry and Johnny disembarked and approached the Christmas tree.

The burly cafe owner, his scraggly bartender, and a surprisingly spry old lady met them at the tree. Many others were huddled together out of the rain, by the cafe entrance. Some were in wheelchairs. Others were being held up, presumably by relatives or friends. There were at least fifty in that bunch.

Larry walked over to the cafe and checked them out. Some were coughing and sneezing.

Others were hacking from their chests. Still others were retching.

Mrs. Wickerstam said, casually, "Hello. I knew you'd make it, despite this murk."

Johnny responded, "Yeah, we made it . . . with some help from our friends. What a great idea that was to bring the Christmas tree out here!"

Mrs. Wickerstam beamed.

Johnny continued, "But what I don't understand is how you trained the dove to do what she did."

Mrs. Wickerstam made a quizzical face.

George stepped in, "What do you mean, 'dove'?"

Johnny looked from one to the other. "Never mind."

Mrs. Wickerstam exclaimed, "Some of the sick folks won't be able to move by themselves, and others don't have transportation to get to town. George here has a couple of snowmobiles that he said we could use."

Directing her question to Johnny and Larry, she said, "Will you help us round them up?"

"Sure, let's go!"

Somehow, they collected another twenty-nine sick residents. Many were trembling in the cold. Several had makeshift "barf bags." Some of them had to be carried to the snowmobile, but others refused to leave, claiming that they'd rather die in their own homes.

The pilots and their helpers distributed masks to everyone and filled the two helicopters to standing room only. Many of the patients were coughing; others fell asleep.

Mrs. Wickerstam said, "Thank you, boys!" to the two pilots. "And please pass on my wholehearted thanks to Cindy!"

"We'll be sure to do so," replied Johnny.

The rain had finally ended, and the fog lifted. The flight back to Reno was smooth and clear—the dove could retire.

Johnny and Larry were delighted to find out later that not one of the "Sagebrush Seventy-Nine" perished in the pandemic.

It was a Christmas Day like no other in their lifetimes. How could they ever forget the little white dove who brought about a Christmas miracle?

A Short Short Story

"The key to writing an effective short story is brevity," the writing instructor lectured the eight students seated around a wooden table in an auxiliary room in the local library. She continued, "After all, that's why it's called a 'short story'—You must practice if you want to become an effective writer. Your motto should be 'reduce, reduce, reduce.' Really work at it. Take your initial draft and cut it in half and so on."

One of the students asked, "How can we fit characterization, plot, themes, descriptions, and dialogue into such a brief story?"

"I wouldn't give you an assignment that I didn't think you could . . . more than handle . . . excel at. It takes practice. I suggest that you keep condensing your story until you reach the perfect balance of brevity and a story that works. You've all done it before for the five-minute read."

The instructor's words were inspiring. Jamie left class that evening determined to minimize the short story of which he had recently finished the first draft. When he returned to his dorm room, he went straight to his desk and withdrew the story from a cabinet. He was excited to get started on the second draft and to reduce the fifteen pages he had written to a number that would be acceptable to the instructor.

Jamie was confident that he had drafted an exemplary short story about curious eight-year-old twins, Hank and Gwen. He carefully edited the draft with his instructor's admonitions in mind. He strained to reduce the number of pages by eliminating many of the descriptions and much of the dialogue between the twins. His diminutive heroes now seemed to be acting in a void, but he plunged on.

He partly solved the dialogue by having them communicate in short phrases. He solved the description problem by making them short, such as, "The sky is blue." The two pages of characterization were reduced to three sentences by "telling" rather than "showing." The plot was shortened, and the themes were eliminated.

The story began in a high-end apartment not too far from Central Park in New York City. The twins' mother and father were recently divorced, and the twins lived with their mother.

The twins were bored. There was nothing good on TV. Hank had played his video games a hundred times. Gwen's doll's attire was worn to shreds. Their mother was shopping downtown and would be gone for hours.

Hank suggested to Gwen: "Let's go exploring in the neighborhood. It'll be fun."

Gwen responded, "I don't think we should do that. Mommy wouldn't let us go. When Mommy comes home and we aren't here, she'll freak out. We'd be in so much trouble. You know Mommy."

They argued back and forth but finally reached a compromise that they'd stay outside for no more than thirty minutes and wander no more than three blocks from their apartment building.

They stealthily went out the front door. The sky outside was blue and the air was fresh and clean. As soon as they began their journey, Hank suggested they hike to Central Park.

Gwen replied, "No way. The park is more than three blocks away. We might get lost." On the verge of tears, she added, "I don't want to."

"We won't get lost. Look at this thing I made."

Gwen looked puzzled, "What's that thing for?"

"Look at this. There's a chunk of heavy-duty chalk attached to the end of this stick. If I drag it like this, it makes a white line that tells us where we've been and how to get home."

Gwen cautiously asked, "What if someone erases it? You know, like the teacher does on the blackboard."

Hank asserted, "Ain't gonna happen—not within our half-hour."

The kids were unaware that a giant truck was washing down the streets and sidewalks in that section of the city on that particular day. They were unaware that wherever they went, their chalk line was erased.

Eventually, the twins discovered that their line had disappeared. There was no guide to help them get home. They began to wander from one neighborhood to another without finding their apartment.

Gwen came to the realization first: "We're lost," she said and began to cry.

Henry protested, "No we're not. C'mon, let's keep looking."

Gwen sat down on the curb and her crying got louder. "I want Mommy. How will we ever get home?"

Henry was not ready to give up. He helped Gwen to her feet. "C'mon, silly, let's go this way."

They walked in a new direction. They soon came upon a movie theater. From the posters it was clear that a horror film was showing. They loved horror movies and watched them at every opportunity. This was just such an opportunity.

Hank wasn't scared, and he knew he could protect Gwen from the monsters on the screen.

They paid for their tickets and entered the cold, dark theater. There were few other patrons.

Gwen had an ominous premonition about the place and wanted to leave.

Henry pointed out that they had paid for the tickets, and they wouldn't be able to get their money back. He said to her, "Now you're really being ridiculous. There's hardly anyone here. The movie is about to start. Just relax and enjoy it," Henry blurted. "The Blob vs. Godzilla. You can't beat that, Gwenster."

Gwen settled in to watch the flick, but she couldn't get comfortable. She had never been in such a dark theater. She strained her eyes but could just make out her brother's form next to her.

After watching the movie for a while, Gwen felt a large, clammy hand on her chest. She sat to Hank's left. The hand could not be his, because her chest was being gripped from the opposite side.

She glanced at Henry and perceived that he was in a panic state. She didn't think it was caused by the movie. She could barely make out the dark profile of a man wearing a gruesome monster mask. She tried to scream, but a scaly hand was pressed over her mouth and suppressed her effort.

She saw another monster grip Hank's arm and begin to pull him out of his seat and toward the exit.

Now the grip tightened on Gwen's own arm. She could see that her assailant also wore a monster mask. He yanked on her arm to pry her out of her seat. She fought hard to maintain her position.

That monster joked to the other one: "I got me a wildcat here."

The other monster claimed, "These kids ain't gonna be easy."

After a struggle, the monsters were able to gain control of the kids and hoisted them over their shoulders like burlap bags of grain. They carried them out to a parked car, forced thick ski masks over their heads, and stuffed them into the trunk. The twins were terrified.

When their mother returned from her shopping spree, she called for the twins but there was no answer. She thought they must be napping so she checked in their bedrooms, but they weren't there.

She called for the maid, Maria, who had been doing a thorough cleaning of the upstairs bathroom.

She asked in Spanish: "Maria, where are the children?"

Maria replied in broken English: "I taut dey were weeth you, Alice."

The mother replied angrily, "No they weren't with me. They must have snuck outside when you weren't looking. I'll deal with you later. Right now we must find the children!"

Alice called her ex-husband at his office. He was in a meeting, but when he was told it was an emergency, he hurried to the phone. She explained what had happened, and he immediately drove home.

They quickly organized a search party among neighbors, relatives, and friends. The twins had vanished!

The parents called the police, who promptly brought in the FBI. Because the twins were only eight, this was not considered a missing person case. The cops promptly called for an Amber Alert. Every effort was made over the next two weeks to find them. All failed.

After the official search ended, the parents kept looking. They always wondered what happened to their precious darlings, but the twins were never seen by their family again.

Jamie was delighted that he had reduced his story to three-and-one-half pages. He was proud of the fact that he had written it within the instructor's parameters. Or was it? Jamie began to have second thoughts. He read the story to his writing class. It took twelve minutes. He glanced at the instructor and thought he saw a look of disappointment and even criticism in her eyes. The students liked the story and generally made positive comments.

Then it was the instructor's turn. She exclaimed, "Jamie, your story is way too long! It could be substantially reduced without weakening the overall impact."

Jamie was frustrated but returned to his dorm and vowed to reduce the current story by one half. When he had done so, he read the story out loud. That's when he realized that he could effectively reduce the story again by half. He wanted to make it a perfect story, so he continued to reduce it by halves.

On the occasion of his next writing class Jamie's instructor inquired about his story. "Were you able to reduce its length as we discussed?"

"Yes. I reduced it substantially in accordance with your standards."

"Oh, good. Class, please pay attention. Jamie's story will be representative of how a short story can be made shorter through careful editing."

Turning to Jamie, she said, "Jamie, please read your story to the class."

Jamie looked up timidly and said, "I'd be happy to, but I lost the piece of paper that the story was written on, and I can't remember the word that was written on it."

The Secret

On their walk to Emily's, she broke the news to her boyfriend, Mark: "Don't be bitter, Mark." She said this like it was a foregone conclusion that he would be bitter.

His mouth turned down and his temperature went up. He tried to keep himself under control, because he knew that an outburst would make things worse. Instead, he played ignorant. At the same time he concealed his growing aversion to her change of mind.

He replied, "What in the hell are you talking about?"

"Don't give me that! I know you. No one can hold a petty grudge caused by jealousy better than you."

"I'm not bitter or jealous, Emmy. Why do you keep changing the subject, which is our plans that we made last month?"

"I don't think what you're saying is true . . . or fair."

"Not fair to whom, Em? I wanna know."

"Whose plans were they, Mark? I'll tell you what I think—they were all yours. You keep saying that I agreed to your plans. I didn't. I merely said that they sounded okay. My new plan isn't okay with you.

"But Em . . ."

"No buts! I won't attend Hayward State or San Jose State later this month just because you want me to. How convenient for you. Close to Berkeley. Close to your 'squeeze.' You want to keep a tight rein on your cute sweetheart, or should I say 'tart'? A school in the Bay Area would make it easy for you to attach me to you on a leash." She was so wound after this speech that she had to take a few deep breaths.

"Wrong, Emmy. All wrong."

"Am I really? When I got my scholarship to attend Boulder University, you faked that you were happy for me, but I knew that you were really going crazy that I'd be halfway across the country for four years. Get real, Mark! If we're really a couple, we have to give our relationship freedom to see what happens. Like with everything else, you are trying too hard to keep control. You always insist we play by your rules. We should give it time and space to breathe."

"Wow, have you changed your tune! Your new attitude is really screwed up. You're not giving any credit for how long we've been together. You're not being fair with me. I'm not some kind of monster. I've always been good to you, haven't I?"

"I guess so—but for your own self-interest."

Mark countered, "Yeah. Now you're making me out to be a controlling bastard who commands your every move and restrains your freedom. You know that's bullshit."

She listened to his increasingly caustic plea and felt he wasn't acting like the old Mark—the guy she fell in love with at the age of thirteen. She reflected, *Is this simply more of his manipulation? I don't know, but it's a matter of trust . . . always has been . . . always will be.*

She responded, "I admit, Mark, five years is a long time. We're practically married. Gosh, I've been on the pill for how long? Over four years."

She looked for a hopeful reaction, but his expression remained as skeptical as a lawyer listening to an adverse witness's exaggerated testimony. She continued in a gentle, less-defiant tone, knowing she wanted the sexual part of their relationship to remain their secret, as it always had been—as she had always trusted him to keep it.

"I admit that we talked about getting married this summer." She sucked in a deep breath and was trying to muster enough courage to proceed with what she had to say. "I know that this is hard on you—in your mind your future plans were settled. Yet, if you love me, please understand my position. Things have changed. I no longer am exclusively yours, at least for the foreseeable future."

To describe Mark as disgruntled would have been an understatement, but he allowed her to proceed.

"You have to recognize that our past relationship is over." She saw him wince. "You have to understand that. You have to let go of me."

He snapped, "Understand? What exactly do you want me to understand?"

"That I haven't known any other life . . . any other men . . . except you since I was thirteen. That's why I want to get away for a while so I can experience a different lifestyle. Everything in life eventually changes. I'm only eighteen, leaving home for the first time."

Her eyes focused on his, flashing uncharacteristic defiance. "I want to experience new adventures in a different environment with various new people."

Mark was crestfallen. It was a feeling he had never experienced with Emmy.

"So, you're dumping me just like that? Our relationship means nothing to you?"

"No Mark, it's not like that . . . you're blowing it out of proportion . . ."

He interrupted her. "Am I? That's exactly what it sounds like. 'Here today, gone tomorrow.' How could you do this to me? I never did anything to hurt you. I haven't cheated on you. I've never criticized you or gossiped about you. Emmy, you know I've always had your back. I've supported you in everything you've done."

She was reluctantly nodding.

"What more can I say, Emmy? I want you to be my wife! Is that so wrong?"

"That's all true. It's what makes this so difficult, but you're missing the point. I want to go to Boulder so I can be free to do what I want, not just what you want. I want to discover who I am.

"I don't want to get hung up in a long-distance relationship either, you know, with occasional weekends at Boulder or Berkeley," she continued. "I don't want to feel obligated to come home every vacation and be expected to spend all my time with you. I know I'll be expected to call you every night and to write long love letters, but I won't want to do that either.

"If I find a new boyfriend, how could I break the news without hurting you? I shudder to think about what your reaction would be."

He flinched at the notion of a new boyfriend and countered sardonically, "Then, what do you want?"

She nervously observed, "I guess you haven't been listening to me. I already was clear about what I want . . . that we always remain friends."

The tension drained from her face, and she began to feel disentangled. She was secretly elated, thinking, *I've actually done it. I've stood up to him.*

Outwardly, her face displayed her typical smile. "We can do that, can't we? There's no reason to become enemies. You've got to honor my wishes—I don't want to go to a school of your choice, and I don't want to get married this summer. We're too young to get tied down like that. Give me a chance to finish college. I hope you understand that?"

His downcast mood again became bitterly defensive. He jabbed, "I know what you want, Emily, you poser! You want to be free so you won't feel guilty when you meet guys and screw them. I bet you're looking forward to doing it with a whole array of guys at BU."

"Mark, listen to yourself. You're so wracked with jealousy that now you're just plain nasty. You figure by hurting me you'll get your way. You've done this maneuver before, but I won't fall for your ruse this time. You've rarely shown this side of you, but now you are out of control. That's the side of you I don't like. You scare me, and I don't have to take it! You're acting ugly."

"Bullshit! I'm not jealous at all."

She regarded him sternly. "You won't accept the idea of me being in love with another man. You can't stand the thought of losing me. You better shape up and be a man, or you're gonna ruin your life."

"Now you're the big know-it-all?"

"Well, I know you're pissing me off! I'm through with you. Don't try to contact me! It's over! I never want to see you again. I sure won't think about you anymore. You're old, stale news to me. Good-bye."

At that point Mark thought, *Should I let her go? There are plenty of girls who would love to . . . er . . . be with a Berkeley man.* He quickly weighed his options. *The problem is that I still love her and have loved her for most of my life. Yet, what is love really? Is it just having fun in bed? If so, then Emmy is awesome.*

He realized that his sullen musing was simply a subterfuge for his real motive: he could not let go of Emmy. He knew it would be an agonizing loss of the control over her he assumed he would have "'til death do us part." It would also be a staggering blow to his carefully cultivated ego. Finally, there would be nothing left from their relationship but a painful, persistent jealousy. He would never be able to get relief from the image of "his girl" naked with another man. This recurring nightmare already sickened and enraged him, and he felt like it would drive him crazy.

Mark couldn't stand it anymore. He had to drive the image of Em making love with another man out of his mind, and the only ways he could think of to do that were by bashing his head into a concrete wall or shooting himself. Neither of these options were palatable, but he had to do something.

What he did instead—he realized almost immediately—was a foolish, immature act. He screamed "NO!" so loudly it caused a startled Emmy to recoil.

She turned her head toward him with a concerned expression, and this momentary pause allowed him to catch up with her.

She turned around, saw him coming with a pained look on his face, and increased her pace. She heard his lumbering footsteps on the asphalt and—as he approached—his heavy breathing. She braced herself for a renewed verbal onslaught. Instead, she felt his hot breath in her ear and his bristly chin rubbing against her bare neck.

"Ick," she uttered and turned to push him away.

Before she could raise her arms to fend him off, he whispered, "I thought you loved me. Now, you're dumping me. No frigging way, Missy! You're not gonna be in such a hurry to dump me, my former loyal girlfriend."

He was revved up now. "I've got spies on the Boulder campus. If I find out that you're screwing other guys or 'dating' a new boyfriend, I'm gonna spill the beans to your parents about what their so-called innocent baby has been up to for the past four years—since she was a middle school fourteen-year-old—and that she's still doing it at Boulder. I'll also tell them that you had an abortion last year but that you plan to keep the next one whether you're married or not."

"That's a lie!" she screamed.

"Yeah, so what? You lied to me recently about going to college in the Bay Area and getting married next summer. News flash: I've just changed my plan. Why not get it over with tonight? If you don't agree to our plans about goin' to one of the state colleges and marriage, I'm gonna tell everything to your parents tonight."

She stopped to consider Mark's threat. Then, she hurried toward her home. Her head was spinning, and she slowed her pace. Mark was still hanging by her ear like he wanted to crawl inside.

In a flat voice, devoid of any emotion and drained of any vestiges of her former passion for this guy, she cynically exclaimed, "Go ahead and tell them. I'm not giving in to your blackmail. See if I care, Mark. You can't hold me back any longer! What did you think I was gonna do at college—only go to class and study? If you did, you're naive."

She turned and grinned wickedly at him.

He pulled his face away from her neck and snorted as his anger reached a feverish state. He was devastated. He figured she was calling his bluff, but he had never been insulted like that. He assumed her diatribe was intended to hurt him, and to his distress, she had scored a bull's-eye.

Emmy's position was that she hoped that he'd accept the obvious, give up, and go home. She thought, *I don't think he has any intention to follow through with his threat, but now I can tell his mood has changed again—from dejected to determined.*

He was still walking beside her. She decided to rub his nose in more shit.

"Gee, Mark, did you really think I was going to spend my time pining away for you? Get real! I wanna go to college and have fun. Do you even know what fun is? I'll only be a freshman once, and I plan to take advantage of it. My dorm is coed, so what do you expect? I happen to know that you've been getting it on with Berkeley girls and probably high school girls too. I've got spies of my own."

She smiled slyly. "You have never been faithful to me, and you won't be loyal even if I promise to be loyal to you. What's good for the gander is good for the goose. Anyway, we're done, so there's no reason to talk about being loyal."

Emmy was painfully aware of the danger if Mark were to tell their secret to her folks. They were ardent churchgoers and so old-fashioned and naive about her sexual activities. She figured, *If they discover the truth, they'll hold me hostage, cancel college, ground me for life, and disinherit me. Under their strict Christian rules, to pay penance I'll be forced to get a menial job as a cashier at 7-11 or stocking shelves at Walmart. I won't be allowed to buy a car or have any friends. They'll keep an eye on me every minute. No doubt they'll confiscate my birth control pills and prevent me from getting any more. I'll never get to enjoy sex again unless I marry some born-again Christian who also works at a menial job. I'll be a hostage chained to a wall in hell.*

They approached her home. She was hanging on the edge of a vertical cliff and about to get her fingers stomped on. There was no escape. Yet, she was too stubborn to give in to his ugly threats. The lights were on in the living room, which meant that her parents were still awake, probably waiting up for her.

She began considering a change in strategy. She couldn't stand to witness the expressions on her parents' faces, which would turn from bitter disappointment to anger to righteous retribution.

She blew up at Mark. "Damn you for putting me in this position. If you really loved me, you'd keep your mouth shut. Why don't you show a lover's compassion for me and keep walking?"

She worried, *If he goes through the front door, I'm dead! I know that he doesn't like change. Once he decides on a course of action, he always follows through. I suspect it is his need for control.*

Her body was trembling while they stood on the front walkway staring at her house. She figured he was stalling with the hope she might accept his "offer." She wavered. Then the unexpected happened . . . she began running down the street away from her home, as if flight would exempt her from her dilemma.

Mark yelled facetiously, "Hey, Em, where do you think you're going? You can't escape your problems that easily."

She stopped, which allowed him to catch her. He placed both hands on her elbow to turn her around and guide her back to her house. The light above the front door suddenly came on, as if extending an invitation to enter.

He whispered, "You're shaking, Babe. I guess my proposed revelations to your parents are getting to you. When the shit hits the fan, don't cry that I didn't warn you. If you don't agree to my terms, kiss off your life."

"I don't care," she spat out. "If I do agree to them, I might as well kiss off my life anyway."

Her mind was made up, and strangely she felt a sense of relief. She figured that the ordeal would hurt him more than her. She saw right through his arrogance and knew in the end she was stronger than him.

With the light shining above, she declared "NEVER!"

The front door swung open, and Emmy's father emerged, his face shining to see the couple. He was adorned in an ugly purple dressing gown.

"Mark, what a surprise. Hello, Emily. Come on in. Don't be shy. Mom and I were just making some cocoa. Want some?

Emmy remained as silent as a corpse, but Mark muttered, "Sure."

They stepped inside.

"Tell me, Emily," her father asked cheerfully, "Did you have a nice day?"

Emmy merely grunted.

Her father led them to the living room. The couple was solemn, almost morose.

Her mom appeared suddenly, as if she had been hiding behind the sofa.

Emmy said, "Oh, hi, Mom."

"Hello, dear." She sensed right away that something was terribly wrong with Emmy. "Honey, what's the matter?"

Emmy didn't answer but glanced dolefully at Mark. Her skin was pale, and her face was wrought with tension, like a soldier waiting for an incoming bomb to hit. Her eyes hurled daggers at Mark, but she knew that it was more likely she was the one who would get stabbed to death. She imagined Mark grasping a stake and thrusting it through her heart.

Suddenly, Mark was ashamed of the abuse they had vented at each other, and he realized Emmy was right. What a dickhead he had become when he learned about her new plans and that she wasn't going to marry him. He recognized that he had become mean, vindictive, and ruthlessly jealous. He knew that his love for her was real, but he had let his erotic desire overwhelm his tender feelings for her. Love had taken a back seat to his hostility and jealousy.

In contemplation of his dirty scheme to scare Emmy, he knew it was time for a complete turnaround. *How could I even think about doing it? Yet, is it possible to get rid of my hostility and regain the sentiment I've had for her? I guess I'll soon find out. I earnestly believe I've always done the right thing for Em. Hadn't she admitted that? Why abandon that devotion now?*

Suddenly, the fun times they had together flashed through his mind: trips to the beach and learning to surf together; hugging while swimming in the frigid ocean; picnics on the meadow grass nestled in the foothills; walking home from school holding hands and kissing; madcap birthday celebrations; making love for the first time—so tender and sweet; and many more adventures.

I know I will never lose these memories, and I never again want to think of her as a conniving bitch. That is simply not part of her character. He further reflected, *She's always been a sweet girl. I've been arrogant, selfish, and insensitive. No more!*

The ugly side of his character surfaced, and it was right there waiting for him to push the button. *I'd hate myself for it. Face it, Mark—you've been a prisoner to your false expectations and engaged too much in the egoism that trapped you since she changed her plans. No wonder Emmy hates me now. Well, I'm getting rid of all that right now.*

He felt on the brink of tears and wondered, *Am I feeling sorry for myself, Em, both of us? The circumstances that have led to this cliff? Do I throw us into the abyss and ruin two lives, or do I walk away? It's true that I have controlled certain parts of her life. Now it's time to take control of mine. When I converted Emmy from an innocent, sweet girl to a passionate, sexual one, was I acting in Em's best interests or my own? Sex on demand, anytime, was my only concern. It wasn't fair to Emmy, and in the end, it was toxic to me.*

The sight of her father's beaming face watching the daughter he treasured triggered Mark's growing doubt in his malicious scheme to ruin Emmy. His conscience was now crushing him, burning a hole in his heart.

He decided what he must do for Emmy and her parents—to step up and be a man for once. If he lost the girlfriend whom he loved, instead of sulking, he could be happy knowing he had made her happy. Ultimately, he cared more about her than anything else. He sighed, thinking, *Caring is the most valuable gift that love can bestow.*

Emmy noticed his smile and wondered, *Is he gloating over his upcoming victory, or is it my imagination that he has changed from the degenerate who had a wolfish smirk earlier? I haven't seen his warm smile in quite a while. Here goes nothing!*

She bravely turned and asked Mark in a flat tone: "Don't you have something to say to my parents?"

Her parents looked expectedly at Mark, who simply said, "Yes I do."

Emmy sat on the edge of her chair, with her head down, her eyes averted, and holding her breath. She mused to herself, *Should I make a break for the door and hitch to Boulder or go ahead and tell them the news myself?*

Mark hesitated, staring at her parents' expectant smiles before he began.

"I just want to say, with Emmy leaving in a couple of days . . ." He turned to Emmy who raised her head but maintained her blank stare: "I love you with all my heart. You make my world light up."

Emmy burst loudly into tears.

They all stared at her with a mixture of sympathy and joy.

He proceeded, "I want you to have the best college experience. Thank you for being so gracious during our friendship. It has meant more to me than anything I could ever experience."

Emmy was still crying, and he was fighting off tears. He prepared to leave but her father asked, "But Mark, I was under the impression that you expected our dear girl to attend Hayward State?"

Mark glanced at both parents, who waited for his response. He turned back to Emmy, busy drying her tears.

"I want her to be happy by going to the school that she, not I, chooses."

Mark accepted warm hugs from both parents and wondered if they'd be his last hugs from them. "I'm sorry I can't stay for cocoa, but I just remembered I have to be somewhere. Good night, folks."

He managed a glance and a polite smile at Emmy, whose smeared face didn't reveal anything. As he left the house, he looked back one last time. He saw more tears flowing, her upper body heaving, and a tinge of hope in her eyes.

As he began his journey up the street toward his own home, he felt happy for Emmy, but at the same time, he was the saddest he had ever been. He was alone in the dark, his emotions in a stupor. The frustrations that were below the surface suddenly erupted and then quickly dissipated as if something had stolen them.

He heard a door slam and an urgent plea, "Mark, wait up . . . please!" He turned around just as she reached him, and she saw something in him she had never seen before. "Honey, you've been crying."

Before he could respond, she kissed him passionately on his lips. "I really mean this. I love you and always will, no matter what happens. What you did in there tonight makes me realize that you really do want me to be happy. It struck me how much compassion and love you have for me. You are willing to let go of me, and that's the purest sign of love.

"I don't know what made you change your mind, but you showed courage and maturity. Mark, you are a man, my man . . . and I love that man. I'll never take you for granted again. I'm gonna miss you more than you can ever imagine. As for 'us', why don't we play it by ear? Write to me, call me, both!"

"Em, I appreciate what you just said. It means everything to me. What I told your folks was all true. I love you for who you are, but my gut tells me that we shouldn't have any contact until we meet next June. In the meantime, do whatever you want to, just don't tell me about it. When I see you next time, we can talk about what our future holds for us."

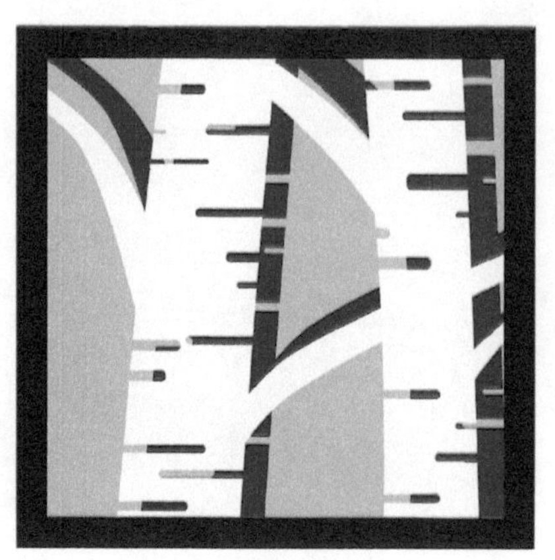

The Smiles
We Left Behind

"Walt Whitman was the best poet America has ever produced," asserted a spirited Agnes. Her face screwed up and was turning crimson, sure signs she was digging her teeth into the argument. "Your claim that it was Robert Frost shows that you don't know what you're talking about. Emily Dickinson was a close second, but Frost was way, way down the list. Face facts, Will—you don't know anything about poetry. I'll bet you've never even read anything by your hero, Robert Frost, except that poem about the road going two ways. Such basic, high school symbolism!"

"Get real, Agnes!" Will hissed with a venom rare for him. "I'm tired of your usual shit. Frost was the best. The American public has said so. You are the most obnoxious know-it-all since Harry Gardiner, that guy who used to live down the street."

Agnes paused and reflected about that for a few seconds. "I remember Harry. Whatever happened to him?"

"He died awhile back—probably of 'know-it-all-itis,' which is what you're headed for! It's a slow, painful swelling of the head."

Agnes would have none of it and maintained her constant, cynical stare. Then she exploded with a burst of sarcasm as if it had been bubbling like magma under the surface.

"Robert Frost! Good God! You've got to be joking, Will. We can dig his book out of the box in the attic and reread it. But I can tell you that his 'Road Less Traveled' was a sloppy metaphor at best, and hardly engendered any serious comment by seasoned poetry critics. You know, Will, Frost's name can't even be mentioned with such American poetry greats as Whitman and Dickinson."

She paused and in a crotchety tone barked, "We'll have no more discussion about Robert Frost in this house!"

Agnes sat down in her favorite chair and picked up the book with the gold-leaf edges from the table beside it. There was an ornate marker placed halfway through Whitman's *Leaves of Grass*. Will peered at her book with a mixture of awe and disgust.

"This is my third reading," she said with pride. "I read some every day like I used to read the Bible." She stared at it lovingly. "You should try reading a few poems in it sometime," and added, with a snicker, "although I doubt you'd understand it."

That got his dander up but not enough to cause an explosion. He contemplated taking the dog for a peaceful walk in the park. He bitterly asked her: "Why do you read so much?"

"It helps me to measure where I am in my life."

"You don't need a book. I can tell you that."

He could feel himself on the edge and wanted to avoid an eruption of the anger that had built up. The last time that happened, it was followed by days of remorseful depression. He was often miserable over Agnes, but she never seemed to get worked up about him.

One of his golfing buddies had asked him once why he stayed with her, advising Will: "If my wife treated me that way, I'd pull the plug on her really fast."

Will had to answer that, honestly, he didn't know. "What should I do?"

His buddy just shrugged, feeling that he had gone far enough and not wanting to be responsible for their break-up.

Will told him: "There was a time many years ago that we separated and almost got divorced."

"What happened?" his friend asked, not looking surprised. "What caused it?"

But Will didn't want to go into it because it hurt too much to dredge up those ancient memories.

"It happened a million years ago," he had said, "and I want to bury it deep."

As his memory of this conversation with his buddy evaporated, he remained lost in thought: *We were so young; we'd only just begun.*

In the present, Agnes was still on the attack. "Will—snap out of it! What were you thinking about? You seemed like you were a million light years away. I was talking to you—pay attention! I was saying that your knowledge of poetry is inferior, like your knowledge of everything else in your life. You have never been willing or able to think things through. It's a big flaw you have. That's what causes you to choose Frost over Whitman. Ha ha! How can I explain to you the beauty that leaps off Walt Whitman's pages?"

"I just don't like some of that stuff you read. It twists and turns me around and seems to intentionally try to confuse me," he defended himself half-heartedly. "Hell with it!"

"Yeah, the only leaves you can handle, Will, are those on your lawn—and those you clean up with a rake because you still don't know how to operate the leaf blower you bought six months ago." She uttered a wicked chuckle. "You owned a garden and repair shop for over forty years, and you still can't assemble a simple blower."

"These things take time, Agnes." As soon as his words left his mouth, he knew they were a mistake, fuel for her inexhaustible store of criticism and cynical comedy of which he inevitably bore the brunt. "Golly, Agnes, you've got your sharpest knitting needle out this morning, and you're poking me with it more than that sweater you're making."

"What are you complaining about?" she asked contemptuously. "At least you're still alive to feel it. Better than poor Bill Sturgess."

Will grimaced at her mention of their retired firefighter friend, who had been fit and showed all signs of living to a hundred. Bill was at least ten years younger and thirty pounds lighter than Will when he suddenly passed away, keeling over on the tennis court during a lighthearted match with Will.

That had been a real eye-opener for Will, but he was not sure as to what. Agnes had used the opportunity to bombard him with an array of health products, advice, and exercise programs. He secretly threw away the products and advice, which were no better than good old common sense. As for the gym exercises, he disregarded them, continuing his twice-a-week golf routine and an occasional tennis game.

All in all, at seventy, Will was content with his life, except when his wife was playing the role of needler, cynic, and custodian of the memories of the family's afflictions. In recent years, she had become pricklier than a desert cactus.

He said, "If you believe the rumors—and, knowing Bill, I have no reason not to—he went out a happy man."

Agnes hadn't heard them and was curious. She asked, "How so?"

"'Cause he had been bonking a thirty-year-old gal twice or more per day, practically under his wife, Dorothy's nose."

"You love that secret love affair stuff, don't you? You know, Will—it's called cheating."

"You're one to talk!"

Will sometimes thought about doing exactly what Bill did—using some retirement money to set up a much younger gal in a "love nest." He might have done it too. The problem was not that he loved Agnes but that he felt a strange, cockeyed loyalty to her. He was willing to sacrifice all the enjoyment and pleasure that a man can have in his waning years out of sheer fidelity to her, with the same kind of doggedness that compels a sea captain to go down with his ship.

Agnes was now up and buzzing around the room, adjusting and rearranging things, a moving target to avoid any of Will's comeback barbs.

"You know," he said, "I'm not gonna argue with you anymore."

"Well, that'll be a welcome relief."

"No, I mean it. The next thing I know you'll bring up music—probably that classical junk—or you'll pretend to be the queen of rhythm and blues. I know that BS is coming, and I don't want any part of it. I'm going to bed and read."

He didn't need to add it, but it was as if he had said, "So there!"

Agnes would not let it alone. "Behind on your comic books, huh? 'Spidey-Man' calls?"

Ouch, he thought, *she's quick. Always has been. I can't keep up with her. She always just turns me into the chump. I'm like a team which is constantly on the defensive . . . So what if I like to read comics, or even just look at the pictures?*

He weakly replied, "There's some pretty good information in them, and it's none of your business anyway."

She scoffed, asking, "What have you ever learned from a comic book?" She didn't let him answer, saying snidely: "Let me guess. How about being a detective and solving crimes from reading 'Dick Tracy'? How about learning how to become a mouse from reading 'Mickey Mouse'?"

"Very clever, Agnes. You love to make fun of me. You never stop, do you? It must give you a big ego boost. No, Agnes, I'm not surprised at anything demeaning you say to me."

"I don't know what you're talking about." She was so used to his hostile looks and barbs that they didn't faze her anymore.

"Sure, you do." Taking a more familiar tack, he asked, "Since you're such a smarty pants, tell me which was the greatest baseball team of all time?"

"That's easy: the 1927 Yankees with Ruth, Gehrig, and a bunch of other great players. Anything else you want to know about sports?" She jutted her jaw and stared at him defiantly.

"I'm not surprised you know all about that team as you were pushing fifty that year."

"Now look who's talkin', Old Folks."

"Agnes, sometimes you make me sick!"

Now that she knew she had him on the ropes, she went in for the kill: "Okay, Sports King, try football."

His feelings hurt and hanging his head, he mumbled, "I'm not playing this game anymore."

"C'mon, Will, don't be that way," she snickered. "Pick any sport. Your choice."

He stood before her with his eyes fixed on the ground, the way a beaten servant appears before his cruel master, and said in a low tone: "You're something, Agnes: one of a kind. You can't go a day without a clever remark here, a bit of sarcasm there, and a full measure of bullyism. You have a need to take control of any discussion to prove yourself—to make sure you always look good. While you're doing that, you make sure that I look like a stupid wimp. I know all about your sneaky tricks, but I can't seem to stop them. I admit I wasn't ever much, but at least I made a living for us for over forty years. And I guarantee that in those days you would not have tried to get away with all your crap."

Agnes perched like a bird on the living room sofa. She noticed him grimace during his diatribe. Will was in obvious pain. It was in his knee from an old high school football injury. He was a big man: six foot three, averaging 240 pounds over the years, which was a lot of bulk for his damaged knees to support. Her acid attack now turned to concern.

"I keep telling you to get to a doctor to have that damn knee checked out. You know, Will, it's not my knee, but it seems to be getting worse."

"And I keep telling you 'til I'm blue in the face—look at me, Agnes. See how blue my face is?—that my knees are fine. There's nothing wrong with them. So, will you shut up about them?"

"Will, don't get mad at me. I was just concerned about you."

He gave her an incredulous expression and the wide-eyed look of the martyr, a role that he had adopted easily over the years.

"You know darn well if I went to see a doctor every time I had a little ache and pain, they'd charge me room rent and for the coffee machine in the reception area. Hey, no one asked you anyway. I don't want you butting into my personal business unless I ask you to."

He glared at her again for emphasis and put this tough, leathery old bird on the verge of tears.

She reflected, *Typical Will; the only time he's mean and aggressive is when I try to help him.* Agnes tried a weak comeback to go on the offensive again: "Your reference to running your shop for forty years surprised me. You're such an old coot I thought you couldn't recall anything more than three days ago."

He set her back by responding in a stinging tone: "You'd be surprised how much I remember from our so-called 'salad days.' It might have been a long time ago, but certain events caused enough pain that I remember them. Oh, yeah—I can never forget them."

Surprised by his bold assertion about the acuteness of his memory, which she had lately assumed to be fading fast, she tentatively inquired, "What memories, dear?"

Sensing he finally had gained a rare advantage, he responded, "A lot of them that show you in a bad light. That's what kind."

He smiled in triumph. He felt he had achieved the moral high ground in an ongoing quarrel that had started years ago.

Suspecting where he was coming from, Agnes skillfully slipped into the role of the innocent bystander, which she had played so many times in the past. She raised her eyebrows in mock disbelief and said simply, "Me?" Before he could say anything, she asked,

"Are you talking about me being part of your bad memories? I don't believe it. Maybe you made them up, playing out some kind of victim role."

Will shook his head. It seemed as if every one of their arguments circled back to the same point: Will's memory was bad, and he filled it in with his imagination of being a victim in a drama that never happened. *Bottom line*, he reflected, *she makes me out to be a liar and a whiner.*

Many of their arguments had their origin in the distant past. He couldn't speak for Agnes, but he certainly didn't engage in these marital slugfests for pleasure. They made him feel like an old and withered elephant warding off a pride of lions as it slowly trudged its final journey to the traditional elephant burial ground.

Just as the elephant's instincts guided it in an incomprehensible way, so Will's and Agnes's instincts, developed from the time of their wedding fifty years ago, guided and instructed them in their fierce daily ritual of argument, put-downs, one-upmanship, slander, and lies. An observer might reasonably infer that they hated each other, but it just wasn't that simple.

As she always did, Agnes reverted to her most effective weapon, the denial: "Never, Will. You're mistaken. I never did anything in my life that would put us in a bad light. You need to get off that kick!" She shook her close-cropped gray head as if by vigorously shaking it, her denial would be strengthened.

Will knew better. His mind was clear this morning. There were no maddening gaps or gray areas between reality and his memory. It wasn't like trying to see through a dense fog.

He boldly asserted, "You'd change your tune if I reminded you of the event with two words."

Agnes was confused—and petrified. Was she about to lose to Will in her own game? She owned him in these word games, and she only had one flaw that they were aware of. Would the old bastard use that flaw now?

Time to counterattack; she displayed a disgusted face, and spat out, "You don't have anything on me! You're bluffing, Will, and I find it ugly and demeaning. You know, Will, I won't stand for it!"

"Bobby Smith."

Agnes froze and turned white as one of the sheets she had just changed. Perspiration immediately appeared in thin beads on the exposed areas of her body. However, she wasn't going to give in yet. Time to defend! *Behind the barricades, Agnes, to fight off his strategic use of the worst episode of our life together, starting in junior high school, a few years before we got married.* She thought, *He brings this up for revenge. My God—thirty years after the fact!*

Despite the sweat, which was now dripping in places, she said casually, "Bobby? What did you say the last name was?"

"I said 'Smith.'"

Her expression was still blank.

"Bobby Smith . . . You know, Agnes—your former boyfriend. The guy you were sleeping with while I was home alone taking care of our young kids."

His thin smile turned to a sour grimace at the memory. He wasn't really enjoying his rhetorical victory as much as anticipated.

"Oh, yeah, that Smith." Her tone sounded like she was reading the label of a vial of rat poison. "What about him?"

"So, you remember him?"

"What did you expect? Sure, I remember Bobby, but I'm surprised you still do."

He looked at her like she was crazy.

"Really, Agnes! How could you say that? The name 'Bobby Smith' will burn in my brain forever. It's like saying the name 'Hitler' to a Jewish fella. It's a name I will *never* forget. The thought of getting revenge on that crumb bum will probably be the last conscious thought I have."

"If you hated him so much over all these years, why didn't you seek your revenge years ago?"

Will figured it was a good question, so he answered with the truth: "For your sake."

"Then why are you bringing up a subject today that is so unpleasant for both of us?" she retorted. "What I think is that it should be buried deep in the realm of forgotten events and burned to a heap of ashes."

"I brought it up because you put down my memory. I admit that my memory has been slipping, especially since I retired. I wanted to prove to you that there are certain memories that I still have and will continue to have as long as . . . That scene between you and Bobby is still vivid in my brain . . . and still hurts."

"If truth be told, Will, my fling with Bobby Smith was really nothing. You know that." She looked at him hopefully, then frowned. "I can't believe it. You haven't brought it up in thirty years. You're just being vindictive, but I don't know why."

It was as if he didn't hear her. He said, "That guy Bobby was really a jerk. He used drugs, drank too much, and almost broke up our marriage."

She knew what he was saying was true, and that he was just warming to the task. Her face turned crimson. "I was just a silly young girl with a crazy infatuation."

"Agnes, quit trying to feed me your line of BS! You still think I'm a Big Stupid. I remember the Bobby thing like it happened yesterday! For starters, you were not still a young girl in ribbons and pigtails. He came onto you when you were at least thirty-five and a mother of three kids. And worst of all, don't you dare soft-pedal the feelings you had for the jerk. You used to sneak off to that dirtbag bar full of drunks to listen to Bobby play his shitty guitar. I know what that scene was like 'cause I sneaked over there one night to see what my wife found so fascinating. It didn't take long to see that her eyes were only focused on the crappy guitar player. It wasn't long after that you left with Guess Who?"

Will's bitterness was dripping like blood from a head wound.

"I didn't know you were still upset about that Bobby thing . . ." she wisely cut herself off.

"Here's the main reason it still bothers me: you were in love with the guy, or at least you convinced yourself you were. You told me you were, even when you came back."

Tears filled her eyes, but really, even Agnes wasn't sure whether they were for the hurt she had caused Will or her long-lost love, Bobby. The two merged in her mind so that she could never separate them anyway.

"'Member that?" He was trying to recall a specific incident, but her mind was still drifting through the labyrinth created by the passage of time, so she ignored him. That didn't help matters.

He commented caustically: "Still hooked on that guy? Can't get your mind off him, huh?"

She nodded but made no other response.

"I can still recall your bags sitting in front of the house," he continued. "You had ordered the kids to their rooms. That asshole backed his old brown station wagon down the driveway and stopped in front of the bags. There was no sign of you. He loaded your luggage into the rear of the wagon and stood out there waiting for you.

"I suppose you were saying good-bye individually to the kids. I heard a lot of crying and begging you not to go, but you were oblivious to their pleas. You came out into the sunlight, hopped into Bobby's car, and he tore off down the driveway. You didn't say a word to me. Not even a wave."

Now his voice was stained with sadness. "No, I take that back. When Bobby pulled his wagon back up the driveway, I saw you stick out your hatless head from the passenger window, but you didn't wave at me or the kids (who had all assembled out front), or smile, or even nod your head.

"You just stared back at us . . . an eerie stare like we were in a museum diorama and you were checking it out—trying to freeze us in the scene like specimens of a lost Brazilian tribe. Or maybe you were arranging us within your picture frame for the classic photo to remember us by while you cavorted around the country with Bobby and his band.

"It spooked me how you could be so frigid to the kids and me while welcoming a virtual stranger with your warm, devoted embrace. The way Bobby had changed you, turned you into a heartless creature with so little compassion for the family who really cared for you. I figured that it was probably better that the kids and I had seen the last of you."

She decided to stick her neck out and ask a question that she hadn't asked in thirty years and to which he hadn't had an answer in that time. "Do you have any love left for me?"

"For you?"

"No, Will, for Batgirl!"

He smirked.

"Of course, for me."

"This may sound harsh, but my answer is . . . not really. I haven't since you and Bobby drove down our driveway, leaving us. That was it for me!"

Now, real tears flowed down her cheeks and she had difficulty speaking. She said softly and with no trace of bitterness: "Despite the complication with Bobby, I didn't know that's how you felt about me all these years. Maybe I just assumed—obviously, wrongly—that you loved me. It was something we never talked about . . .

"None of the kids have ever held it against me. Did you know that the first morning we were together, I told Bobby that it wasn't going to work out, that I couldn't leave the kids with you?"

"That doesn't sound right, Agnes. It sounds like you were telling him that you believed I was incapable of raising the kids by myself."

"I guess that I meant something like that—that I didn't think their dad had the right tools and enough time to raise them properly. By coming back, I thought I was doing you a favor. I also felt that the kids needed their mother. It took me a couple of days to fully realize that I was in the wrong place with the wrong person, even though I loved Bobby. I was certain that returning home to the kids was the right thing to do."

"You know, Agnes, I never was sure why you came home to us—why you didn't just keep going with him. That's what you wanted . . . It wasn't the kids and it certainly wasn't me."

She wanted to respond, to talk about the importance of motherhood, the family home, and loyalty, but he didn't afford her a chance.

"Don't get me wrong—I understood why Bobby felt so hurt when you reversed course and came back to your family. You were in your midthirties, a very attractive woman, with a good sense of humor and intelligent. In other words, you were a desirable woman to be with."

"Look at me now! I no longer have any attractiveness nor any charms. I'm not any fun to be with. I'm a shrew with a nasty attitude toward everything except my kids and grandkids. I certainly no longer have a sense of humor, except maybe a cynical one. Will, you should have dumped me a long time ago. In fact, you would have been better off if I had just stayed on the road with Bobby."

She paused to take a deep breath and asked, "So, where are we now? We don't have many years to go. If we're going to set this right between us, we'd better start pretty soon."

Will looked at her and thought about what she had said. He agreed with most of it. The only real question was whether, at their age, it was worth it. He realized it would take considerable effort.

He finally said, "You're sixty-eight and I'm no spring chicken at sixty-nine. You always remind me that I'm as dumb as a juvenile male goat whose idea of fun is bashing his head into a wall. But what about my good looks?"

"You've never been a Paul Newman," she laughed. "And you're not sixty-nine. You're 70!"

"Okay, then, let me ask you something. I'm an old goat; whatever modest good looks I had disappeared over the years. I'm dumb as a doornail. I can't tell Walt Whitman from Walt Miller our garage mechanic. And I haven't been frisky in bed for you for many years. So, why have you stayed with me all these years, except for your brief fling with the infamous Bobby? Please make some sense of this for me."

She kept her eyes focused on him, trying to figure out why he was asking this question—what was his angle? Her smile was the same thin smile she had when she asked him last night whether the Royals beat the Twins.

He noticed her shallow, aloof gaze and said, "It shouldn't take you long. My list of accomplishments is short, and my outstanding traits are nil—at least compared to a class guy like Bobby. So, I again lay it out there for you—a pitch right into your wheelhouse—go ahead and smack it out of the ballpark! Why have you stayed with me?"

"Lady's Choice—you tell me why you've stayed with a cranky smarty-pants like me? A gal like me who cheated on you. Who hurt you? Who went about indifferently destroying your pride?"

"I've got a one-word answer for you: Sex. The notion of not having it was—as the kids say—a bummer."

His answer stunned her. She reflected, *Most women love to hear from their partners that they're good in the sack and not simply taken for granted. I guess I'm not an exception.*

Will realized he had hit the mark and hoped he could politely end their conversation. But he then made one of those statements that was equivalent to the goat butting its head against the wall.

As she was getting up to go to the kitchen to fix something for them to eat, he said with a faraway look: "I remember our bedroom activities during our go-go years like they were yesterday. During those years, you were . . . how should I put it? . . . wild in bed. We were all over each other. I thought I had gone to heaven. Our sexual antics led us to do it anywhere. I remember one time we were doing it in a dark corner of a movie theater."

His blunt recollection wiped out the floating feeling that the pair had been enjoying, popping a bubble that had enveloped them with a renewal of their warmth and goodwill toward each other. Agnes's embarrassment was bursting out in a face becoming redder and angrier, but he wouldn't shut up.

"Yeah, we were goin' hot and heavy 'til the usher found us in the beam of his powerful flashlight," he said. "That kid was cool, though. He never shone the light on our faces, sparing us the embarrassment in our small town. He didn't even kick us out of the theater."

Agnes laughed despite her embarrassment. She was able to set that aside, thinking it was fun to reminisce about their early sexual exploits, which Will wasn't ashamed to glorify, depending on the incident. It provided her with a feeling of immense satisfaction to know that all that sexual gratification had led directly to their four wonderful kids. She decided to chime in.

"I was glad he kept the light on our lower extremities since I didn't have any make-up on. The face of a sixteen-year-old girl trapped in a bright beam of light that exposed all her guilt and frustration, I can assure you, would not have been a pretty sight. I'm sure it would have looked ghastly, as the pimplefaced kid posing as an usher in that God-awful uniform could have attested. Bless his heart that he didn't flash our faces."

"That experience was such a close call that, if I remember correctly, it scared you off any sex for a month," Will added. "You wouldn't do it anywhere, even in the back of your brother's van, which was usually a safe space for us. Man, was that month frustrating!"

"Was it really that long?'

"Yep. Seemed like three years!"

Will was pleased. They hadn't taken a stroll down memory lane in a long time. It was fun, and he had forgotten how funny Agnes could be once he wound her up. Her personality was sharp and irreverent. He reflected, *She sure as hell ain't no church marm.*

He knew that her rebukes could sting the innocent and guilty alike. Even her children weren't exempt. She called them "zingers," but he just called them mean, and he had seen her targets brought to their knees. On occasion she might apologize later, but that didn't always happen if she felt justified in her action.

Television was becoming more popular, and Agnes was almost always at home watching it. The news programs were her favorite, and she switched from channel to channel to catch the weather girl in action. For unknown reasons, Agnes was fascinated and at the same time disdained the poor weather girl on each channel. She would call up and even write letters to the station to complain about weather girl antics during the reports. She especially scorned what she called "sexual suggestiveness: or manteasing." The caked-on make-up and beehive hairdos drove her crazy. They were all "material girls" to her, and she spewed a steady stream of wicked commentary about them.

Will, on the other hand, tried not to pay any attention to "Queen Crabby," as he called her, because he enjoyed checking out the weather girls' shapely bodies.

Will hoped for a little peace between them for the rest of the day, so he changed to a more lighthearted subject: "Why do you think we had four kids together . . . at least I think we did?"

She made an expression that asked, "What are you trying to imply?"

He shrugged innocently.

She said, "If you're trying to say that one of our children is from Bobby, you're dead wrong! For one thing, Mr. Paranoid, the timing was way off. I only saw Bobby for four months, and I know I didn't get pregnant during or following that time. In the back of my mind, I knew you always worried about that possibility."

"You're right about that." Secretly, he thought, *I was almost sure of it, and that's another thing that has been ripping me up during all these years. Now I find out that they were sneakin' around and fuckin' for four months, and not just the one month I've always believed. Holy shit!*

Outwardly, Will looked skeptical and slightly ill.

But Agnes said in an uncompromising tone: "There's just no way Bobby's sperm could have made one of our babies. Three of them had already been born, and Becky didn't come until long after I had said good-bye to Bobby."

She pulled a typical Agnes move; she pointed her tongue straight at him like a sharp dagger aimed at his heart. He quickly raised his hands there as if she had plunged it in.

She continued, "Look, buster, it was your sperm that impregnated me four times to produce four perfect kids. Next question?"

"Maybe so, but along came Bobby! What did he have that I didn't? That's a question that's bothered me for thirty years. Was he working with bigger equipment? Satisfying you where I couldn't? What was it, Agnes? I never asked you before because I was afraid to. I was out of my mind with jealousy, and I was afraid of what I might do to Bobby . . . and you."

"But, Will . . ."

"Don't you 'but' me, Agnes! The worst part was imagining you lying with that creep and him rolling over on top of you, doin' it over and over with him, shrieking in joy that you never had with me."

"Stop, Will!" She looked at him, panic in her eyes. "How did you know we made love a number of times?"

His eyes narrowed to slits, and he bellowed at her furiously: "Because you told me!"

All she could think to say was: 'Will, at least give me a merit badge for honesty."

Her wry smile indicated she was ready for a volcanic eruption. By candidly admitting her full amorous relationship with Bobby and revealing that their affair had actually lasted four months, she wondered whether she had pushed Will (them, really) to the collapse of their house of cards. No matter how much she might want to pick them up and rebuild the house, she knew it couldn't be done.

With a somber tone now, he said, "I wish you had never told me anything about your lovemaking, that you had kept it secret from me. Your leaving me and the kids was bad, but your having sex with another man—and probably loving it—really hurt.

"I was a man; I thought that's what I always meant to you. But your . . . fling . . . with Bobby destroyed that image. It made me feel like a failure as a man, and that's the way I've felt ever since . . . I tried to compensate by working hard in my shop, you know, bringing home the bacon. I barely made it, and we almost didn't survive as a family. I blame lots of things for that."

"You blame my affair with Bobby—don't try to put it off on anything else."

"Okay, Agnes. How was I supposed to feel? You tell me."

"Will . . ." She tried to reach out to hold him, but he rudely pulled away with a jerk.

The thought of her touching him was nauseating. Three hours or thirty years, it didn't matter to him . . . the notion of that guy's greasy fingers all over his wife, and the notion of his . . . oh, my God, inside her, giving her the pleasure she sought . . .

He couldn't stand to talk about it anymore. Contrary to what they promoted on the TV talk shows that had been springing up, no amount of talking was going to help deal with the pain he felt. He needed to shove it into a hole . . . into deep hiding . . . until he died, which, frankly, he hoped was soon.

But, in Agnes's fashion, she wouldn't let it go. "You know, Will, I don't think you were a failure at your shop. It was tough to make a little place like that go, and you did it. You can be proud of that.

"And then, there are your kids! What's not to be proud of about them? Becky out west at that big university. Your little Becky, a scholar, soon to wear a black robe, being handed a diploma. Your other three with good jobs, promoting wholesome values, raising families."

"Agnes, you bring up some good points. You know how to put paint on a pig to make it look pretty. But let me tell you a few things. I think that ever since the Bobby affair, you—and maybe even the kids, due to your guidance—have considered me a fuck-up. Everyone joked I couldn't hit a nail on the head, I couldn't mow a straight trail on our lawn, my grass would never grow green, only brown. My attention span was so weak, I couldn't get through a newspaper or magazine, let alone a book.

"I drank too much and too often, and I wouldn't get help for the so-called 'problem.' I spent too much time at the shop and not enough time with you and the kids. I was frequently too tired to give you the loving you needed. I was guilty of this conduct, but I complained if you nagged me about it. I've always thought that part was unfair to you."

"With Bobby," Agnes responded, "I had to follow my emotions where they were telling me my destiny lay. Initially, they told me with him."

"I think it was something different, Agnes. There is such a thing inside us as a conscience. Most people have them. We all might fantasize about such indiscretions, but I know that my conscience, in the end, would never have let me do what you did."

"C'mon—I made one mistake. You've let it drag you down for thirty years. When are you going to finally resolve that it's over and move on? When are you going to forgive me?"

"After your affair, I thought about it a lot . . . you know, trying to understand it."

He was staring in the distance as if trying to see the ocean over two thousand miles away. Turning, he fixed his gaze on her eyes. "Finally, I realized I couldn't understand it, and it's haunted me ever since."

Agnes was so impressed by his profound sorrow that she felt paralyzed and could not speak.

Will went on. "At that time I was shocked that one act of disloyalty, one shitty deal of the cards, could cause all of them to . . ."

"Collapse," she finished his sentence for him.

"That's right. That's exactly what happened, at least in my mind." He stretched like he was ready for a nap, but then said, "I always admired your many fine qualities. The kids and grandkids love you. You shine as the brightest star in the sky for them. I guess I'm all alone in wondering . . . after thirty years . . . I've tried and tried, but I still can't understand it, and most of all, I can't understand why your conscience didn't stop you."

Will heaved a deluge of tears while Agnes looked on sympathetically. It sounded to her like his world finally had come to an end, and maybe it had. She felt there was nothing she could do for him.

For some crazy reason, she thought of Shakespeare's tragic talk of romance and "star-crossed destinies." She had just read the classic play *Romeo and Juliet* and contemplated the couple's irrational love for each other, which ultimately caused their deaths. She thought about the themes in the play—what the Bard was trying to say about such universals as devoted love, loyalty, family ties, friendship, and how much we can really rely on them to make our decisions for ourselves.

She considered the centuries-old themes of prejudice, jealousy, and revenge that existed between the two families and for which the moderate prince put them to shame in the end. Agnes thought that the play had a full plate. Then, she compared it in a very minor way to Will's and her situation. She wondered whether their own destinies were going to take them to their deaths—like Romeo and Juliet—without ever making things right.

Maybe she was just kidding herself? She realized that when she had left her "true love," Bobby, she did so for the kids but not for Will. She knew when she was still with Bobby that, if not for her kids, she would have stayed on the road with him, playing at jazz clubs across the region. She had a decent singing voice and he encouraged her to get out in front of his band with the microphone and sing. But she made the decision to return and submit to thirty years more of an apparently loveless marriage.

She mused, *Now Will insinuates that I had no sense of loyalty, no conscience. Bullcrap! The truth is that Will is the one with no loyalty; it was he who didn't love me well before I met Bobby. It was he who abandoned me emotionally. His heart left me and never came back to me. Whereas he claims not to understand about me and Bobby, I do understand about why Will stopped loving me: jealousy. And he's still jealous of me to this day. There are many elements to that, but the one that stands out most is his jealousy of how much the kids and grandkids favor me. The only exception is Becky, our gifted 'late-bloomer,' now a senior at UC Berkeley. She absolutely idolizes her father. As if she has reverse X-ray vision, she sees all the qualities I saw in him during our early years.*

Will tapped her on the shoulder. "Wake up, Agnes." When her eyes adjusted, she scrutinized him. He said, "Don't scare me like that! I thought for a second you were having the Big One!"

"No, Will, you couldn't get off so lucky."

"I should have told you my true feelings long ago."

"True."

"But when Bobby dropped you back at the house, you were sobbing, proclaiming that Bobby was your 'soulmate.' I didn't know what that was at the time, but I got a pretty good idea later on."

Agnes was quiet, but she thought, *That's it! I'm sick of all this 'Bobby stuff.' After thirty years, it's time to give it a rest! This is all just a vessel for him to launch a revenge on me. But revenge for what?*

Ignoring her role in it, she assumed it was for all the petty hurts, jealousies, and failures that Will had suffered throughout his life. *Things haven't gone the way he wanted them to, so he feels the need to blame someone else, and that's me. Well, enough is enough. Will hasn't brought up the Bobby subject in a long time. Why now? If he wants to use it as his excuse for no longer being interested in sex with me—fine. I have no problem with that 'illogic.'*

She was working herself into a frenzy and got out a glass decanter of Jim Beam Kentucky bourbon. She never drank in the morning.

Unheard of. But she was so worked up she pulled down a highball glass from above the bar and—without offering a drink to Will—she poured herself a stiff one.

He stared at the brown liquid in the tumbler and then at the half-full decanter with a mix of desire and apprehension. He knew that Agnes couldn't handle her liquor, and he was concerned that she was getting into the sauce so early in the day. He considered taking the glass away from her and dumping it in the sink. Of course, he was aware that he'd have to take away the decanter too.

She read his mind and before he could move, she reacted, glaring at him, and snapped. "Go ahead, try to stop me!"

She gulped down what was left in her glass, grabbed the decanter before he could, and poured herself four inches of the amber spirits. Will turned his back on her, as if to say, "You're on your own."

When she was halfway through her second tumbler, she tried to get a fix on his eyes, but they shifted everywhere but upon her.

She slurred, "C'mon, Will—we need to change the subject, or we might come to blows."

He was aware from some article he had read that there's a place in our brains where we store memories of the ups and downs of our lives. He gloomily reflected, *In my life, it's been mostly downs.* He had heard there was a place where unpleasant experiences die in the shadows, and where secrets that should remain buried were placed in a hole and covered like a corpse. This place had no bed of roses. Its stench was strong and tried tenaciously to slip back into our present lives to destroy them. That's what these denizens of the dark corner of our mind are good at: creating depression, unhappiness, and weakness—but they are best at destruction. They seek death, and that's what they often achieve.

It bugged the shit out of Will that in thirty years he had never been able to get a straight answer out of Agnes as to why she had favored Bobby over himself. It wasn't even close because she was willing to abandon three kids too.

He glanced over at her beginning to get sloppy drunk. She was now into her third tumbler.

He thought, *Let her. I don't care. I'm tired of rescuing her from her mistakes.*

He almost drooled when he looked at the decanter within his reach and her sloshing another big gulp down her throat. He longed for a drink, but his quack doctor had forbidden him from taking another sip of alcohol or it could be his last.

He had reluctantly complied, although there were times that he felt like flicking it in and devouring himself in a series of shots and beers. He was too old and his chronic bad back kept him from playing his favorite game, golf, anymore. Four years ago, he shot 107, lost $25 to his buddies, and decided to hang up his clubs for good.

They didn't have a dog for him to walk, although they once had a lab who lived to twelve and died in his arms. Will told Agnes at the time: "Maybe old Jinx's death is telling me something."

Movies at the theater were too expensive. Concerts on the Green were too boring. That left reruns on the boob tube. It was no wonder he was itching to drain the bottle.

And I probably would, he reflected, *but Agnes hovers over me when I'm in the house, making sure I stay away from the booze cabinet. That might be all that's keeping me alive, but it's keeping me from any fun too.*

It began when I came home from the doctor's and made a fateful mistake, due to my inability to lie. Agnes naturally asked me what the doctor had advised. I often speak without thinking and thus muttered to her: "No more drinking."

"None?" she asked.

"Nope—not a drop." I immediately realized my mistake in telling her. In fact, it was one of the stupidest things I've ever done. She's been like a bulldog guarding the saloon doors ever since. And she takes perverse pleasure in it. She even advises me to go to see a quack

chiropractor to straighten out my back, so I can get back to the golf course again. That's Agnes! Always looking out for me in a way that humiliates me!

Back when Agnes learned that the doctor had declared Will officially off the booze, she danced in delight to her inner music. She pronounced her own "second opinion" about his drinking: "I told you so." She had reflected, *Topping Will in anything is like shooting fish in a barrel with a shotgun.*

She had turned to him and gloated, "Your drinking days are over . . ." Then, with a wry smile, she had added, "May they rest in peace."

Now, Agnes carried her tumbler along to the bathroom. It was almost empty, and she was thinking of pouring another. "Why not?" she chirped to herself. "I've got nothing else going on today."

She looked in the mirror, and right away she knew it was a mistake. What she saw was a small, formerly beautiful face now scarred by endless wrinkles and blemishes, especially the grooved crows' feet around her eyes. She thought, *No amount of plastic surgery could fix this face, and anyway, where would we get the money—rob a bank?*

Age suddenly felt very heavy on her. The only word she could think of was "hideous!" She felt like getting a scalpel and tearing off her face to "repair" it. She regarded the tumbler with disgust and thought, *I'm sure that booze is not helping to block my aging process.*

Yet she went back to the bar and poured herself another stiff one, saying out loud, "That's four, but who's counting?"

Standing there for a few moments, she held onto the bar for support. Her eyes glistened, and she didn't know whether she was going to get sick or not. She wobbled to the sofa and sank down, her small body almost getting lost in the cushions.

The phone rang, touching off at least a temporary truce between them in the continuous feud. "Goodness gracious," exclaimed

Agnes. It was one of her favorite phrases, but this time she slurred it. "I wonder who that could be?"

Will's only thought was, *Saved by the bell*. Then, upon reflection—*I like this reversal of roles: this time I'm the sober one—in complete charge of my faculties—and Agnes is dependent on me! If she keeps drinking, she'll be the incoherent one.*

"Don't answer that," he barked. He never liked answering the phone. It increased his anxiety, as bad news was on the other end more often than good news. Not answering was his practice for years at the shop to avoid tax and bill collectors or irate customers complaining about late deliveries.

The phone continued to ring, and that bothered Agnes to no end. It was a dentist drilling her teeth! She couldn't stand it any longer, so, drunk or not, she picked it up, jerked it up to her face, and flashed a furious look at Will.

She didn't know who it was but guessed it was one of the women from her Bible Study group. She had been remiss of late in attendance and had been thinking about dropping out. This Bible-thumper was probably poised to launch an attack. Agnes thought, *My sounding drunk may convince her that I don't fit with the religious zeal and staunch morality that the group sponsors.*

However, a cheery, most-welcome voice greeted her: "Mom . . . Mom—is that you?"

Agnes realized suddenly that she had made a big mistake by boozing this morning, and she was about to compound it by speaking to Rebecca in such a bad condition. Her daughter was an expert in booze, drugs, and partying and would recognize the condition right away and probably call her on it. *What can I say if she does?*

Will was sitting silently (reveling in this twist?). Agnes thought, *The daughter on the phone is the light of his life.*

Although Rebecca had come very late in their reproductive period—in their forties—she was no "afterthought." She was desperately wanted by both of them, and they both did their best to raise her right in an increasingly difficult modern era.

Becky was and had been a modern and freedom-seeking girl. As she was completing high school, her parents had urged her to stay close to home and attend a conservative Midwestern college, but she insisted, "That's not me. I'm tired of Republicans, Bible-pounders and 'safety first' folks." Her parents argued, "The University of California is physically dangerous, wildly liberal, and stresses individual freedoms over societal structure and religion!"—to which Becky responded, "Amen!"

Always on the alert for a good argument, Agnes had countered, "Fires, earthquakes, rapes, and murders right on campus—riots, fraternity partying gone wild, the drug capital of the U.S. and wacko politicians like Jerry Brown . . ."

Rebecca was sweet and honest, but she was one tough cookie, more of a fighter than any of their other kids. In that regard, she was a nice combination of Agnes and Will. She fought to get into Berkeley, and she fought to stay there. On one occasion, she fought off a would-be rapist on the way to her housing unit. The campus police were impressed that she had overcome the guy with a series of karate moves.

She was also nobody's fool, achieving top grades in all her classes. Now, she was going to graduate in May with honors. She planned to stay in the Bay Area and attend grad school—one of the first women in her field to do so.

When Agnes had heard these plans, she told Will: "Did you know that Becky is planning on staying in the Bay Area when she graduates? She's not coming home and wants nothing to do with the Midwest."

Will's response had been predictable. "Can't say as I blame her. Let her find her own way."

"Yeah, but she doesn't even want to get married. She claims it's like being chained to an oar in a Roman galley. I think she wants to go to law school and has been saving money for her tuition, room, and board. Can you imagine my little darling a lawyer? In court? Meeting with all those nasty clients?"

Will said, "Not only can I imagine it, I know that if Becky wants to do that, she will, and she'll be a helluva good lawyer!"

Agnes had confided to Carol, one of her Bible study friends: "Rebecca, our youngest, is a headstrong girl in every respect."

Carol had responded, "Rebecca is a very beautiful girl—the best of you and Will—but I feel that maybe she's too beautiful. Her beauty may give her too much pride. It might also lead her into an overconfidence that could get her into trouble. She'll think she can handle anything without a man, but she's wrong there. It's contrary to God's commands."

Agnes often pondered many of the same questions that she knew Will had. He wondered how such an all-around pretty, gifted girl could have been produced by his genes, which were more apt to produce an ugly right guard for the high school football team who barely passes school.

He told Agnes before Becky was born: "Our marriage is worn out, cheerless, and on the skids headed for the divorce court." Yet, after the birth, things improved. Her little soul became a light that glowed for them as well as for herself.

Will now observed, "I don't know exactly how she did it, but she helped to patch our marriage to where we could live together. It was truly a mystery."

Agnes adopted her know-it-all face again and said, matter-of-factly: "It wasn't a mystery at all. From the time that little girl came home from the hospital with that cute, sunshine face, you were in love, Will, maybe for the first time in your life, and you would do nothing—not even divorce me—to deprive yourself of full custody of her. You couldn't dump me for fear of losing her."

He knew she was right and just nodded his head. *Now, his girl was on the phone! And Agnes—drunker than a skunk! Ha, Ha.* He just hoped

Agnes didn't say anything to screw things up with Becky. He motioned to her to put him on the phone, but she ignored him, smirking.

Becky apparently detected that something wasn't right with her mom. "Mom, are you all right? You don't sound too cool. Mom, why do you sound so different from usual?"

Agnes tried to sound calm, at which she was a master. "Look, Becky dear. I'm fine." Will again moved to take over the phone, but Agnes turned her back on him.

Becky said, sympathetically: "You sound like you've had a few nips this morning. That's totally unlike you! What's going on? You haven't been fighting with Daddy again?"

No response.

Becky continued with honest concern: "I'm worried about you. Dad quit, but it seems you've been drinking more. I think you ought to quit too."

"Don't worry, dear."

"Mom—you didn't answer my question. How are you and Dad doing? Are you fighting again?"

"Just one bloody battle after another in the long 'Civil War of the Flints.'"

"Oh, Mom, please don't talk like that. It makes me so upset. So many other good things are happening in my life, and I don't want family squabbles to bring me down. Anyway, I don't think I can take anything you say seriously." Becky added, with disgust, "You sound really drunk!"

"Huh!"

"Can you listen to me? I mean, really listen and not just focus on your petty crap at home?"

Agnes didn't answer. She knew her daughter well enough to recognize that if Becky had something she believed was important to tell them—anything from a "hot new belt" from Macy's to the seductive wink she imagined she got from the young Comparative Religion professor—she would do so.

But the last subject Agnes wanted Becky to discuss and feed Will's never-ending arguments against was Agnes's own drinking. She preferred to be the example of harmony within the family. For the most part, her deceit had worked with their other kids, but she was aware that Becky was a special case and existed in her own world of values, standards, and lifestyles.

Agnes suspected that Becky was sleeping with a variety of men, and all she could do was pray that Becky didn't contract a venereal disease or get pregnant. She knew Becky was on the pill, which gave her some assurance against unwanted pregnancy—but it also encouraged promiscuity. As for protecting against disease, the principal method was to use a condom, which she suspected Becky's men did not use. She prayed that her daughter would find the right guy.

The other element of Berkeley life that Agnes found repugnant was the heavy drug use. Agnes had read up on the effects of this scourge on a personal user and on a societal level. She didn't know all about it, but she did know that she and Will had lived through an entire generation without using drugs—so why couldn't Becky?

Becky had endured the rancorous arguments and fierce in-fighting between her parents on a daily basis up until the time she got on the bus for the West Coast. Agnes rationalized, oddly for her: *Maybe she's seeking "harmony" in ways that my generation didn't, and we were even too afraid to try.*

Agnes was not attending to the loquacious Becky. Once Becky got wound up, Agnes usually let her fly, like a jet plane off the runway or a chatty parrot on the wing.

"Mom! Are you even listening to me?"

This was the question Agnes feared in a telephone conversation with Becky because it went right to the heart of the matter. Chances were that Agnes might have been listening to her voice but not really concentrating on the words Becky was saying. Although she felt bad, she didn't blame herself for her inability to keep up with the avalanche of words.

"Mom, I can't tell if you're even listening to me," Becky repeated. "What I've got to say is important . . . Hello?" This last exclamation was a typical tactic by Becky to redirect their attention to her, and it usually worked.

Agnes slurred, "I am, too, listening. Give me your news, and I'll pass it on to Daddy."

There was a long pause. Becky was rethinking her strategy. Agnes was hoping the call would end abruptly.

Agnes asked, "What's your big news?"

"Why don't we forget it, Mom. You'll never believe it."

Agnes reflected, *She's got that right,* but made no comment.

Becky plowed ahead: "I have a new boyfriend," she said melodramatically, as if she owned the Triple Crown winner or had just received the Pulitzer Prize for Literature.

Agnes was unruffled by the news. She not only could believe it but received it as she would if her grocer called to tell her she left a quart of milk on the check-out counter. She knew that Becky had conveyed the same information to them at least six other times during her senior year alone.

Agnes thought, *Her pace has been accelerating. There was a new boyfriend just two weeks ago! I'd be shocked if she* didn't *have a new one every two weeks.*

She put her hand over the phone, and as a courtesy to Will, told him, "Your daughter's love life is a revolving door."

Will didn't like how that sounded and wondered about its sexual implications.

Agnes knew there was a sexual component to Becky's relationships, but her imagination ran wild when she thought about what her daughter and her assorted boyfriends actually did with each other in those shabby coed dorms. Fleas and bedbugs? Heavily stained sheets and mattresses? Showers together in plain view of other students? Water pipes to get high and increase the pleasure of their unfettered copulation? Shallow suggestions of a hippy-style love that could mean anything—but probably meant nothing?

It was important for Agnes's sanity and avoidance of daily drinking that she exorcise these wicked images from her mind. She had to remind herself that Becky was more than two thousand miles away and she was going to do whatever the hell she wanted to do, with or without Agnes' approval. This was natural for a child breaking away from her parents' hold, like a baby bird flies out of the nest and is gone.

She thought, *Becky is free! Hopefully, we raised her in such a way that she'll do the right thing. All these boyfriends are simply her way of expressing her freedom, so when she calls to announce the news of her new boyfriend to us, she's making a cry for her freedom. She's shouting out to the skies that she's flapping her wings and flying.*

Agnes was concerned, however, that her obsession with making Becky happy would prevent them from ever having a commonsense mother-daughter discussion. Becky was, according to Agnes, "always in the clouds." She knew that she needed to say to Becky: "We sent you to college to learn and to form the beginnings of a career. We did not expect that you'd become the Whore of Babylon!" But Agnes was afraid to confront her like that—afraid to lose Becky forever.

"How exciting, dear," Agnes said tepidly.

There was a long silence. Agnes could only hear Becky's breathing but knew she was still on the phone.

Becky had rambled on and on earlier without saying anything that mattered. That was not unusual for her. She was a "yakker" and not a communicator. After an earlier call about a new boyfriend, Agnes and Will felt they knew less than at the beginning of the call. So, Agnes suspected this was going to be one of those forgettable conversations. Becky was certainly not an idiot, but when it came to men . . .

Becky now gabbed about the new boyfriend in such glowing terms that he sounded to Agnes like a sure thing for the country's next president. "And he's so handsome and kind and loving. And, Mom, here's the great thing—he loves me! Can you believe that . . . he really loves me!" She ended with a deep sigh. It was as if she had driven to the pinnacle of the hill and suddenly ran out of gas.

Exhausted, she waited before continuing, gravely, "Mom, I'm dead serious." Becky seemed chagrined—why? Agnes couldn't fathom a guess.

Becky continued, "This man is perfect. He is the love of my life, my soulmate."

Agnes had heard her daughter use that same phrase about a few men in her life. This didn't bother Agnes, but it might disgust Will. He would never admit it, but he was often jealous of Becky's boyfriends.

Then Becky slung a zinger that she had never mentioned before. 'We're gonna get married . . . not right away, but someday."

Agnes was aghast, but had the presence of mind to ask, "What's his name?"

Becky giggled, "It's Freddie."

No last name, but Agnes figured that would be revealed later . . . *unless*, Agnes snickered silently, *she doesn't know it yet.*

Agnes had felt socked in the solar plexus and stunned by the marriage news, but, like any experienced fighter, she reacted with simple dignity. "Rebecca—I am so thrilled for you. What an exuberant time in your life! Your father will be . . . uh . . . overwhelmed."

She was thinking about how to play Will—perhaps avoid telling him until it all blows over, when Becky finds herself yet another boyfriend. If she ever got around to actually marrying this Freddie fellow, it would be long after Will had passed on to the garden shop in the sky.

Becky took a wild guess at what her mom was thinking. She couldn't have been further off, but, teasing, she asked, "I'll bet you want to know his last name."

"Well, dear, that would be nice." She thought that this lover situation was going to hit Will hard—his special girl being ripped from him by a "Freddie." Agnes maneuvered to find out more about this fling, and asked Becky: "Is he from a good family?"

However, Becky didn't take the bait. She had been fishing with her father too many times not to recognize a hook, line, and sinker. As with all her boyfriends, Becky preferred to give away as little information as possible. She didn't know why she was so secretive—it just felt like the right thing to do with her mom and dad always swarming around her.

In truth, she knew very little about Freddie's family; they could have been axe murderers as far as she knew. She deflected her mom's question, saying, "Isn't that name, Freddie, completely frightening?"

Though Becky chuckled, Agnes was not about to be spun around regarding such a crucial issue. She awaited more information. When it didn't come, she said, "It seems, dear Becky, that all of your boyfriends frighten your dad and me in one way or another."

Having thought about it for a moment, Becky said, "Gee, Mom, I don't know enough about his family to form an opinion, but if they're anything like Freddie, I'm sure they're wonderful folks."

Agnes took in this dodge and realized that, with Becky on her game, Agnes wouldn't get anything out of her. She wasn't sure why on earth Freddie's first name was supposed to be scary or why Rebecca was so enthralled with a connection between his name and something scary that it was all she could talk about.

Agnes wasn't worrying about Becky, though. *She can take care of herself*, she thought.

The memories of her own life bothered Agnes—how it had spun out of control when she—as a married woman—had hungered for another man so much that a serious upheaval of her marriage resulted. That was thirty years ago, when Bobby was really a mere boy. Thinking about Bobby in the present (while still on the phone with her daughter) brought on spasms of fear.

She didn't know whether it was something Becky had said or whether her memory was jogged by the flash thought of Bobby. Now, another glimpse into the past had Bobby grasping her and pulling her close. A second spasm enveloped her. She tried to block the amorous scenes and the flood of thoughts: *What if he could appear in the present? What would he look like? Would he still find me attractive? What would he say? Would he blame me for leaving him or would he forgive me? More terrifying still, what would I do if given the chance to renew our connection?*

Becky shouted, "Mom! Are you alright? You're not saying anything and it's worrying me. Are you getting drunk in midmorning?"

"Maybe I'm not okay now," began Agnes. "I lived long ago—way before you were born. Maybe that's when I was happy. Maybe that's when I lost my purpose, the direction in life everyone seeks!"

"Mom, you're loud and talkin' crazy! Now I know you're drunk! Let's get back on track—you know, about Freddie."

A little hesitantly, she continued, "I want you and Dad to meet him. It's important to me that you approve of him if I'm gonna marry him."

Agnes thought, *This is a switch. Maybe she's maturing, as Will suggested.*

Now that she was back on the "Freddie track," Becky talked in such rapid-fire chatter that Agnes had difficulty following.

"Christmas will be insane with all the families and their new babies underfoot. Laurie will be ranting her shitfits about everything under the sun. I swear she acts worse than the goddamned Grinch sometimes. The house will be a disorganized mess with boxes, wrappings, ribbons, and fallen tree ornaments scattered everywhere. The 'men folk' will be forced to cling together in front of the TV to watch football games, one after the other. Freddie doesn't like football and would feel uncomfortable. He's into soccer and plays on the intramural team. He realizes that many of the guys on campus call him 'freak' because of this preference. He prefers wine to beer.

He's gotten used to being called 'Druggy' and 'Hippie' due to his long hair and love of getting high.

"Anyway, I'm getting off the subject (stick with it, Beck). I was hoping that Thanksgiving would be better for our get-together."

Agnes responded, 'What get-together is that, dear?"

"Mom! The one we've been talking about! When I'll bring Freddie there at Thanksgiving to meet you and Dad. It'll be the perfect time: the big family dinner will be at Laurie's, and then we can have a nice quiet snack together at home. What do you think?"

Agnes was slow to process. "About what?"

"About the Thanksgiving arrangements. We'd only be home a couple of days—three at the most."

"It's okay, I guess, but does that mean you'll miss Christmas Day with your family? That would be the first one you've ever missed. We always found a way to get you back here for the Big Day." Agnes was reeling as if she'd taken a sucker punch to the face, knocking her senseless.

"I know I've always been home for Christmas, but there has to be a change of tradition. I recognize that traditions die hard, especially those involving holidays. But Freddie has a big family in Oregon, and we're already committed to go there for Christmas. That's carved in stone—we can't change it."

"I see what's going on," snapped Agnes. "You're already dividing up families like married couples do. I get that. It'll be Thanksgiving with us, but your Dad has to approve these arrangements. Let me ask you a question."

"Sure," Becky replied with trepidation.

"Before my question, allow me to say something. You've just recently met this Freddie. You've had many short-term boyfriends since you started at Berkeley—several of them just this year. I'd call it a steady stream, with none of them lasting more than three or four weeks. You'll have to ask yourself why that is. But don't you think it's too early in this relationship to bring your boyfriend to meet your parents? After all, you've already conceded that the two of you are not getting married anytime soon."

Will was trying to follow the conversation, from Agnes's side. He also tried to grab the receiver up to his ear several times to hear what Becky was saying. He did hear the part where Becky said something about "perfect time" and "soulmates."

Will despised this term so much that when he heard Becky use it, his skin began to crawl. Then it felt like it was boiling. He went into a "cussing frenzy," his face turning a blend of red and purple. He began snorting like a bull.

Agnes was alarmed. She wasn't concerned about his elevated blood pressure killing him, but she was worried that his rampage would turn physical and he'd break up furniture and furnishings, as had happened before. If Will were a bull, that simple word, "soulmate," was a red cape waved in front of him.

Will's brain had been imprinted with decades of despicable images of his naked wife writhing under the body of a stranger—a person she had called her "soulmate." Now Becky had a "soulmate." This would drive him crazy!

Over the years, Will had carefully erected barriers in his mind to keep out the hideous images of Agnes and her "soulmate," as if they were barbarians trying to storm his sanctum and only through force of will could he keep them at bay. What he didn't realize was that the core of those defenses was his own rage, an emotion that was so fundamental, so violent that it could upend everything in his life. He had chained this beast in a dark dungeon for thirty years, but upon learning that he might be losing Becky to some flaming asshole hippie she called her "soulmate," the monster freed itself and emerged from its dark cave with destructive power.

Agnes saw what was going on with Will. He reached to grab the phone from her, and she ordered him to "take a few deep breaths." She noticed his right hand clenching and unclenching.

This reminded her of the prizefighters on television, gearing up to charge the opponent.

She reflected, *Will's opponent is on a campus two thousand miles away, and yet he'll do the most damage against an innocent bystander, his daughter—if I allow him on this phone.*

Will's heart doctor had advised him that whenever he felt a fit of rage coming on, he was to think of something pleasant and peaceful. Agnes cupped the phone and said, "Think of something pleasant, dear. Fill your heart with its image."

His stare at her was similar to his stare at his snickering buddies when he missed a one-foot putt with all bets at stake.

"The hell with that! No doc-babble is gonna help! I'm really mad, and it's my anger, not to be dumped off on some pleasant image. I haven't had any 'pleasant images' in thirty years!"

"Remember, Will—the doctor advised you that if you feel angry, just think about your kids, and that will settle you down."

"That's just great! It'll work for sure! The problem is that when I think of my kids, the first one who comes to mind is Becky—and that leads to her 'soulmate'—and I'm right back where I started!"

"Mom! Mom! What's going on?" Becky's voice asked from the telephone receiver.

Will regained some control and made a deft move to grab the phone from Agnes. At the other end, Becky, awaiting a response from her mom, was unprepared for the assault that was launched by her father.

Trusting she was still on the line, Will said evenly: "You know, Becky, I love you so much! More than Mom . . . more than my own life. And I'd do anything for you. You know that, don't you?"

"I know I'm your girl," she answered cheerfully but warily.

"Then please, for me, dump this Freddie fellow. Today! Not over coffee tomorrow. The longer you put it off, the harder it'll be for both of you."

"Why would I do that, Dad? I think I love him."

Sobbing now, but still in control of her voice, she said, "I know that at least I like him. He makes me laugh and we have fun together. It's better with him than with a lot of those guys who just want sex from me all the time. I get bored with that."

Will winced at hearing about his daughter's sex life, but at least none of those "predators" was her "soulmate." He was still incensed at this "Freddie thing." He wanted to treat it as a pesky fly and swat it out of existence, but it wasn't going away. He was about to enter the explosive stage of his emotions—when he would lose control of his actions or words. He was standing on a ledge, all too ready to jump off.

He snarled at Becky in a tone she hadn't heard before. "Don't ever bring that 'Berkeley Bum' to our house! Ever! Have you already slept with him—WAIT—don't answer that, it'll kill me to know. The best fatherly advice I can give you is DON'T DO IT! This Freddie is bad news, honey. If you produce a baby with this creep . . ."

He could hear her sobbing.

"I'm sorry it has to be this way, but if you don't drop him, I don't want to talk with you or see you ever again. You'll be banned from the family, I guarantee it! I especially don't want to ever hear you refer to this Bozo as your 'soulmate.' That's the ultimate outrage against me. Do you understand?"

Agnes had run to the bathroom to shield herself from Will's assault on their daughter but returned in time to hear his final blast. It was an insult to Agnes too. Her frail hands were shaking so badly she dropped her drink.

She didn't think she could stand any more but stood transfixed—how could she stop him? She tried to grab the phone away, but he resisted.

Becky was broken and sobbing uncontrollably. She was livid, too, and shouted into the phone. "Daddy, I can't believe you're saying these things! This is so unlike you. What's gotten into you?"

She paused and delivered the clincher: "Freddie is really a nice guy, a bit of a free spirit, which is why I wanted you and Mom to get to know him."

Across the country, Becky dropped her face into her hands. She felt as if she had been talking to a frying pan without a handle.

In Will's natural scheme of life, however, a "nice guy" could not coexist within the same body as a "soulmate." Impossible! And Freddie had already been declared the latter. Once combined, he and that label couldn't be separated. It was like a bad piece of fruit. Once it began to rot, you had to toss out the whole thing. You couldn't eat it nor put it on the pantry shelf. It would spread its rot to other fruit.

Becky told herself that she was a tough bird, of the same flock as her mother. *I can make it through this. I can get Daddy to accept Freddie, if not love him.* She smiled a big Becky smile to herself and launched into another effort: "Daddy, give him a chance. Just this one time. I promise that I'm not just a flaky college chick . . . Please let me bring him home. It'll mean so much to me."

She made this last appeal with so much emotion that Will was stunned and dropped the receiver. Agnes rushed in to retrieve it, but either they had been disconnected or Becky had hung up.

"Nicely played, Mr. Ambassador! How could you lose your cool with your favorite daughter and your wife of forty-six years in a five-minute conversation? Very smooth, dear. An Academy Award-winning performance."

Her tone was malicious, but he seemed impervious. With all they had been through, Agnes hadn't felt hatred for Will, but this stubbornness had changed that. She didn't care what he did to her, but she couldn't abide his abysmal treatment of Becky. It was an abomination!

"I'm leaving you, Will. You can have the house and everything in it. You can reach me at Laurie's if you need to." Her movements were quick as a ferret now that she had made up her mind.

"Darn it, Agnes, I know I didn't handle that very well. I don't need you to tell me. I got really pissed. I'm still upset about her diddling with that Freddie, her so-called 'soulmate.' We all know what's going on here—what's he's doing to her. He's taking advantage of her to get free sex. Just like Bobby did to you!" he shouted at her, as she was heading upstairs to gather her things. "There's no love there, and 'soulmate' is slang for free sex. That's what makes me angry: he's taking advantage of her and will get just what he wants from her."

Agnes stopped on the stairs and asked him: "Are you sorry for what you said?"

"When you said I lost Becky, that hit home. That really hurts. Yes, I'm sorry for all of it, but I can't put the words back into my mouth."

"Well at least you're sorry. That means a lot, especially from a stubborn old cuss like you. I spoke in haste about leaving, but you better lighten up on Becky. Was it really so wrong for her to use the nickname, 'soulmate?' What if she breaks up with Freddie like she does with all her boyfriends?"

Will responded, "What difference would that make? Isn't being 'soulmates' a lifetime thing?"

Agnes answered cautiously: "No way. You can be soulmates one day and never want to see the person again the next. I suspect that's what will happen with Freddie."

Will nodded. That's just what he had been hoping for.

Agnes continued to make her point, "Remember that "Fickle Frank" fellow during her freshman year?"

Will gave her a quizzical look, trying to remember the circumstances of that dude. He guffawed. "Yeah, I kind of remember she was in the freshman dorm. I imagined it was a crystal palace, a big Party Central with unlimited sex. No more Midwestern values or lifestyle."

"You got it. Fickle deluded her into having regular sex with him. Lucky she didn't have a baby because I don't think she was on birth control yet. Anyway, my point is that she thought they were going to get married, but Fickle had no such plans."

"Boy, was she in for a shock!"

Agnes laughed, "That's probably gonna be the same result with this Freddie. So, Will, I don't think you have to worry about Freddie being her soulmate."

"But what I'm worried about now is getting her back. I think I've lost her for good."

Agnes thought he was going to cry. He hung his head, as he was apt to do when events were overwhelming him. It seemed like the space just above his forehead was clouding over. Could lightning strikes be far behind?

If he failed to patch things up soon with Becky, Agnes feared she would also lose *him*. She reminded him: "Remember that good-looking guy—I forget what year it was—whom she fell head over heels for? He was the sportsy type from San Diego. They were very much in love and headed to the altar. She flew down to visit his parents in what she called 'La La Land.' He even taught her how to surf. I'll say what I wouldn't ordinarily say: I thought they were ideal for each other."

"You recall this stuff better than I do."

"It wasn't very long ago."

"Yeah, but I try to put it all out of my mind."

"I know, but it helps to look over the photos once in a while. By the way, she never did tell me why they broke up. I speculated about it, pumped her with questions. In a way it was best because they were really too young to get married. That surfer from San Diego was named Jared."

Will admonished her more vehemently than he meant to: "But, I say, watch out for this Freddie character! She never called or referred to Jared as 'soulmate.'"

"Will—you need to get over that. A name, or in this case a nickname, is nothing more than that. Next week she might pass him on the campus and pretend not to know him. That's the way a girl's mind works. That old adage, 'Here today, gone tomorrow,' could very well apply to this affair too."

Will reflected, *Thank goodness my wife was always the wise one*. Yet, he replied with less enthusiasm: "I hope you're right, ol' gal."

"I'm pretty sure I am. Remember what a handsome guy you were when we met? You were an entrepreneur and an independent businessman. I was captivated. I was aware you liked me, but you had a lot of competition. The guys were all licking their chops over me, but, secretly, I couldn't think of anyone but you. From the first at-bat, you hit a home run."

She paused but wasn't finished. "You know when you meet the right one—you just know. That's how love works. And that's how it was with us. Our wedding day was the happiest day of my life. Take a peek at our wedding photos, you'll see. Then, the birth of our first child! Each birth was an event. Those were the best days of my life!"

Will remembered and was in awe. He nodded in agreement, speechless.

She said, "If you look at the pictures of Rebecca's birth, I guarantee you'll be overwhelmed with joy. Or the day when she popped up in her crib and began talking, 'Dada, Mama.' And she's never stopped. Oh, Will, remember her first steps?"

All Will could do was think back and nod.

Agnes studied him and noted the profound mood he was in. Unusual for Will. She added, "Those were good years, huh, kiddo?"

"Yeah, the kids always made me so happy."

Agnes reflected: *He was surely implying that I didn't.*

Then, Will floored her with an astonishing statement about their lives together. "I gotta admit that I loved you more than I ever told you. I should have told you and shown you my love more often. You deserved a lot more love than I was willing to share."

He pondered that and said, softly, "I guess that's why you had the affair with Bobby. You lost your 'soulmate' because he neglected you, and along came a new one."

Agnes thought, *He's got it partly right, but he still doesn't fully understand me, and there's no need to be crossing swords on a fine point.* She simply responded, "Yeah, probably."

She continued, sympathetically, "For as long as I could remember, our burdens—financial and otherwise—were tough, and you had to work too hard. It all wore you down. I was the last one you had time or energy to keep satisfied. You really didn't have time for the kids either. To ease your guilt and your pain, you began drinking too much at night and eventually at the shop during the day. You began to make mistakes. You lost customers to your competitors.

"It was a bad time for you. That's when you began to hit me when you were drunk. My guess is you blamed me for all your failures, all your burdens, and your own dissatisfaction with your life.

"During the worst of those times, I met Bobby at my church. You didn't go, so you missed the origin of my sin. You claimed you had to work on Sunday, but I knew you were out drinking. It's ironic, in a way, that the man you blamed for all your troubles in reality came into my arms because of your problems and the harsh effects they were having on me and the kids. I sought shelter from the storm you had created. And the man whom you hated as a wife stealer and family wrecker was actually a kind, gentle, religious man—everything you weren't at that time. He . . ."

Will put up his arms as if he were under arrest, but it was his signal to stop her from continuing on with the "Bobby Story."

Agnes forged ahead anyway: "I was saying that Bobby became a tranquil island surrounded by raging storms and violent seas. I know it's an overused cliche in stories and songs, but I found a home in his arms."

She sneaked a look to see how her "Bobby Story" was affecting him. Not well—which was exactly the effect she intended. In fact, he looked pale and even a little green in places. She envisioned him running to the bathroom. Well, she was almost finished.

"You assumed that I was abandoning the kids when Bobby and I drove off that day, but that was never my intent. Bobby and I planned that as soon as we were settled, I'd come back and relieve you of the kids, whom I perceived to be in some danger with you. We planned to fight you in court for custody if we had to.

"Instead, I returned home because I thought it was in the best interest of the kids. They would have missed you too much despite all your problems. They would have missed their home. If Bobby and I had to be on the road too long, they might have become disoriented, missed school, and missed their friends. Neither you nor Bobby were a factor in that decision.

"I believe the kids all turned out pretty darn well, don't you?" she said, flashing her wide Agnes smile, then sobering. "Anyway, at least you didn't hit me anymore after I came back. If you had, I would have left you for good."

With her long explanation ended, Will appeared like a large white stone lying at the bottom of a clear pond. As his wife was telling the last part of her story, he might well have been that stone, because her voice sounded miles away and dull, as if transmitted through layers of concrete.

Agnes thought he looked helpless and ready to break down—but, for once, not for himself. This time his emotions were for her and their children.

He lamented, "I'm 70 years old, and what do I have to show for it? I'll tell you . . . nothing! I've accomplished absolutely nothing for myself or our family. My life has been a big zero. If not for the kids, I might as well not have lived. Maybe I've been an okay father, but I'm afraid I've been a crappy husband for you."

Agnes looked at him and patted his shoulder. She saw a sad, tired old man. She had known this man for almost her entire life, but she had never seen him look this wretched. He looked defeated—the lowest she had ever seen him.

With her husband faltering so badly, Agnes felt the ball was in her court and she needed to do something to help—make that "save"—Will, to make his pain disappear. A shard of an emotion began to emerge. It had been nagging her for a long time, but she had elected to keep it buried. Now, she saw no benefit in covering it. She reflected, *Any longer and I might forget it's there. If there were ever a time it was needed, it is now.*

The unrevealed sentiment? *I actually love this big, occasionally unpliant lug, and I'm gonna miss him after he leaves me.*

She turned to him to express this out loud, but the moment had been lost.

Will was flailing his arms and murmuring inanities, laced with obscenities about Freddie and Bobby.

"I know Freddie is a complete flake. All her boyfriends in the past have been. I hope I never have to meet the SOB. And Bobby, that asshole! He should never have messed around with a married woman. You'd think if he spent so much time at church, he'd know better than to take her away from her home and loving children."

All that verbal garbage was burning her ears, so she interrupted him.

"Will, calm down! I've got something to show you." She suddenly grasped both his hands in hers and led him down the hallway to the trapdoor that came down from the attic.

Will, perplexed, wondered what was in the attic that was so important for him to see.

After the ladder came down, Agnes climbed it as nimbly as a spider monkey. Will lumbered up behind her, and they squeezed together into a small space that was all angles. Fortunately, there was a utility table in the attic, where they could examine documents.

Agnes knew exactly what she was doing; Will had not a clue. She took a large box off a shelf and handed it to him.

He set it on the table and asked, "What's this?"

"A lifeline."

They began to withdraw yellowing photos from the box and study them. The several hundred photos were not organized but lying randomly in the box. Some depicted friends of the family and their children, but the vast majority were of their own nuclear family.

Will focused on each photo in awe, but he didn't linger very long over any one of them because there were so many. He was silent as he gazed, as if he had discovered a new island to explore for himself.

As much as she wanted to chat, to encourage and urge him on, Agnes realized that now was not the right time. So, she backed away and observed. What she saw was a man—whom she sometimes called a lughead—transforming. As he looked at the succession of photos, he didn't show tears or sadness. His demeanor was that of a gentle wistfulness, seeming to round off the sharp edges of his face and leave an extraordinary contentment. Agnes was certain Will had never experienced this state in his life—a form of euphoria few are lucky enough to feel. She didn't need any verbal explanation of what was happening to Will: it showed in his eyes.

Each photo he looked at triggered a sweet or powerful memory of the event itself: for example, a picture of Laurie wobbling along the sidewalk on her first bike reminded him of teaching her how to ride. At the time, that had been a joyful experience, only he just hadn't realized it. He had grumbled about what a slow learner she was and how much time it was taking—time he could have been at the shop trying to make money. His bitching had hurt Laurie at the time, although she was already used to his ways.

What he now realized, as he looked at the photo, was that teaching Laurie the skill of riding a bike had been a joyful event. He was proud of her for successfully accomplishing it and proud of himself for helping her. Looking at the photograph enabled him to relive the event and bring back the hidden joy.

He realized there was another benefit. He was able to feel anew the profound love the family members in the photos had had for each other—his love that he had been unable to express over the years, the love he had buried so deep inside, the love that now was able to rise to the surface and shine like a thousand searchlights.

"Feel any differently about these dusty old photos?" she asked.

He looked up but didn't need to respond. She didn't expect him to. His expression was as if a doctor had just told him that a lethal cancer was gone, disappeared without a trace. Agnes suspected that this new state might remain with him.

He found a number of photos of Agnes wearing a beautiful flowing white dress, her hair styled the way she liked it for special occasions, and flowers everywhere.

"Our wedding photos," he exclaimed with a smile.

He noticed the silver tiara in her lovely chestnut hair. He thought, "Dude! We really got decked out to get married!"

She had been the star of the show and was in almost every photo with her bright smile. In the photos depicting the two of them together, Will noticed mutual expressions of love, respect, and devotion, virtually engraved on them. He hadn't expected that. The contrast between then and now was eerie, but he didn't say anything about that to Agnes.

The photos were as varied as they were precious. Will Jr., was involved in all sorts of sport and outdoor activities, seeking Will Sr.'s approval and kudos. Comparing the photos, it was obvious that Will Sr. had spent more time with his son than with his daughters, but that wasn't unusual for that era.

Another photo was of Lu Ann, the creative member of their family, dressed in a tutu and standing in a line of girls in a fifth-grade classroom. They were rehearsing for a ballet recital, and Lu Ann looked to be a half step ahead of the others. The photo itself didn't show it, but Will remembered that, a split-second later, the entire line had broken out in laughter at Lu Ann's antics. Will chuckled.

Lu Ann had been a girl for all seasons. He came across another photo of her in sixth grade dressed in her softball uniform, warming up to pitch for the win in the league championship game. Will's arm was around her, but he looked stiff, unable to express his love.

Agnes saw now that his love had been there, lying just beneath the surface. She didn't need to say anything (to do so might be harmful), but she knew this to be a poignant moment. He finally had insight into the emotional neglect that had been his scourge in all his relationships. She reflected: *When Scrooge breaks free of his hardness and cruelty in Dickens's* A Christmas Carol—*and dismisses the ghosts that tormented him—he races into the street on Christmas morning, beaming a smile, announcing great tidings and joy for his transformation. And Scrooge becomes a different man.*

Agnes wondered whether the same would happen to Will. *Will the photos act similarly to Scrooge's ghosts? Can they truly change him? At least in regard to Lu Ann, it seems to be working!*

She could almost see the lightbulb clicking on over his head when he realized that there were no photos of Becky in the box. He looked like a man whose pockets had just been picked.

"Where are the photos of Becky?" he asked in a challenging tone. "There were lots of them and not a single one is here!"

Without a word, she handed him a separate album overflowing with more recent photos. He checked out some of them to confirm his suspicion that they were all taken from episodes in Becky's life. He began to look at each page carefully and turned to Agnes. "Why are all her photos in a separate album?"

"You wanted it that way. You bought the album for her. Something about 'nothing too good for my girl,' and when she was here on vacation, she separated out all of hers. You don't remember that?"

"Nope, it's news to me. Agnes—could you give me a little time to look at these by myself, please?"

"You betcha. I'll just be down below."

The photos had already been organized in chronological order, making viewing easier. The first one was a shot of Agnes pregnant, her belly protruding over the waistline of a pair of jeans. Will was in the picture, too, playfully patting her belly.

Then, of course, there was her birth, with doctors in green scrubs all around and Will in the middle of the action, helping Agnes do her breathing control. First words; first steps; being cradled and loved by her much-older siblings.

In the car; in the park; with an ice cream cone in hand but most of the ice cream all over her face. Birthdays; holidays; vacation trips. Lots of sports—the winning soccer goal; striking out (with a painful look of disappointment); hitting the walk-off home run (with a radiant look of triumph). At high school; helping her dad at the shop; first date; high school graduation. First day at Berkeley in her ratty freshman coed dorm. The photos were all there, and they accurately told the story of this outstanding young woman's life up to now.

For the first time, Will was genuinely absorbing the photos of his family members and trying to correlate their meaning to his own life. In the process, he recognized how his involvement in each of their lives had made a positive difference each step of the way. He realized that now. It had been a long time coming.

Still alone, before he left the photos and descended the ladder, he took a closer look at a photo of Becky after she had grown nearly as tall as him. She had her arm wrapped around his shoulders. She flashed that big, photogenic smile directly into the camera, her expression screaming THIS IS MY DAD. He decided that this was his favorite Becky photo. That was odd, because in the photo he was crying—tears of joy or tears of sadness he couldn't remember.

With Agnes patiently calling him from below, he began to cry again, and he knew that these tears were heralds of the wistful yearning that nostalgia evoked from the past.

Something unrecoverable, he reflected, *in all our lives. We can't go back. Our lives have only one direction and there are no do-overs.*

You screw up something and move on. You get something right; you rejoice in your success—and you move on. I got it right with my kids—why I haven't rejoiced has been a crying shame. But I'm still alive and it's never too late to change.

He had begun to shift himself to make his descent down the attic ladder when he suddenly realized one additional fact: *One thing in my life that has been a constant has been my love for Agnes. I was sixteen years old when I fell in love with her. But something else has been constant: I've never expressed my love for her, especially after the Bobby affair. I should have let her know that my love would always be there. I held her affair against her for thirty years. She bore my anger because she blamed herself for the fling. But it wasn't her fault. It was my fault—the whole thing. If I had treated her better as a wife, companion, and lover, she wouldn't have needed to seek solace in Bobby.*

I don't know for sure—I'm not a shrink—but it occurs to me that Becky was trying to do the same thing: running away from me into the arms of the first man—Jimmy, Johnny, Mack, or Freddie—who would accept her.

Down from the attic, Will shouted "Agnes! Hey, Agnes, I'm coming down!"

There was no answer. He replaced the ladder and cruised into the kitchen where he expected to find her. Sure enough, there she was, preparing something to put into the oven. She smiled, "Quite a trip back on Memory Lane, huh? Help you?"

He gave her a nod, a small smile, and said, "I cannot believe all the smiles our family left behind. They happened at the moments in each photo and represented our family's happiness. Then, they disappeared somewhere."

Agnes smiled more broadly. "Yes, one of our poets might have written that the smiles were left behind but never forgotten, thank God. Some of them were captured by our cameras, and many more of them were captured in our memories. A songwriter once wrote:

'What's too painful to remember, we simply choose to forget.' That's fine. Forget it all if we can, but we can cherish the smiles and laughter that we didn't leave behind—because, in the end, they're all we have."

Will mused, *She's right, of course.*

Just then the phone rang, and Will ran to it like he was busting through the line with the pigskin.

Agnes smirked, "That's the fastest I've seen him move in years!" There was no second ring.

"Becky!" Agnes heard it and wasn't surprised by the urgency and desperate longing in his voice.

Will heard the bright, youthful voice at the other end: "Dad, is that you?" Her voice sounded emotional. He thought she must have been crying.

"Becky—are you all right?"

"I am now. Dad, please don't interrupt me, okay? I want to say that I'm sorry for what I said on the phone earlier with Mom. I said some things that I regret like . . . forget it. I don't want to repeat them. They weren't fair to you and Mom."

"Stop right there, Becky! You didn't say anything wrong. I was just about to call you to say I'm sorry for acting like an ass and to ask for your forgiveness. I promise never to act that way again. Now, I hope we can just drop it."

"Thanks for your apology—it means a lot to me. By the way, you'll never be an ass in my book . . . maybe a 'horse's patootie.'"

"Yeah. Becky, one more thing before I forget."

"What is it, Dad?" She was concerned that the other shoe was about to stomp on her.

"Will you be bringing 'Freddie Krueger' here for Thanksgiving dinner? If so, be sure to tell him: 'None of your movie antics!' He's got to be on his best behavior."

"With pleasure!"

The Women's
Track Club

They say in long-distance running—more than any other sport—"Don't give up; keep going; you never know what will happen." I know it's just a slogan, but it occasionally comes true. I experienced this firsthand at The Women's Track Club.

When I entered its story, Kate Bradshaw had dominated The Women's Track Club in Pasadena as its reigning "queen" for three years. She had previously run as the star of the UCLA women's team. Upon graduating, she returned to her nearby San Marino home. Only twenty-five years old, she appeared to be in great shape and was still a strong runner. Her specialty was the two-mile distance, but she was nearly unbeatable in any race. She had run all the distances, except the marathon, at meets around the country. In college she had even tried the steeplechase, but she didn't like getting wet.

Kate was a dynamo on and off the track. The members all agreed that she was the strongest runner in the club. Many of the younger women respected her prowess and all but worshipped her. They regarded her as a mentor because she occasionally helped them with their technique.

After Kate joined the running club, she determined that its power would not be shared with anyone. She stated, "This club is not a democracy." She mostly ignored the other members, but when she did take notice, she was condescending and rude.

My name also is Kate. It's Kathleen Skyler, but I've always preferred Katie. For me, it was a strange coincidence to have the same first name as the club's superstar, but for her it was an insult.

I'm from Orange County, south of LA, but I attended college at the University of Oregon. I successfully ran track in high school at Fullerton High, so I tried out for the Oregon track team, the Ducks. I was rejected. Based on the time trials, I just wasn't fast enough. Through a series of telephone calls, my supportive mom helped me cope with the resulting depression.

That was the year that the Ducks' women's track team won the NCAA championship. I didn't know Kate then, but I heard of her fame as the winner of the 440, mile, and two-mile at the NCAA championships—and one relay. I read in *The Oregonian* that Kate accused her UCLA teammates of losing the championship by not putting enough effort into their training and lacking the desire to win. The paper quoted her saying, "The loss to the Oregon Ducks is a disgrace!"

I was the top runner at my high school, a "big fish in a small pond." At OU it was the opposite: "a small fish . . . etc." It was frustrating to fail to make the team during my first year at Eugene.

In my freshman year, I attended all the Ducks' home meets but only as a spectator. I trained vigorously on my own. My new friends on the team monitored my progress and assured me that I had substantially improved.

Thus, I tried out for the team again at the start of my sophomore year. All the stopwatches clicked my times, and they didn't lie. I was thrilled when the coach informed me that I had not only made the team, but I would be one of its featured runners. That was the beginning of a decent but unspectacular three-year college career.

After graduating, I returned to Fullerton to work at whatever. I wasn't sure. I just knew I wanted to continue my competitive running, so I moved into an apartment in Pasadena, home of the nationally renowned Women's Track Club, which I applied to join. I figured the club would be a perfect way to maintain and hopefully improve my times. I thought I might even try out for the next Olympics, but mostly I wanted to have fun running competitively against a capable group of women.

I met the other Kate on my first day of practice. She made a point to check out the newest member, confidently introducing herself as the club's leader. Of course, I knew her by reputation as the mighty Bruin track star. When I told her my name and what college I had attended, she sneered at me.

She sarcastically uttered, "Oh, you're the Duck. I thought I heard quacking in here. I've heard they call you 'Lil' Katie,' but to me if it looks like a duck, quacks like a duck, and smells like a duck, it must be a washed-up Oregon Duck. Tell me, Lil' Katie, does water roll off your back?"

"Nice to meet you, too, Big Kate."

Some of the other girls snickered. Our initial exchange suggested that Kate and I were going to be adversaries.

After I had been in the club for a while, I discovered that our premises weren't a place for fun and games when Kate was around. I had learned from Amber, a sprinter who was my best friend on our team, that not long after Kate arrived, she aggressively assumed the club leadership from Sue Rafferty, a former superstar at San Diego State. No appointment, no vote, no formalities. Sue had peaked and was on the downslide. Her times were increasing. Kate felt that the club had no further use for Sue. Somehow, Kate managed to dump her without the support of any other member.

After driving Sue out, Kate began setting the training schedules for each athlete and demanded compliance, with a threat of being eliminated from the club. She insolently threatened several long-term vets. Members were uncertain whether she'd carry out her threats, but they were afraid to challenge her.

I admit that I, too, was initially afraid of Kate. I worried that her fierceness and deliberate condescension might break up the club. She possessed a vicious mean streak and was vindictive and prone to bullying members during the practices.

If Kate found fault with a member's technique, she charged over and got right in her face. She then called the offending member out like a Marine drill sergeant, so that all the other members heard Kate lashing out. On those occasions Kate's face got red and her voice level increased by several decibels.

One day she all but throttled sweet Amber as if she was trying to shake a better technique out of her. Fortunately, I was near enough to them that I could have intervened if Kate tried to inflict any additional physical harm on her. On another occasion I witnessed Kate get so angry that she pushed a tear-choked member out of the starting block to show her a better stance. The young girl, Ashley, stumbled to the track and bruised her knee. Ashley quit our club that day and joined a rival club where she became a premier runner.

Kate carried a notebook at all times. When she saw what she perceived to be a violation of her rules, she yelled at the violator and wrote about it in her notebook. Once she caught Julie smoking behind the bleachers. That infraction, according to Kate, was a ground for Julie's immediate dismissal from the club. Julie was one of our best quarter-milers, and a number of members protested to Kate, but she would not relent. She insisted that it was a serious violation of club rules and required severe discipline.

The real reason for her bullying was that Kate was a fierce competitor who hated to lose. She feared that to back down from any of the members would be an intolerable sin. If a runner threatened to beat her, she first yelled and then pushed her off the track.

Kate also relished taunting the younger members and considered reducing them to tears to be a victory. There wasn't a single member who didn't hope that Kate would sustain a career-ending injury, but we all accepted her decisions as law.

My bell was rung one afternoon in the locker room via a nasty blow from Kate's elbow. She immediately claimed it was an accident but didn't bother to say she was sorry. I didn't believe her accident excuse, but I couldn't prove it was deliberate either.

I felt blood running down my chin, so I hurried to the restroom. The mirror revealed my lip was gushing blood. I was fortunate not to lose any teeth. I admit that I broke down in the restroom and cried due to the pain and my shame that Kate had taken advantage of me.

It was the first time I could recall shedding tears since fighting in junior high with MayBeth Olson, the class bully. MayBeth stunned me with a left cross to my cheek in a sneak attack for allegedly stealing her boyfriend, Andy Cutler. However, I had never liked Andy and wouldn't hang out with him for anything.

When I peeked at my face in the track club mirror, there was also a sizable bruise below my eye. I washed the blood off my face and figured I'd have an embarrassing shiner. I secretly wanted revenge against Kate such as I eventually got against MayBeth. I had never hated anyone as much as Kate—not even MayBeth and her nerdy boyfriend. My anger erupted when I looked into the mirror. *Katie, you're pathetic!* I scolded myself. *Get your act together!*

Kate had pushed me too far this time. I was familiar with the slogan: "Don't get mad, get even." I urged myself to make that a reality. As I turned away from the mirror, I wondered whether I had the guts to do it. I also wondered how to get my revenge. I was not a devious person, but I had to develop a plan and keep it secret from the other club members.

A week later, after my bruise had almost vanished, I took my first step to activate my plan. I approached Kate in the locker-room, and she smirked, "How's your eye, Lil' Katie?"

I ignored her question and retorted, "You know, I'm sick and tired of you boasting what a great runner you were at UCLA. You've ridden that reputation to take over this club. All that's ancient history. It's crap! What have you done lately other than bully the members and abuse them into leaving the club? I want the chance to prove that all the stories about you are obsolete myths."

This was quite a speech for being so nervous.

"Hah! You're full of shit, Lil' Katie! Why don't you elevate your pathetic ability and put it where your mouth is?"

"That's exactly right," I agreed, thrilled that she had fallen so easily into my trap. "I propose that we race at your favorite distance—the mile. I'll beat you for sure."

Kate barked, "You are a ridiculous little pipsqueak, Katie-o."

She pronounced my name as a slur. "You're just a lil' runt that I can brush aside whenever I choose, like dirt on my shoes."

"You think you're such a hot runner. Did you hear me? I proposed that we run a one-mile match race. If I beat you, you'll immediately resign from the club and never show your face here again. If you beat me, I'll do the same."

"There's no 'ifs' about it, but I have a counterproposal, you spiteful little bitch. Make it two miles and you're on."

Kate must have known that in a one-mile race, I had a decent chance to win. It was my strongest distance, and my latest times had been lower than Kate's career best at the mile. She undoubtedly was aware of my advantage.

However, Kate had a distinct edge at two miles because of her height and long stride. She was the NCAA individual champion three years in a row at that distance. She busted all the collegiate records. I would have two strikes against me before the starter's gun popped.

"You're on!" I responded confidently, unwilling to back down now.

Some of my girlfriends were stunned. Amber whispered, "You're getting in over your head."

Others went further and intimated to me: "You must be crazy. We're gonna miss you."

My friends shook their heads and tried to get me to back out even as they spread the news about Kate's and my locker-room exchange to the other club members.

I mused, *Maybe I'm crazy but at least I'm willing to take risks. Racing against Kate at her signature distance is clearly high-risk.*

I envisioned myself walking out the exit with tears flowing and my countenance shadowed by shame. In my vision I was slumping as if my workout bag weighed two hundred pounds. I could see myself turning around to take a farewell gaze at my friends and saw that they were all waving and some were crying. Kate was not there, having vacated the locker room for the track. I appreciated the members' loyalty, but I felt that I had let them down. I was sorry for being so gloomy and realized that I had to lift myself up, not put myself down. At least I had tried.

With this depressing vision in mind, I heard the members around me start referring to our pending match as 'The Race,' as if it were the only one worth talking about.

As I strolled out to the track, trying to act confident, I observed that cheering club members had formed parallel lines for me to walk through, like at a high school football game. Even the women running sprints interrupted their training to gather around me.

Kate had the effrontery to grab a strap of my tank-top and pull me aside to ask, "When are we gonna get this massacre started?"

She turned to Amber, who was hovering nearby, and ordered her: "Go get some mops and a bucket, so we can clean the blood off the track."

Amber's dirty look was a clear sign of the degree of some of the members' animosity for Kate.

I calmly responded, "No better time than the present."

"I concur," Kate said with a ruthless smile.

I was already doing some stretching and warmups. She snidely asked, "Are you about ready?"

I was aware that one of Kate's prerace strategies was to call her opponents insulting names to confuse them and distract their concentration. Thus, I was not surprised when she asked me: "Hey, Shit-for-Brains, have you psyched yourself for the most humiliating loss in your putrid, little life?"

I was also careful to neutralize her slickest trick—to start running before the starter's gun went off while her opponent was still warming up.

She barked at Amber: "Hey, scrub, fire the gun when I tell you to."

I reflected, *It's clear that Kate barks orders and insults to those around her to boost her own ego. She tries terribly hard to maintain an aura of invincibility and isolation. Her adversaries are like bubbles which she pricks with her putdowns.*

I quickly glanced at Amber, who raised the gun up so high that I had time to prepare. As I expected, Kate took off early and to a five-yard lead before the gun went off.

The sharp discharge was a stimulant for my legs to start churning. I used a sprinter's burst to pull ahead of Kate, but I worried that I had already used too much energy, which I usually preserved for my final kick.

I maintained a slight lead and gradually increased it to four strides. It really wasn't a shock that I was ahead at the mile marker. I glanced over my shoulder, and it appeared that Kate was running smoothly and not winded at all. She obviously was biding her time for her big kick.

I sensed that my own body was laboring. I looked back again and saw Kate's long body straining to catch up. I assumed that she was beginning her patented breakaway, which had always decimated her opponents.

Yet, a slight smile materialized on my face. I felt that with a quarter-mile still to go, she was sprinting too early due to panic. I told myself not to panic if she passed me.

I could hear her gasping right behind me. She was so close I could almost feel her sweat on my back. Her acceleration closed the gap between us, as I figured it would.

I felt like a thoroughbred when the jockey holds him back for the final stretch kick. I glanced sideways and was not intimidated by her gloomy countenance. Instead, I was incited by her leering smile that proclaimed, "You may be even with me now, but watch me zip by you to break the tape well before you stagger in."

Amber told me later that during the height of her breakaway, Kate appeared more like a racehorse than a human, that the scene was like a lioness running down an antelope. That's the effect Kate had on people. Amber said, "It looked like she was about to pounce on your back and go for your jugular."

I previously heard some of her former UCLA teammates describe her in similar terms.

When she burst by me with three hundred yards to go, I controlled my anxiety but still worried that Kate was living up to her reputation. The thud of her track shoes as she passed me was the worst sound I ever heard. Surely, this was her final dash to crush me. It felt like I was standing still.

When she pulled into the inside lane directly in front of me, her sour sweat was cascading off at me. I could smell its distinctive odor.

That stench was another motivating factor for me to race around her. Yet, Kate was increasing her lead. I imagined she began her kick so early "to get rid of that pathetic Duck nuisance from the club." She must have assumed she possessed the stamina to maintain her sprinter's speed to the tape.

Other than her silent leer, she didn't gloat, so I figured she was saving her boasting for the clubhouse. I imagined she expected me to flop to the track as I crossed the finish line from sheer exhaustion while she erupted with a belly laugh. Only a shamefaced Amber would run onto the track to support me in my hour of defeat.

It was not my imagination that while Kate was several strides in front of me, I could hear a strange snorting coming from her—the kind of noise you hear from a pigsty. I could see her labored breathing, indicated by her upper body slumping. I figured she had used up all of her extra energy to pass me. These were encouraging indications that I could overcome my aches and the growing burn in my chest.

Kate looked behind to see where I was. She must have seen that I was gaining on her, but she had used up her energy in her frantic effort to pass me. There wasn't much left in the tank. It appeared that my staying power had wiped away her cloying, sadistic attitude, which had now transformed into a different emotion—fear.

It was obvious in her bulging eyes, a shorter stride, and that unearthly stench. Despite my own burning lungs, slumping legs, and overall pain, I was determined not to give up.

For inspiration I said to myself over and over, *Katie still has fuel in her tank. Let's show them!* Just inside a quarter mile, I began my kick. I also began another silent mantra that seemed to reverberate throughout my body, energizing it. My will was aroused to achieve victory from the jaws of defeat:

I may be small but I'm powerful; I've got this race!

My face in the mirror before the race had reflected this determination and reminded me of the humiliation Kate had inflicted on me with my own blood. I not only desired to win the race for myself but for all the track club members under Kate's tyrannical rule. It would be a victory for all underdogs everywhere and would hopefully encourage women not to ever give up. It would also end the image of Katie as the waddling duck.

My legs went into overdrive, seemingly by their own volition. I could see that I was gaining on the lagging Kate. I could again hear her desperate gasps for oxygen, which were louder than before. It was as if she had resorted to sucking air into her lungs.

Her gaunt body was getting closer with every one of my confident strides. We came around the final turn, and I was so close I could reach out and touch her heels. The white tape across the finish line was now in sight. I could faintly make out Amber screaming and imploring me—to victory.

I passed Kate without a glance with one hundred yards to go. A cheer erupted from the women lining both sides of the track. I accelerated my pace, doubling my lead. That was when I heard Kate's moan. I supposed she now recognized the inevitable.

I glanced back at her retreating body; it appeared she was attempting to mount a second kick. It was too little, too late. The "racing machine" was finally defeated, and she knew it.

Amber said later that Kate's expression was of "exasperation and defeat." It had dawned on her that I was the better runner and that there was no way in hell she was going to catch me. It was an awesome sensation to burst through the tape well ahead of the dethroned queen and into Amber's open arms. The rest of the club members rushed to embrace me and slap high fives with the winner.

Moments later I heard a loud thud behind me. I looked and saw Kate sprawled face first on the track. She wailed once in anguish and then was silent, as if her defeat was sinking in.

She started to rise and stubbornly refused help, rudely pushing everyone's hands away. It appeared that she had already decided to have nothing further to do with the club. She dusted herself off and vanished from the scene.

The entire club gathered around me, clapping, cheering, and offering congrats. I was humbled, but I felt an inner glow of satisfaction for a job well done.

Amid all this hoopla, I caught sight of a dog lying in the grass on a knoll above the track. Amber tapped my shoulder and pointed, "She watched the entire race and never moved." The dog suddenly stood and looked at us and wagged her tail. That's when I noticed that she only had three legs. I thought, *Talk about an underdog.*

Amber and I approached the furry spectator. I exclaimed with embarrassment: "Yep. Three legs."

The dog stared at Amber and me and at the track. It appeared to me that she was lost to memories of bouncing across open fields or in sand down at the ocean.

She hobbled over to me like she recognized the winner. She tried to raise up to greet me but almost toppled over. So she rubbed against my leg and then sat on my track shoe. I tried to pat her head, but her wet, red tongue met my hand and gave it a happy lick.

Amber and I walked back to join the celebrants. I hoped the dog would follow us.

Instead, she vanished as if she had been an illusion all along.

I asked Amber: "Where did she go?"

Amber shrugged her shoulders and said, "I dunno; maybe she's got a home somewhere."

The club members huddled around me like I was a football coach. I almost expected the crowd to bend down in prayer.

Instead, they started singing, "For she's a jolly good runner . . ."

I said, "Stop, please! This is embarrassing."

I had a final glimpse of Kate pushing a shopping cart across the parking lot like a vagrant, though it was probably filled with her gear. She failed to say "Goodbye" to anyone. I was sure that she felt whipped and bitter, but a farewell to the club would have been a class act. That's not the way Kate operated, though. I felt certain I'd never see her again.

We found the three-legged dog curled up in the locker room. She seemed to be resting before the onslaught of excited runners came charging in. Jenny went straight to her locker and withdrew a full bottle of Captain Morgan's.

I stank and needed a shower before celebrating. By the time I emerged in a white tank top and jeans, the rest of the women were crowded into the locker room, passing the Captain around and playing enthusiastically with the dog, who seemed to happily relish the attention.

I remarked, "Why is she here?"

Amber responded, "I talked with several of the members, and we hoped to adopt her as our club mascot . . . you know, the underdog."

Already a bit sloshed, Jenny asked, "What do you think, Katie?"

"Let's take a vote," I suggested. 'How many in favor, raise your hand."

It was unanimous. So the three-legged dog was crowned the mascot of The Women's Track Club, but she still needed a name.

'Tripod' was rejected as uncouth. Amber suggested, "Let's keep it simple. How about 'Under'?" Everyone agreed.

I expressed my thought aloud, "Isn't it ironic that our club has a three-legged dog as a mascot?" That brought a hearty laugh from the giddy members.

I guess it made sense that, even though I didn't ask for it, the women voted me captain of our team and president of the club. I vowed that I would "conduct our affairs differently—and hopefully better than—our recently deposed leader had."

Two years later, I turned over the reins of the club to a younger but competent member. Under was present at the ceremony, wagging her tail, of course.

I was happy to be relieved of all the duties and to return my concentration to racing. The two-mile distance became my specialty.

Sadly, Under died not too long after that. Not a single club member missed her dignified burial ceremony.

The Confessional

The confessional door swung open, and a young man sat. "Father, bless me, for I have sinned . . ."

Father O'Flaherty sat uncomfortably on his side of the booth. Listening to confessions and grinding out absolution had always been an important part of his duties as a Catholic priest. Yet, it was his least preferred. Part of the problem was that occupational ennui had seized him during the past few years regarding his duties, particularly working the confessional booth. After all, he had been doing the same chore for more than forty-three years. He felt his parishioners would understand his burn-out.

On this day the priest was already feeling a bit tipsy because he had imbibed several "nips," as he called them, and it was not yet noon. He brought his bottle into the confessional even though it was strictly prohibited by diocese rules. He was aware from long experience that if he continued to sip his Jameson's Irish Whiskey throughout the afternoon, he'd need an early nap and would have to take the bus home, which he had done many times before.

Sometimes he regretted drinking so much alcohol, but he had been doing so for over fifty years, since he attended a Catholic boys' high school as a child. He couldn't recall the reason he started drinking or why he drank so much as a youth. Now, in his old age he simply drank out of habit.

His overindulgence of whiskey had taken its toll on Father O'Flaherty over the years: his beak-like nose had turned the color of blood; veins popped out of his pale skin, which was heavily wrinkled; his weight of 140 pounds on his 6'2" frame had dropped below unhealthy levels; and his once-prominent eyes had retreated deep into their sockets, like they had become exhausted from gazing too long at a disintegrating world. They were perpetually bloodshot like a bloodhound's and dazed, as if the images they perceived were invariably askew.

The Father didn't expect many confessees to show up today. The parish population had been drifting steadily downward, partly because the crime rate in the vicinity of the church had soared during the last few years, and "white flight" had chased many of the long-term parish families to the suburbs. Anyway, he was so confident there wouldn't be anyone else that he had considered closing early.

That was when the young man stepped into the booth and sat down across the shaded grill from him. The man seemed to Father O'Flaherty to be unusually agitated. His dark brown hair was disheveled, his black eyes were darting around impatiently, and even his hands were shaking in a manner inconsistent with his youth. Overall, the priest thought his parishioner was a mess, but he wasn't particularly surprised by that. *After all*, he reflected, *sin has a heavy price to pay sometimes.*

The man appeared to have an intense need to make his confession and then hurry to somewhere that had more priority for him than confessing, as if the booth was a quick stop on his delivery route. The priest felt like he was taking orders at the drive-through of a fast-food joint, and this guy was just another hungry customer.

In his befuddled condition, the priest at first failed to recognize his confessee. However, a closer second look revealed that it was Buddy Armistead. His voice confirmed it. Father O'Flaherty remembered him now: an Irish neighborhood tough, white kid—there actually were a few of them left.

Buddy made infrequent visits to Saint Mary's with his long-suffering wife, Molly, who was a regular churchgoer. Father had heard that after many years of futile and frustrating efforts, Molly was now in the early stage of pregnancy. *Good for them*, thought the priest. He had noticed that Molly seemed excited about the upcoming arrival.

Buddy began his confession, but Father O'Flaherty was becoming increasingly deaf due to his advancing age. He asked Buddy to speak up.

"Yes, okay, Father. No problem, Father, bless me for I have sinned real bad."

It looked to the priest like Buddy was going to jump out of his skin. "Relax, my son. What did you do?"

"You remember my wife, Molly?"

The priest nodded.

"I just killed her a short while ago."

At this point Buddy's face showed signs of extreme distress. He could have been viewing into the deepest place in Hell, where he already expected his home would be forever.

The Father motioned with his hands for Buddy to calm down and get control of himself. Then, he said in a soothing voice: "Calm down, son. Tell me if there's anything else sinful you've done."

His chest heaving and fighting sobs, Buddy blurted out, "It is not what else I've done, Father. It's what I intend to do."

Before the priest could advise him that future sins—those acts which are merely planned but not committed yet—cannot be forgiven, Buddy snapped, "I'm gonna murder my wife's cheatin' lover—that snake, damn him!"

"Tell me, son, what's his name?"

"Don't worry, Father. He's not one of your parishioners."

"I still need to know the name of this reckless sinner."

"I understand, Father. I'll take your word for it. His name is Bill Considine, and you should know, that baby that Molly was carrying was his."

"You shall be absolved for the murder of your wife and her unborn fetus, but regrettably I cannot forgive you for a crime you haven't yet committed. You must do penance for such a crime. You must turn yourself in to the authorities and serve your time in prison under the secular laws . . . I urge you in the Lord's name to go forth and sin no more."

"It's not really gonna matter," responded Buddy, "'cuz when I blast that bastard's head off, I'm saving a bullet for myself. Father, I'm sorry for doing what I have to do, but I can't live in prison!"

Without giving Father O'Flaherty time to respond, Buddy bolted from the booth and was gone.

The priest was left alone on his side of the booth completely stunned. He had received confessions from murderers before, even spousal killers. Yet, he had never heard a confession from someone who had not yet carried out his mortal sin. It was a troubling new experience which left him dazed and confused.

Sucking on his bottle of whiskey all morning had rendered him dizzy, but it was the bottle where he sought solace once again. He withdrew it from the drawer and tugged a long one. His Adam's apple bobbed as the whiskey gurgled down his throat. He sensed the pleasant warmth of the spirit as it made its journey to his gut. As he often had in the past, he felt it was acting as a tonic for the woes of the decision he knew he'd have to make.

Father O'Flaherty wasn't sure at this point whether he could even stand up. He was mortified by his inability to act and felt that even if he could, he was not sure what action he should take.

The priest was firmly aware that church ethics prohibited him from reporting what he was told in the confessional, but that rule applied to past sins and crimes that had been confessed to him.

He was confused as to what the professional ethics prescribed for confessed future crimes.

He wrung his frail white hands and opened the Bible to no specific page. He glanced at it but didn't read a word. He had no clue as to what chapters and verses could help him in this dilemma. He reflected, *This is a modern problem. They didn't have Canons of Ethics back in biblical times.*

Now he stared at the places on his robe that were soiled. There were many, and he closed his tired eyes. He had a notion that he needed to wash his robe.

He felt a low-grade headache starting in his left temple lobe and was relieved that no one else came into the confessional. He could no longer ignore his feeling of alarm. His conscience insisted that he should notify the authorities about Buddy's confessed plan to murder Bill Considine, and the logical starting place was to dial 911, but he agonized over what to tell them.

With his confessional duties completed for the week, he rose shakily to his feet, regained his balance with difficulty, and locked the booth.

He thought, *Maybe God will know what to do. I don't know whether I need to somehow tell God or whether He will know on his own what's happening and send a sign to me.*

As he rushed into the church, his next thought was comforting, *I pray that God can prevent the disaster from happening!*

Then, he did something he rarely did anymore in his daily life. He couldn't recall when the last time was, but it was many years ago. He dropped to his knees at the altar and prayed.

"Father, I don't know what to do. Please help your unworthy servant. Shed some of your healing light to help me find the way to do what's right in dealing with your wayward son, Buddy. Please give me a sign. Thank you, Lord, for your kindness and mercy."

The priest decided to wait another ten minutes for the Lord's sign. During his wait, he almost passed out, but when he snapped to, he checked all around the church for the expected sign.

As he sat by the altar, he had great confidence that the sign—maybe in the form of a voice from Heaven since there were no bushes around to burn—would come. He was sure the Lord would furnish the help he requested. He looked and listened with all the alertness that a drunk could muster. His head sank lower and lower as time elapsed and he realized that there was no voice—from on high or anywhere else.

Then he was bitter: *God is leaving it up to me to decide what to do. And I'm not surprised. During my fifty years as an adult Christian, I can't recall a single occasion when my prayers have been acknowledged by God or even an angel. They certainly have never been answered. I know this is sacrilege, especially corning from a Catholic priest, but sometimes I wonder whether there's really a 'Big Guy' up there.*

He slowly rose from his knees so as to prevent straining himself, left the church, and slipped back into his small, cluttered vestry office. He thought, *It's time to make the call even though I still don't know what to say. A hefty shot of courage is needed to do this.*

He removed an unopened bottle of Jameson's with the seal still on it, which he kept in the lowest drawer for such a stressful occasion as this one. He unscrewed the cap and took several sips of the rich, searing liquid straight from the bottle, dispensing with the filthy glass he normally used.

He could feel the familiar burn reach his stomach with a satisfying splash. He felt a momentary sense of happiness replacing the moroseness and anxiety that had swamped his brain. Thus fortified, he reached across his desk and tremulously dialed 911.

The operator answered in a clear, strong voice: "911, what's your emergency?"

Father O'Flaherty began talking in a low, shaky voice, barely above a whisper, "My name is Father Frederick O'Flaherty of Saint Mary's Church."

That was a lot for him, so he paused. He tried to gather his courage and contemplated taking another gulp.

"Yes Father, what is your emergency?"

"I wish to report a murder . . . and another one that is about to take place . . . at any moment!"

"Do you know the name of the person who is about to be murdered?"

"Yes, I do. It's Bill Considine. I don't know anything else about him."

"Then how do you know he's about to be murdered?"

His courage was peaking, and his nerves were a bit steadier now. He replied, "Because the killer is a parishioner of mine—my church, and he told me in the confessional exactly what he intended to do, He said he was going to do it because his wife was sleeping with this Considine fellow."

"Do you know where Mr. Considine lives or works?"

"No, I'm sorry I don't."

"Who is the person who told you about the murders?"

"Buddy Armistead. He's our parishioner. I'll get you his address. Wait a sec . . . my Rolodex is just out of reach. Please hang on."

"You're not computerized, Father?"

"No. Not yet. I couldn't run this church without my Rolodex."

There was silence on the line, except for some paper shuffling in the background. "Father?"

"I've got it . . . hang on . . . here we go. Buddy lives at 2339 Honeypot Lane."

"Before you go, Father, what about the person who told you he had already committed a murder?"

Father O'Flaherty, in his befuddled condition, responded without thinking: "Same guy. Buddy. He told me that his wife Molly was at their house lying dead."

The priest had had no intention of violating the sanctity of the confessional, but the information had slipped out. Unlike a genie, there was no way to get the words back in the bottle.

After the call clicked off, the priest sat in his comfortable chair paralyzed. He recognized right away that he had breached his professional ethics by reporting what Buddy had confessed. His brain was fuzzy, but he concluded that this violation wouldn't cause any harm.

Really no problem: Molly's dead; if Considine is alive, it's due to my action; and Buddy is either dead by his own hand or he's safely hiding somewhere, or in prison for life.

He took a satisfying pull on his bottle, and it helped momentarily to settle his nerves.

After an hour more of steady drinking and gazing down at his robe counting the stains again, he heard the phone ring from a place far away. It took some effort to locate the phone.

In a tentative voice he said into the receiver: "Saint Mary's."

"Is this Father Fred?"

He had to pause for a moment to recall that this was, in fact, his name and then slurred, "Yes, it is."

"Father, this is Detective Jay Ramsey of the Chicago PD, Homicide Division . . . Father, you don't sound right. I imagine that it's been quite a day for you, huh? Are you feeling well enough to talk right now?"

The priest didn't respond, so Ramsey proceeded with his spiel, "I'm sorry to report that we've found Buddy Armistead."

The priest was confused. "Gosh, Detective, that's good."

"'Fraid not, Padre. We found his body at Bill Considine's house. It appears that this Buddy creep murdered Mr. Considine and then turned the gun on himself. They're both dead. We also know that Buddy killed his wife, Molly, earlier. It's been a tragic day . . . three dead."

"Oh my!" was the priest's only comment.

"We're gathering evidence from Mrs. Considine. Do you have any idea why Armistead committed these murders and took his own life?"

The priest tried to explain in jumbled words what Buddy had told him in the confessional.

"Thanks, Father, for helping to complete the picture here. You know, putting together what Mrs. Considine told us, it appears that Chicago PD received that citizen's 911 call just a few minutes too late. We checked with the supervisor and found that, if 911 had received the warning a mere ten minutes sooner, we might have prevented the deaths of Mr. Considine and Buddy himself. How 'bout that, Father? Bad timing, huh'?"

Detective Ramsey's words of farewell now sounded somewhat sarcastic to the priest: "Have a nice day, Father."

Father O'Flaherty didn't say anything. He let go of the receiver, and it fell off his shoulder and tumbled onto his desk. He realized—like being zapped by an electric shock—that it was he who had made the tardy so-called "citizen's 911 call."

With the guilt of two deaths on his hands, he understood that he had shamefully delayed making that call. He knew, just as surely as if he had murdered them himself, that he was directly responsible for an innocent stranger's death, as well as the suicide of one of his own flock.

A wave of guilt and remorse staggered him like nothing ever had before. He felt like a giant tsunami struck him as he walked on the shore.

The priest angrily ripped the telephone cord out of the wall. After a few minutes of trying to calm himself, he found the telephone directory and looked up the listing for Bill and Maxine Considine. He started to dial their number, then stopped when he realized that there was no dial tone.

His body trembled as he sat immobile in his chair. He downed several more swigs of the only source of courage he had. Irritated and unhinged, he removed his collar and wondered if that removal would be permanent.

He slumped over his desk, half asleep, but his red bloodshot eyes were open and haunted. He was aware that his real suffering had just begun. He felt much older than when he began this day.

"Maybe I'll call her after mass on Sunday," he said to no one in particular, as if he were giving himself permission to put off another unpleasant task.

The Man
Who Didn't Exist

I recently returned to the States after a tedious stint in Afghanistan. This was my first tour of duty in that forlorn country. The experience was unpleasant, and that's an understatement.

I am impatient by nature, so waiting at the base for something to happen was unbearable. The skirmishes and nighttime firefights with the Taliban, our enemy, were few and far between. During the rest of the time, the fellas and I drank beer, played cards, and slept.

After the 9/11 terrorist attacks, I volunteered to fight for my country in Afghanistan. To me, the Taliban was an enemy that had to be extinguished to gain freedom for the Afghan people, especially the women and girls. When I was deployed to Kabul, the capital of the country, I was gung-ho to kill as many of the Taliban as I could. However, my first experience as a "fighting soldier" exposed the reality of war to me, and my focus soon became my survival.

When we left the base on patrol, I was not thrilled about shooting at people, even though they were shooting at me. I don't know to this day whether I actually hit anyone. My guess is that I missed all of them. I was a crappy shot on the range, where they used stationary targets. It would have been a shock if I discovered that I killed someone.

War is a two-way street though. Worse than killing a total stranger would be the enemy's bullets whizzing by and following tracers at night right into my buddy's body. The first time I could actually see the enemy's bullets, I realized that they were trying to kill me. That's why I subsequently ducked for cover whenever I heard enemy fire.

On the next-to-last day of my tour, however, one of those bullets hit me in my shoulder. I was on the base at the time. I wasn't sure whether it was fired by a Taliban sniper who had infiltrated our perimeter or a ricochet from the rifle of one of our own—possibly an inebriated trooper. A drunk soldier with a loaded M-16 is an accident waiting to happen. It's called "friendly fire," but there's nothing friendly about it.

While in Afghanistan, I heard that there are more casualties by friendly fire in the battle zone than is officially recognized. The generals try to cover them up by disguising them as war casualties, or they contend that these men and women never existed. For that reason, loved ones are never notified of the tragedy. There is no body in a box draped with an American flag; no passionate eulogies; no elaborate caskets; no small children bawling as the dirt is tossed into a hole; and no new widow trying to appear stoic but shattered on the inside. The dead soldiers' names are never included on casualty lists, and their loved ones are shuffled from one bureaucrat to another as they try to find out what happened to them. The unfortunate soldier simply vanishes from the official record.

My injury, which wasn't too serious as war injuries go, was recognized by the Army. Our company commander assured me that I was "lucky." I felt like responding that I would have been luckier if the Army had sent me to Germany or kept me at a home base in the States, but I wisely kept that opinion to myself. Instead of being discharged on schedule, I was shipped to

Germany, and I was stuck in an Army hospital during my entire "recuperation period."

They finally released me, and I returned to my parents' home in New Jersey. Not long after, I received a Purple Heart in the mail. I was disappointed not to receive a form letter from the form-letter guy in Washington expressing my country's official "thank you" for my service, but I figured I was fine and no worse for wear, except for a purple scar on my shoulder.

It was time to move on with the rest of my life. The owner of the first company where I applied for a job told me that I must have a current, valid driver's license to work there. I knew that would be a requirement at most companies.

I hadn't driven a motor vehicle as a civilian for four years, so I called the local DMV. The lady who answered informed me I needed a driver's license to drive in the State of New Jersey. I had questions, but she clicked off. When I tried to call back several times, all I heard was a recorded message.

I needed the license because I needed a job for money, and I needed money to survive. That's the way it is for most people. I had to face the obvious. It was time to apply for a license at the local DMV. Even though a trip to the DMV is generally regarded as equivalent to a root canal without a painkiller, it had to be endured.

It was freezing when I rode a bus to the DMV office on the outskirts of our city. The bus's heater must have been faulty. The driver told me that it hadn't worked in three years. The obvious question was, "Why hadn't the bus company fixed it?" but I didn't ask. I guessed that all the buses lacked functioning heaters, so there was no point in changing buses or even complaining about this bus's lack of heating. I had only worn a light jacket, so I froze my butt off all the way.

It wasn't far from the bus stop to the low-slung DMV office, but as I walked, my breath turned to frost. There was a brisk wind blowing, and by now my teeth were chattering. I rubbed my hands together like two sticks in a meager but futile attempt to warm myself. I said a silent prayer that the office would have the thermostat set to 'toasty.'

The building was the color of wet cement, and I didn't see a single window. I strolled through the glass entryway and had a vague notion that I was entering enemy territory. The entryway didn't have any heat, so I continued to rub my hands together. It seemed silly to do so, but I supposed it was merely out of habit.

When I was in high school, the DMV was not my favorite place. Every time I had to go there, the lines were long and moved at a snail's pace. They were even slower than the post office lines. No matter how long the lines were, though, they always failed to open an extra line. If anything, they'd close one, so that all the people in that line had to scurry to the ends of the remaining open lines. I was convinced that these delays were deliberate, but I couldn't figure why. Maybe it was the nature of a bureaucrat to use his or her petty power to punish ordinary citizens, or it was simply for saving costs.

In high school I failed the written driver's test once and the behind-the-wheel test twice, which necessitated five extra trips to these excruciating DMV lines. I'd rather do a second tour of duty in Afghanistan than make another visit to the DMV, but this one was a matter of my life or death.

Somehow it was even colder inside the building than outside. Each breath generated a frosty cloud, which seemed to have its own icicles.

I spotted an elderly man standing next to a vent in the wall. He looked frigid, of course, but also frustrated and weary. I asked him, "What are you doing? Can I help you?"

At first, he appeared not to hear me. His chin was buried in his chest, and his eyes were fixed on the dirty linoleum floor. I figured that he might be a foreigner who didn't understand English. When I finally got his attention, he gazed up at me in a dazed and confused state.

"I'm waiting for heat . . . heat! I need heat and it'll come from there." He pointed desperately to the vent.

There wasn't any air—hot or cold—coming out of the vent, but I didn't have the heart to point that out to him. I, too, was becoming frustrated. With little hope of a rational response, I asked him: "What's the deal with this place? Are they trying to freeze us to death?"

His eyes showed little comprehension. Either he was, indeed, a foreigner, or he was too confused by the cold to process my question. I noticed for the first time that his lips were blue, and his entire body was shaking.

A middle-aged lady emerged from the backroom. There were gray streaks in her hair, which was tightly wrapped to her head in a bun held together by a series of bobby pins.

I pointed to the old man and asked her: "Were you aware that this man seems to be freezing to death?"

"No, not really," she answered. "It's not my department."

"When are they gonna turn on the heat?"

I hoped she would pick up on the edge in my voice, but she simply turned and walked away. I heard her caustic remark over her shoulder: "He's not the only one who's cold."

That was true. Just about every person in the long lines was either blowing into their hands or blowing out frost trails. We were all shivering and stamping our feet. One notable exception was a smug-looking fellow wearing many layers of clothes, which made him resemble a Kodiak bear.

Another elderly gent, who apparently overheard my conversations with the foreigner and the DMV lady, approached me. This fellow seemed to be more stable, so I asked him why it was so cold.

He replied that he had been told by an employee that the building's only space heater was broken and could not be replaced due to lack of funding.

I asked, "How long has it been out of service?"

"Let me put it this way; I was here last winter, and it was out of commission then. I was told that they were working as fast as they could to repair it." He winked at me with a twinkle in his eyes.

I sarcastically remarked, "Yeah, I bet they were."

His impassive stare preceded a silent shrug, as if a defective heater in a public building, like on a public bus, was normal. Producing bitter cold for the customers and employees alike was acceptable to the DMV higher-ups. He closed his remarks by saying, "I'm sure the DMV is sorry for the inconvenience."

I stood at the end of one of the long lines that I picked at random. I was visibly shivering when the guy in front of me, wearing a thick coat, a ski hat, and woolen mittens, turned and asked, "Can you believe how cold it is in here?" He must have heard my teeth chattering.

Guys like that really get me. He's as warm as toast; yet he knows I'm freezin' my butt off! He still asks me a stupid question like that. After a pause, I spit out an irritated, "No I can't."

I sought out the second elderly guy I had conversed with and asked him how he could stand the cold.

"You mean because I'm so old? Unfortunately, I'm here every weekday, and I know that the heater bonked out at least two years ago and has never worked since."

"Why are you here so often?"

"'Cuz I'm the daytime janitor, but most days I'm sure I'm that creature, you know . . . the abom . . ."

I finished for him: "Abominable Snowman."

"That's the one! Anyway, I'm ready to quit. My friend told me to sue the state. What do you think?"

"I'm not a lawyer, so I don't know what to tell you."

He appeared to be disappointed. "What do you do?"

"I was a soldier. Now I'm looking."

He showed no interest, so I said, "About your lawsuit against the state, just go for it if you think you've got a case."

Even though he didn't know if he had a case, that's what he wanted to hear. He cracked a broad smile and said, "Thanks."

I was at the end of what appeared to be the shortest of four very long lines, so I tried to feel lucky. I was surprised that so many people could fit in the building. At least twenty ordinary folks were packed tightly between me and the counter. In that each customer took an average of ten minutes, I figured it'd take me three hours and twenty minutes to reach the counter. I groaned.

The people in line shuffled forward with bored expressions. Each customer left the counter with a look of relief. I could feel a slow burn rising somewhere inside me and, despite the cold, my forehead was dripping. I realized that there was nothing for me to do except wait.

I spotted with envy a man ahead of me reading a book. I assumed he must be a DMV vet and figured that he could polish off *War and Peace* by the time he reached the counter. I began to regularly stick out my head so I could see each customer being served and the employee behind the counter. She was a young woman who was very pleasant to look at . . . there were not too many like her in Afghanistan. I could tell that she was efficient and friendly. She even smiled at each new customer.

Then, with sixteen customers still ahead of me, the friendly clerk was replaced by a woman old enough to be my grandmother. She had a sour expression—like she was mad at the world embodied by the couple dozen people in her line. As she slowly scrutinized and then processed each customer, she vanished regularly from the counter, as if the strain of standing there was too much for her. Each time she exercised her disappearing act, I heard several groans from the people standing ahead of me.

The guy at the front was probably relieved when he finally reached the finish line. But he fell to the ground just shy of the counter. I figured his legs were numb from standing there so long. He began crawling, but the elderly lady in line behind him tried to lunge around him to go next. At that point, the old clerk decided to take another break. The man whose turn it was managed to stand by pulling himself up by the edge of the counter. Then he elbowed Granny back behind him and pounded the Formica in an outburst of understandable rage. He shouted at the slowly retreating clerk: "Get back here and do your job!"

I sympathized with the guy but thought, *A lot of good that's gonna do. Yet, his situation could be mine in a couple of hours.*

The office wisely didn't have a wall clock, but my watch told me I wasn't gonna make it before closing time. "Swell!"

When the guy at the counter banged his fist and yelled, I heard a cheer from some of the unhappy souls in front of and behind me. The clerk finally returned, and the guy at the counter could barely contain himself. He derisively muttered, "How could you take such a long break with so many people waiting?"

It sounded like a reasonable question, but she stared at him the way a grandmother gives the evil eye when the kids under her care get a bit too rowdy. Then she looked past him and calmly said, "Next."

The summit of this character's head almost erupted like Mount St. Helens. His face was the color of a beet. Hair rose on the back of his violently shaking hands. He was hysterical. I was afraid he might go postal and was thankful he didn't have a gun.

The clerk must have noticed that he was ready to blow and shatter into a thousand pieces all over the linoleum. She said with a bit more edge in her voice: "Back of the line."

He yelled, "Do you know whom you're talkin' to?"

He obviously was full of himself and refused to move.

I facetiously wondered, *How could he defy a state bureaucrat like that? That's not possible, is it?*

When the counter clerk spoke, it sounded more like a croak. She looked at Mr. Big Shot with daggers thrown from both eyes. It was a game of chicken, and my bet was on the clerk. He wisely decided he had had enough and turned toward the door, spouting out a stream of invective which would have made my drill sergeant blush.

Oh well, at least I was one person closer to what I thought of as the finish line.

The clerk kept up her disappearing act, and many of the people behind me were panicking and bailing out to other faster-moving lines or for the door. The folks ahead of me didn't budge, probably because they had already invested so much time in this line, or perhaps they were praying for the pretty clerk to return. She didn't.

I overheard two women line-dwellers in front of me gossiping about our new clerk.

"I wish I'd brought a tent."

"Yeah, and some beer and hot dogs too."

"Make a party out of it . . . what's the deal with this old gal? She must feel entitled to all her breaks because of longevity."

"You bet—one hundred years!"

"Either that or she's a pee-aholic."

"What's that?"

"Think about it. Someone who has no control over her bladder and has to pee all the time. We had one in our college sorority. She attended PP meetings every week, but her bladder gave out even at those meetings. She had to regularly make a run to the bathroom, and she couldn't drink coffee, a staple of those PP meetings."

"What do you think about that guy going ballistic?"

"I don't blame him. I'm about ready to go in that direction myself."

"Just don't let her hear you say that, or you'll be sent in shame to the dreaded 'back of the line.'"

"Just like the first grade, huh?"

The women got me thinking about pee-aholics. We had a boatload of them in the service. We dreaded to get some in our platoon because they were nuisances in the field. They regularly whined that we had to stop because they couldn't hold their "water" any longer.

So we were constantly taking breaks, making us sitting ducks for the Taliban snipers. And they never had to take a pee break at the same time. One would have to go, and we'd ask the other one, and he'd say, "Nope, I'm good." Ten minutes later he'd have to go.

Finally, one abrasive sergeant told the whiner that he didn't care whether the guy peed and shit in his pants. The platoon wasn't stopping.

Another way for me to pass the time in line was people-watching. I'd spot a distinctive customer in one of the other lines and follow his or her progress to the counter. After a while I'd see that customer at the front of his or her line or leaving the building with a satisfied smile. That's when my fun ceased and frustration took over.

I figured that the DMV could have opened two additional lines but apparently chose not to do so because they didn't have enough clerks to man those extra stations. Thus, as I wasted time, I became more and more irritated. As the hours went by and the croaker's breaks became longer, some of the customers in front of and behind me began to sit on the floor. It was like a college sit-in. I didn't join them. The floor was so dirty that I figured they were risking their lives in a battle with germs.

A few late arrivals actually attempted to cut into the front of the line, but the existing folks there vehemently stood their ground and fought off the intruders. A few angry words and some pushing were exchanged, but there was no serious damage.

When I could stick my neck out far enough, I could view the old crone behind the counter. She barked at customers who didn't have their paperwork in order, although there weren't any instructions posted anywhere as to what order they should be in—or even identifying the required papers.

I noticed that she appeared to be suffering physically and correspondingly took more frequent and longer breaks. I also noticed that she shuffled papers in an increasingly haphazard manner, as if her eyes had stopped functioning and she was operating on auto-bitch. Finally, it appeared that she remembered her specs, which she had left on the counter. They seemed to slightly speed up her work.

I was fairly sure that the documents she was reading were forms that she had seen ten thousand times before, and yet, she scrutinized each one like a scientist studying a new species of insect under a microscope. At first I thought she seemed like the type who considered herself above engaging in conversation, but then she surprised me with how much time she spent conversing with some customers and answering their endless questions.

As I inched closer to the counter, I noticed that her remaining teeth were heavily stained yellow, her index finger was also discolored, and she shook like a sapling in a windstorm. It didn't take a genius to conclude that our counter person was a heavy smoker and her lengthy breaks were taken outside the building to smoke. She probably was able to survive the cold because her skin was as thick as an elephant's.

I overheard an anxious customer behind me mention to her companion that this office closed at 4:00 p.m. I was ninth in line and again worried that I might not make it before closing. This meant I'd be forced to undergo this ordeal again tomorrow. I'm not aggressive by nature, but this situation was starting to get my attention. It was 3:05, and the clerk was taking another break.

I was in good Army grunt shape but had been standing on the hard floor for a long time. I was hurting. My knees and lower back were crying "Uncle." In addition, my recently injured shoulder was throbbing.

When the customer in front of me reached the counter, I prayed that the visibly worn-out clerk would not take a break. Then, for no particular reason, I began holding my breath, which lasted two-and-a-half minutes. I blew the air out in what might legitimately be called my last gasp. I finally reached the counter, DMV's version of the Holy Grail, and with two minutes to spare.

The granite-faced woman on the other side of the counter smiled with glee in saying, "You are my last customer, so make it fast!"

Before I could state my case, she glared at me with her beady, little red eyes. "Well?" She dropped her smile and angrily barked, "I'm gonna close this line in five seconds unless you tell me why you're here. Come on, spit it out!"

She then hinted that I was a troublemaker and the principal cause of any delays in her line. She obviously was designating me as the scapegoat for her failure to serve everyone before closing. Why was she targeting me? I had no clue. At that point I reached over to touch the counter to check whether this was real or all a bad dream.

"Now, what are you doing here?" she smirked.

"You wouldn't understand . . ."

"Stop it!"

"Can we just get on with this?" I was losing my patience . . . tired of her game-playing, but I knew I needed to control my anger. I tried to explain what I wanted, "I'm here to . . ."

She suddenly exclaimed, "Be right back."

I stood in front of the empty counter for eight minutes until she returned. I tried unsuccessfully to avoid her nicotine breath.

She said, as a challenge, "See this watch?" She removed it from her pocket and placed it on her side of the counter. "I usually do not work past 4:00 p.m. I have a life too. So I'm going to give us five minutes to resolve your problem. Then, my lane is closed, and you'll have to come back another day. Comprende?"

I glanced over at the empty lines without clerks and nodded. All of a sudden, she took off again. I saw her confer with one of her coworkers and then waddle back to her station. She appeared surprised that I was still there. She looked at her watch again and said, "You've got three minutes."

"Hey, hold it right there. You said I'd have five minutes . . ."

She interrupted me and croaked, "Now you've got two."

A few of the stragglers in line behind me started to grumble and release some of their pent-up frustration. Somehow, they, too, thought I was the cause of her numerous breaks.

Her icy stare went right through me, as if she was trying to connect with the next person in line. When I began my explanation of what I needed, she ignored me and called out, "Next!" Her two-minute limit apparently had expired.

The woman behind me appeared to be one of those persons who make their way through the world with a sense of entitlement. She was a big, matronly type. She tried to push me out of the way, but I wouldn't budge.

The clerk seemed to be bemused by the shoving match that was taking place in front of her. She finally slammed her fist on the counter and barked to me: "Get out of this lady's way. I'm workin' overtime, which I detest, and I don't have the time or patience to do anything for you."

I thought, *So this is how it's gonna' be.* I snapped at the counter lady. "I've been waiting for over three hours. You're gonna listen to me and do what needs to be done for me, or I'm gonna have a word with your supervisor."

She snickered, "Ha! Okay, buddy, you have three minutes. What can I do you for?" A wry smile replaced her usual grouchy expression as if to say, "Listen to how clever I am."

I said defiantly, "I need a New Jersey driver's license."

"What happened to your old one?" she asked suspiciously.

"I don't know. I got it when I was a teenager. I haven't seen it for a long time."

Her phony smile disappeared and was replaced by a frown. The heavy wrinkles on her brow and neck deepened into grooves. She paused as if to control her nerves and gather strength for an all-out assault on me. "What do you mean, you don't know?"

"I was in the Army the last four years fighting in Afghanistan."

"Where the hell is that?" Then she quickly changed her mind. "Forget about it . . ."

Her blank expression told me she was mulling over whether I was a wacko terrorist. I figured she was having graphic flashbacks of the news coverage of the terrorist aircraft attacks by the suicidal pilots: the collapsing buildings; the dust swirling around into a mammoth cloud; a large part of New York City turned into a desert storm; frantic people rushing out of the buildings and running for their lives; desperate screams of the poor souls who couldn't make it to safety; the jumpers from the upper stories with no chance to live; sirens blaring; car alarms reverberating in the streets that would soon be buried by massive chunks of fallout; and store windows shattering as if a violent mob riot had just broken out.

I reflected, *That's why I enlisted! Could this bitchy bureaucrat actually be suspecting that the guy in front of her with the hopeful expression was really a terrorist sympathizer, who at that minute was devising a fiendish plan to bring down America?* Then I caught myself. *I can't worry about what she thinks of me! I know who I am and what I've done to help my country.*

She made a half-hearted effort to paste a smile on her face and asked in a facetious tone, confident that she already knew the answer, "Do you have any type of identification?"

"Let's see . . . I have my Army ID card. Will that work?" I didn't wait for her to respond and quickly fished it out of my wallet.

Her cynical expression answered my question. She snatched it out of my hand and scrutinized it vigilantly. I sensed that she was trying to find some way to prove that it was fake, a key item of evidence proving my participation in a terrorist plot. I read her intent to expose me as a criminal using a false ID to manipulate the system.

"It says here that your name is Kent Wilcox. Is that, in fact, your name?"

"Right. It's been my name since birth."

"Look, buster, don't get smart with me! I can play that game too." Then in what seemed like her "aha moment," she snapped, "Have you ever used any other names? C'mon, give it up." She sounded like a loyal fan of TV's "Law and Order."

"Nope."

Her beady little eyes remained fixed on mine, like she was thinking that if she stared hard enough, I would crumble and confess the truth—that I was a liar, a fraud, and a terrorist sympathizer. She punched some keys on the keyboard attached to her computer. Her grin and her humming flaunted her determination to expose me. I could hear the keys tapping as if she was moving in for the kill.

Then, a slip. Her mouth drooped. More key tapping. She paused and then made a breakthrough. I could tell whatever she had found was going to go against me. The coup de grace. Her expression turned to triumph, and I thought she'd scream, "I told you so!"

Instead, she spitefully declared, "There's no Kent Wilcox on my computer. I checked it twice. That name doesn't appear anywhere in the U.S. The computer is always right. Kent Wilcox doesn't exist! You'd better come clean, buster. What's your real name, and why are you using a false name to obtain a driver's license?"

This accusation hit me like a hard slap across my face. I felt ashamed even though there was no reason to feel this way. I wanted to debunk her accusation to those people standing close enough to hear her question. My attitude changed from fear of not getting my license to a panic that I could not fully explain. The concept of my vanishing from the DMV's computer was maddening and, at the same time, scary. I wondered where I was in this bureaucratic maze. Had I been temporarily "misplaced" or permanently deleted?

To drive the last nail in my coffin she jovially called out over my shoulder: "Next!"

I wouldn't budge. I held my ground as only someone can who knows he's right. It was the way we held a hill during battle.

The mouse-faced matron was adhered to my backside with her pig-tailed two-year-old tugging on a leash attached to mom's belt.

The child was squalling up a storm. My ears ached, and I felt like grabbing the kid and shaking her.

The matron apparently decided to nudge me out of the way to get to the counter, but I had waited longer than her, and I was not about to acquiesce to her maneuver.

The woman behind the counter fired bullets at me with her piercing eyes that said, *You're guilty as hell*. She snapped, "Get out of her way! What you're trying to do is a crime punishable by years in prison. Leave the building right now! You're trying my patience, and I'm about to call security."

"Look at me, ma'am! I clearly exist! You've got it wrong. Your computer is wrong! I'm breathing; my heart is pumping blood; I'm alive! I survived a bloody war in a foreign country. I was fighting under the name Kent Wilcox. I was fighting for you! Kent Wilcox is still my name. I'm entitled to a New Jersey driver's license. If you won't issue one to me, I'm ready to—as they say—come undone.

"Maybe this will make sense to your avaricious nature: no license, no job. No job, no way to support myself. No earnings, no payment of taxes, and I'm entitled to life on the dole."

Then I beat a retreat toward the exit. As I hustled to get out of there, I shuddered to think of what my final words had actually accomplished, if anything. Disgusted, I turned back toward the counter clerk and shouted, "What are you trying to do, kill me? Well, if I don't exist, I'll never have to pay taxes again."

I figured she'd just ignore my blast, but I saw her out of the corner of my eye conferring with two security guards in navy blue uniforms. They began striding toward me. I had to admit that the crazy clerk was feisty.

She yelled over their oncoming assault: "You can't get away with your scheme! Not in my department! Not on my turf; not on my watch, fella!" She followed that with "Officers, take that man into custody."

I had to get the last word in, so I yelled, "How can they arrest me if I don't exist?"

It turned out it wasn't the last word, though. She bellowed, "Shut your mouth, buddy, so I can serve some real people!"

I could hear the customers who were still in line cheering and clapping at my ouster.

The glass exit door now had a "Closed" sign pointing outward. I was about to slip through it when I felt a heavy hand on my wounded shoulder. I exclaimed, "Ow, that hurts like hell!"

"What's the problem, buddy? I didn't grab that hard."

My anger and disgust at the counter clerk almost carried over to punching the security guard. However, I took a deep breath and readied myself for the confrontation.

The guard who grabbed me calmly said, "Take it easy, Kent."

Boy, was I shocked—like I'd been bit by an electric eel. My name!

"You called me by my name," I said excitedly.

"Don't get too wound up. That's the only name we have for you. Yet, according to Batty Betty and our ancient computer system, you don't exist."

"Batty Betty?"

"Yep, that's her nickname around here. Others call her 'the ol' battleaxe.'"

"Right on!" I added, "Am I in trouble?"

"Hell, no. If you were involved in some crooked tax scheme, would you have picked the line with that ol' gal at the counter? Your so-called scheme was applying for one driver's license? Give me a break! Let me see your military ID card."

I showed it to him, but I was anxious he'd claim it was forged.

"Looks fine to me . . . you know, I was in the Army too. I was born too late for Vietnam. I applied for overseas duty, but they confined me to a fort here in the States. My assignment was office clerk. I never fired a gun in anger."

He looked distraught, but I wasn't about to set him straight.

"I admired and respected you guys who fought overseas, especially the GIs who came home wounded—you know—who got a Purple Heart."

"Nah, it wasn't what it was cracked up to be."

"Did you get one?"

"One what?"

"What we were talkin' about—a Purple Heart?"

"Oh yeah, I'm sorry . . . yeah, I got one . . . for my shoulder. A Taliban sniper got it."

"I'm sorry to hear that. I guess after that, your stateside problems, such as Batty Betty, must seem like a piece of cake."

"Hum, not exactly, but I can't do anything about it here."

"Well, I'll let you get on your way." He offered his hand and I shook it.

"Thanks."

As we walked away from each other, I could hear him say, "A word to the wise: Try to avoid Betty's line next time."

As I hiked to the bus station, I felt a bit better. My anger subsided, but I was worried about my future more than ever. I knew some guys in the service who took the position, "Let it flow; everything will work out." I was not built that way . . . sadly.

When I got home, I figured that the next step in getting a driver's license was to formulate a new plan. I could try a different DMV office. Another possibility was to travel to another state to apply. New York State and Pennsylvania were the logical choices. If that failed, I could tour all the states until I found someone who believed me—damn their computer. They would come out and say it—the words I longed to hear: "You exist as a living person."

I had heard of a relatively new crime called "identity theft," which I believed was what Batty Betty did to me. I had also heard in a movie—or was it a book—of "a man without a country." I even heard of the "invisible man."

But I had never heard of "the man who didn't exist."

For a veteran of the bloodfest known as the Afghanistan War, this problem seemed like it should be "a piece of cake" for me. Perception can be different from reality, though, as I discovered in my battle with the DMV.

11

A Father's Tale

My father has never been much of a talker, and he has especially avoided talking about the war he fought in . . . World War II. Growing up, my brother and I would ask about his experiences in the Pacific theater, but he would brush us off with vague excuses like: "That was a long time ago. I don't remember much," or "I don't have time to talk about it right now."

All of this changed one recent evening when my mother came downstairs carrying a thin, ragged piece of metal about the size of a pillow. My name is Josh, I'm thirteen years old, and this is my father's story about the battle for the Japanese island of Okinawa.

Brandishing the homely hunk of metal, Mom asked Dad pointedly: "What do you want to do with this . . . I won't call it 'junk,' so let's say it's a relic?"

The rest of us were sitting at the dinner table. Dad and my younger sister, Kacie, were still eating. My sixteen-year-old brother Jeff and I had cleaned our plates but had not been excused. Dad liked to run a tight ship, and we were all expected to remain at the table until everyone had finished the meal.

Normally, Mom followed this rule as well, but she had been on one of her cleaning kicks all day and apparently couldn't wait to get back to it. I wondered later if she picked that moment to come downstairs so she could ambush Dad while he was still at the table.

"It's been in the closet for years collecting dust," she said, her voice full of disdain for this mysterious object. "We've gotta throw it out."

We kids were wide-eyed with mystery and awe, suspecting that my father's sentiment for the filthy-looking piece of metal must have been deep if he had saved it for so many years. My father had never been a collector. As far as I knew he had not kept any photos from the war or his youth on the East Coast. That's why I was so surprised when he spoke.

"I'm keeping it, Liz," he informed her simply. "It's important to me."

My mother was tenacious and impatient. She didn't give up easily about anything. I heard her once yelling at a patch of tomatoes to grow faster. So, she wasn't going to back down over a useless metal scrap. She demanded, "Why do you want to keep that old piece of junk? It takes up space we need for other things."

My father turned to all of us, "Gather around," he said. "It's about time you heard the story behind this piece of metal. Maybe then you'll understand why this souvenir means so much to me."

We kids sat in a semicircle on the living room carpet with our backs to a roaring fire. Dad sat down in his usual reading chair in front of us. Our mother glanced around fretfully for a moment—probably reluctant to abandon her closet-cleaning project—before perching on the edge of an ottoman on one side of the fireplace.

"Kids, I'm going to tell you a story about this piece of metal that you've never heard before," Dad said. "Mom, you may remember some of this tale."

He didn't have to tell us to listen closely. The mystery of the metal artifact combined with a rare storytelling moment from our father had riveted our attention. When he began to speak, we were all ears.

"It was the spring of 1945. Our country had been at war with Germany and Japan for over three years. Germany was already defeated in Europe, but the Japanese were hanging tough and holding onto heavily fortified islands such as Okinawa, the closest island to mainland Japan.

"I had been stationed on a Navy destroyer ship in the Pacific Ocean for all this time, racking up one victory after another. Our vessel cut through the water like the Pacific bottlenose dolphins that constantly swam in the wake behind us.

"I was only twenty-three years old but still the veteran of our crew. A sailor or soldier ages fast during wartime. My shipmates and I were weary of war, but we still had a job to do. My team was in charge of the gun on the aft deck. From there, we could fire effectively but were an easy target for any Jap planes who evaded our defenses."

Jeff interrupted, "Isn't that word 'Jap' slang for the word 'Japanese'?"

Dad answered, "It is the name we used to call our enemy."

"Yeah, Dad, but isn't it offensive to the Japanese people these days?"

"I suppose so. Kids, don't ever use the word 'Japs' in public. Got it?"

We all agreed, so he continued in his composed, even manner.

"I often stood next to the long barrel, surveying the horizon. As I gazed across the calm water on the day I'm telling you about, I saw an awesome sight: hundreds of gray hulks bobbing all the way to the horizon. They looked like logs on a still pond. It was our invasion fleet. They gave me the warm feeling of being protected.

"As I stood by myself on the deck, a golden glow seemed to envelop me. Other than the dying sun, I couldn't figure out where it was coming from. Anyway, the glow seemed to chase away my fear of the upcoming battle. I figured that no enemy could defeat such an armada. I felt a power that fostered confidence in my crew, our ship, the armada, and myself. I knew we were all led by the indomitable Admiral Halsey, and that strengthened my confidence.

"The ships were making long shadows across the water. I figured there was about two hours of daylight left. Then, it suddenly got dark. The tropics are like that. I could just make out some carriers and wondered which one had the head skipper aboard. I also wondered which of the ships, including ours, would survive the battle."

My father paused to look around at his family. We were all alert and, I believe, eager to hear more. He smiled broadly—rare for my dad—and continued.

"My buddy, Seaman Bobby Heck, joined me at the railing and asked the same question that was on my mind: 'Which ship do you think Halsey's on?'

"I glanced at my pal and replied, 'I wonder. I'm sure it's not info that the brass would advertise. Just pick any of those carriers.'

"Bobby, who never missed a beat, said, 'Oh yeah, that narrows it down to . . . what, six? Where do you think we're headed?'

"A couple of the crew who had been eavesdropping leaned in a bit closer to hear my answer.

"I said, 'We've assaulted every one of the islands up the chain toward Japan's home islands, and we've conquered every one of them. There's only one group left: Okinawa. But it ain't gonna be no piece of cake. Those bastards fought hard to hold onto every one of them—a no-surrender policy. I heard that the land battle on Iwo Jima was a horrible ordeal. We lost thousands of our land forces. I guess the brass figured that we couldn't afford to bypass any of those islands.'

"'Were you at Iwo Jima, Jack?'"

Jack is Dad's name.

"I nodded and elaborated, 'Our guns joined those on the other ships to pound the jungle that lined the beach. We also joined our fighters in protecting the skies so that a Jap dive-bomber couldn't drop a bomb or launch a torpedo. Capturing Iwo Jima was a slugfest.

We lost many of the ground forces, planes, and even some ships. It was shocking to see our boys getting mowed down on the beach by the Jap machine-gunners hiding in the jungle.'

"Bobby noticed that I was tense describing the battle for Iwo Jima, but all he said was, 'I know it's gotta hurt. Smoke, Jack?' Bobby was always offering me a cigarette. He'd forget I didn't smoke, or he wanted me to start."

Jeff pointed out, "Maybe you should have smoked on the ship. It might have settled your nerves."

"You know, almost everyone on the ship smoked," Dad replied. "I was tempted. It was the era where men were expected to smoke. Ol' Bobby was persistent too. 'With all the crap that's about to hit the fan, it's as good a time as any to start,' he pressed.

"'For the last time, it's gonna take something bigger than a war to get me to smoke,' I told him.

"Someone mentioned the Japanese home islands, and that diverted our attention.

"Bobby said, 'Okinawa will be nothing compared to their home islands. They're gonna be a bitch!'

"Not pulling any punches with these guys, I responded, 'They're gonna fight us over every inch of their home soil. Balls to the walls for all the Japanese troops, planes, and ships. They're tough. Don't forget that our supply lines stretch over four thousand miles. But we can't get ahead of ourselves. We have to capture Okinawa first.'"

I looked over at Mom when he said "bitch" and "balls to the walls." She frowned her disapproval but would never criticize him directly for it, and Dad was too immersed in his tale to notice.

"Bobby asked me, 'What is Okinawa like?'

"It was a mysterious place to me, too, but I told the guys what little I knew about it: 'The Nips have been on Okinawa a long time. They're well dug-in. I've heard that they've occupied and fortified every high point and every ridge. It's gonna be a suicide mission for our advance forces.'

"Bobby responded, 'I guess we got no choice, Jack. If the brass didn't bypass any of those other islands, they sure as shit ain't gonna bypass Okinawa.'

"'Yep, there's no way they can,' I agreed.

"The rest of the crew concurred. I added, 'The Japanese still have plenty of planes, so it'll be tough for the fleet. Their zeros and dive bombers will target the destroyers first. We're gonna have our hands full out here on the perimeter.'

"There was a slight tremor in Bobby's voice when he said, 'I hear ya. When their planes are attacking our ship, guess which part of the ship they're gonna go after first?'

"One of the other members of the crew exclaimed, 'They'll come at our gun. We gotta be ready for them!'

"The sun was taking its sweet time sinking into the ocean. Twilight is the scariest time for a naval ship at sea, as it is for an ocean swimmer. The creaking and moaning of the ship were amplified, as if ghosts were coming out to play. The massive ship's engines churned and chugged. The sirens were silent, but the bells were loud in signaling a shift change or chow. The sounds of the waves lapping against the hull were unusually loud.

"I noticed that the wind stiffened, causing the flags to flutter. Could a storm be on the way? Waves were breaking on the sea all around us, creating whitecaps. They sounded like rifles firing in a series on a range. Distant ocean swell looked like gray mountains advancing toward land. I imagined them gathering strength until they crashed over the reefs and rolled onto the sand."

"Just like on our beach, huh, Dad?" commented my sister.

"That's right, honey."

Continuing his story, Dad said, "Even above the relentless chop, we could hear the seagulls flapping above us, fighting the wind in order to remain even with our ship. They occasionally swooped down and dove below the surface to snare a fish.

"Bobby and I made eye contact but quickly looked away. We both knew what the presence of the gulls meant—the ominous fact that land was near and so was the enemy, setting the scene for the inevitable battle. With it came the chance of dying.

"At first light, the Marines will be landing in their crafts that plow through the shallows right onto the sand, I reflected. The enemy planes will be overhead and taking their toll on our troops. My imagination was running wild, but I was smart enough not to share these thoughts with my crew. I figured there was no sense in rattling them before we even began to fight. I couldn't help but think that it would be a terrible shame to come this far and to fight in so many battles, only to die in this lonely expanse of ocean."

My father winced and said, "A knot formed in my gut as I stood at that railing gazing at the horizon."

I glanced at Dad in this unheard-of moment of vulnerability. My father never showed or even talked about his feelings. From his example, I had always understood that stoicism was how a man was supposed to act. I figured it took a lot of tension and sadness to cause such a momentary breakdown.

I saw Kacie wince too. She also appeared excessively wrought by the tale. I silently considered that the upcoming part of Dad's narrative had the earmarks of a horror story for my nine-year-old sister.

Personally, I felt chilled even though I was sitting by the fire, and I asked myself whether I was succumbing to the stress of the tragic events that I was sure Dad's story would entail. I thought it might be a case of nerves that would go away in a few minutes.

In that moment, though, I identified with Dad and the poor souls on his crew. We all have duties to our family, our country, and the people around us at work or school. We also have a duty to ourselves merely to survive.

Dad continued, "I heard a scratchy announcement on the ship's aging sound system that ordered all officers and crew chiefs to report to the main mess. Bobby flashed a nervous smile and called out above the din, 'That's you, Jack!'

"'I know it. On my way.'

"I double-timed it to the ship's main mess. The captain was up front with some of the senior officers. When he was satisfied that everyone was there, he stood up and began his pitch:

"'This is it, gentlemen. We're steaming toward the Japanese-held island of Okinawa. It is heavily fortified on the beaches and on the inland ridges with over one hundred thousand Japanese troops. It's going to be a tough slog for our ground forces. It's up to us to back them up.

"'There shouldn't be any Japanese naval forces, but here's the rub; their air force is still functioning. They'll be coming from airstrips on their southernmost island. There's a reliable rumor that they'll be supplemented by suicide planes called kamikazes. The only way to defend against them is to shoot them down before they make their final dive toward the ship. Understood?'

"'Aye aye, Cap.'

"'Any questions?'

"A gun chief stood and asked, 'Sir, how will we know if the incoming plane is a . . . What's it called?'

"Someone shouted, 'kamikaze!'

"The chief continued, 'Yeah, one of them.'

"There were a few snickers.

"The captain sternly said, 'Knock it off.' Then he explained grimly, 'Chief, if the plane headed at your gun mount keeps flying at you, it's a kamikaze. If you wait too long to shoot it down, you'd better duck.'

"There were more snickers around the mess hall, and the chief's big, round face turned red.

"The captain announced in a more upbeat mood, 'Ok, boys, sounds like you're ready. Dismissed!'

"I rejoined my crew in the rapidly diminishing twilight. Bobby remarked, 'It's a beautiful night.' I smiled but didn't answer him.

"I gazed at the first stars twinkling in the brilliant clear sky. As tranquil as it was, I had a bad feeling about tomorrow, so I decided to hit the sack early to avoid recurring thoughts about the upcoming battle.

"Although I didn't sleep much, I still woke up feeling much better. I looked around and heard the snores of the seamen and their talking in their sleep. Even here in the bowels of the ship, I could still sense the ship's movement.

"As I made my way to the main deck, I thought, *They're getting the fleet set up in front of the largest island by now. The Japs are not gonna like that. They're gonna do everything to sink all our ships. Their air force is bound to strike first and furiously.* I moved quickly to take my position at the gun mount.

"The rest of the crew trickled out of the mess hall. It was daybreak, that early morning time when the sun's first beams burst through the fog. Stars still twinkled overhead, as if they were saying their good-byes until nightfall."

For a guy who rarely told stories, Dad sure was painting some vivid pictures for us. I wondered where he had been hiding this talent and if we would get to see more of it in the future.

He continued, "I couldn't see Bobby among the guys. Case of nerves? Ill? I didn't think so. Bobby was too experienced fighting in battles such as our upcoming one. He relished the feeling of his gun blasting away; the roar of the enemy planes overhead; the crash of the bullets ripping into metal all around us; and the shouts of our crew. None of it fazed Bobby. He wouldn't miss this assault for anything. So, where was he?

"No sooner had these thoughts gone through my head than I spotted Bobby sprinting across the deck. He looked embarrassed but still managed a smile upon reaching the crew. He scanned the horizon to make sure the battle hadn't begun without him. 'I'm sorry I'm late, Chief.'

"I replied, 'This better be a good one.'

"'I was late getting to the mess,' he said sheepishly. 'I wanted to fill my stomach so I'd have something to heave when the Jap planes began crashing into our gun mount.'

"I wasn't angry with my friend. I said, 'Okay, enough chatter. Let's go through our prebattle routines.'

"By then the final traces of mist and fog had lifted, and I saw something white, green, and brown over the far railing. Land! The island had finally come into view. The pristine sand stretched around its perimeter, and the aqua water gently lapped onto the shore. It looked like a tropical paradise, but of course, looks can be deceiving. The sun was peaking above the horizon. Its rays glistened off the calm water and used the ship to create a long shadow.

"I was appreciating this scenery when I heard a hum that was easily distinguishable from the ship's engines. This noise sounded more like an angry hornet—one who was trapped in a kid's jar and seeking a way to escape. I pondered how an insect could get this far out, but my thoughts were interrupted by some Jap zeros protecting three dive bombers flying out of the bright sun. It appeared that they were targeting the nearest carrier. Our job was to protect the carriers.

"I could hear an alarm loud and clear over the loudspeakers and a voice yelling, 'Battle stations. To your battle stations. This is not a drill!'

"Bobby yelled, 'See them, Jack? I've got a bead on them.'

"The crew was in position to let them have it. The reload crew also stood ready to feed another shell into the chamber as soon as Bobby fired, so I yelled, 'Commence firing!'

"The gun made a loud crack. The smell of gunpowder was oppressive.

"I panned the sky with a powerful set of binoculars. There had been three bombers escorted by four zeros. Now there were only two bombers. Bobby had hit one of them. However, there were still four aircraft heading toward the carrier.

"Then I heard guns fire from the carrier, and two zeros splashed into oblivion.

"Bobby screamed with a twisted smile, 'I got one of the bombers. Did you see that, Chief? I'm gonna get me another!'

"I yelled at Bobby, 'Two o'clock!' He fired. I scoped in on where I thought one of the remaining two bombers was. Sure enough, Bobby hit another, and it was spiraling toward the surface trailing a plume of black smoke. I yelled, 'Good shot, Bobby!' but he was already searching for the third bomber."

Kacie was listening to the story attentively for someone so young. When Dad paused to catch his breath, she asked him: "What does 'two o'clock' mean? I thought that was to tell time."

"Yes, sweetie, it tells time, but it also tells direction by using the clock dial. Two o'clock as a direction means the plane was flying a little bit to the right of 12:00, which was straight in front of us."

"I see. Kinda like the vane on top of our house tells which way the wind's blowin'."

"You got it."

Dad resumed the tale:

"Bobby fired again, and I could hear him curse so I knew he missed. If the carrier was blown up, I knew Bobby would blame himself.

"'Hell, you missed, Bobby! Wait! What's that coming out of the tail of the bomber?'

"'Well, I'll be, Chief. You're right! Hell, that's black smoke! Three for three! Not bad, huh, Chief!'

"'Look, Bobby, it's dropping faster than a stone in a pond. You are an ace!' I exclaimed.

"We didn't get to celebrate for long. The next squadron came right at us. Someone obviously had alerted them to knock us out before they bombed the carrier.

"They were in formation but spaced out and coming in fast and low. Machine gun bullets from the zeros hit all around us. The unnerved crew members naturally sought out shelter. Fortunately, no one was hit.

"After they flew over us, Bobby shook his fist at the sky and yelled, 'Damn Japs!' Now kids, remember, that's a term that we used for our enemy during the war, but you must never use it. The Japanese are now this country's friend.

"I pointed out urgently to the crew, 'That's what they're gonna do every time if we let 'em. They're trying to neutralize our gun while other squadrons do the same to other destroyers and cruisers. Except for our air support, their bombers will be free to go after our carriers. I know there's a lot of risk being so exposed out here, but we've got to hold our position and shoot them down. We can't let them neutralize us! Any questions?'

"Bobby replied with the whole crew in mind, 'Don't worry, boss. We'll stay right here and fight.'

"I smiled and said, 'I just wanted to make sure we were on the same page.'

"There was a chorus of 'aye ayes.'

"The squadron with three planes left that had just flown over us seemed to have disappeared. The Japs adjusted to the failure of their last raid and amassed about twenty zeros and bombers in formation. Naturally, they were headed directly toward our ship.

"'What next?' I murmured to Bobby.

"I focused my binoculars on the island, which was closer now. The fleet's big guns were ruthlessly bombarding the green areas on the edge of the beach. They were so loud that I was happy to put on my earmuffs. I wondered how anyone could live through such concentrated power.

"I reflected that it might be a futile shelling. I had heard just that morning that the Jap soldiers and artillery might be buried underground in an immense network of tunnels and bunkers—like honeycombs all over the island. Supposedly, their lairs were impenetrable to even modern artillery and bombers. If this were true, our troops would have to enter the bunkers and root out the Japs . . . a very dangerous prospect.

"Before I turned back to focus on the airplanes, which had veered off and probably would fly out of the sun's rays, I swept my glasses across the island and saw explosions and fires scattered all over the terrain. Impressive . . . but effective? I trusted Halsey's team, but how precise was the information furnished to them?"

Jeff asked, "By that do you mean that naval intelligence believed that the Japanese forces were in the jungle, but really they were in bunkers and tunnels on the inner part of the island?"

"That's exactly right, son. I was worried that our fleet was wasting its heavy arms on vacant areas of the island.

"All of a sudden, the big naval guns stopped firing, and our jets returned to their carriers. I had no clue where the Jap squadron flew off to. My ears took a few moments to adjust to the relative silence. I wondered again how anyone could live through such a mighty pounding, unless the rumor was true that the enemy was secreted in bunkers and tunnels further inland.

"Fires were scattered throughout the jungle at the places that had been thumped by heavy artillery shells and bombers a few minutes earlier. It was quite impressive, but I wondered again whether it was effective or just a waste of ordinance.

Jeff asked, "What did you mean by that? How could a bombardment be a waste?"

Dad responded, "Remember, the shelling was directed to the jungle just beyond the beach. If there were no Japanese troops there but instead they were inland, the shells would not be hitting anyone.

"About five minutes after the shelling stopped, I saw landing craft filled with Marines being lowered from our troop carriers. I pointed them out to Bobby: 'Look, our invasion force!'

"He looked at where I was pointing and nodded. We had to be especially careful now because our Navy fighters were back in the air and engaged in dogfights in the sky above our heads. It was less likely that our fighters would be able to help the ships, as they were involved in their own battles with the Jap zeros. If we tried to help them, we might hit our own planes, an example of 'friendly fire.'"

My sister asked, "What's that?"

"When our side injures or kills by accident one of our own soldiers," Dad explained.

"I gazed toward the troop carriers and saw a hundred or more landing craft skimming across the surface toward the nearest beach. They had to weave their way through the coral reefs and contend with the medium-sized breakers before they ran the boats onto the sand.

"I assumed that there would be savage fighting over the thin strip between the beach and the jungle, with the Japs trying to repel the Marines back into the sea. I had seen film clips of beach landings on the Normandy coast in '44 and the slaughter that ensued. Those men were gallant and never lost their focus on what they had to do. I assumed that the Marines I was watching would do the same.

"However, there were no beach battles. Not a single Jap appeared. Not a single shot was fired. This was a big relief but also mysterious. Where was the Jap army? Maybe the rumor was true—they were concealed inland, waiting for our troops to show up.

"The Japs must have learned from their defeats on the other islands that a beach defense was futile. When the Marines got a toehold on a beach, they held and expanded it until it became a tactical base. From there they could move their operations inward. That's why on all the islands before Okinawa, the Marines had met heavy resistance before they captured the beach.

"While I was looking for beach battles that didn't materialize, our fighters were outmaneuvering the Jap planes. This portended good news and bad news. The good news was that there were now fewer enemy planes attacking our ship and specifically our gun mount. However, the bad news was my prediction that we would soon be under extreme danger from the kamikazes.

"As if they were on a strict time schedule, I spotted them coming in low and fast right at us. I was sure that they were kamikazes because they were flying in a straight line, making no effort to evade the antiaircraft fire. They might have been planes left over from Japan's Chinese campaign in 1937. The pilots were hand-picked young men from a pool of eager volunteers. Their goal was obvious: take out our guns on deck by crashing entire planes into our ship.

"With the kamikaze aircraft acting as frightening bombs, our ship would sink in a few minutes. This would open a pathway for their bombers to blow up the carriers."

He paused, perhaps to give us time to understand what he was saying. I had heard of kamikazes before but never as a danger to my own father. The firelight illuminated his face, giving it an otherworldly glow. Suddenly, I realized that if he had died in the war, my brother and sister and I would never have been born. Dad was speaking again, though, so I let that thought go.

"Our ship was on the fleet's perimeter, so we were the logical target for their kamikazes. It was clear that we had to shoot them down before they accomplished their goal. The question was how.

"One member of our crew, nicknamed Squirrelly, was small in stature but had a big heart. He wore thick, black-rimmed glasses and had wild, uncombed hair. He didn't look like a Navy seaman at all.

"Squirrelly barked out, 'They're coming low right at us!'

"I'll tell you, he was a brave little squirt. He didn't allow anything to prevent him from doing his job, which was feeding shells into the big gun as fast as he could. When I ordered him to take cover, he shook his head and kept loading shells. After a few moments of silence, he said in my direction, 'I've got a job to do.'

"I think my ears are still ringing from the sound of that kamikaze crashing into our ship. Mom accuses me of not hearing half the time. The sound was like I'd imagine a full dump truck going seventy-five miles per hour would make crashing into a concrete wall. I was sure it could be heard all the way in Sydney, Australia.

"I caught a quick glimpse of the pilot before impact, and he looked crazy, like a zombie. The weird part was that he didn't appear to be in any kind of wild frenzy. He looked calm, as if his suicide mission was something he was destined to do. Killing Americans was his immediate goal, but it was more than that. It was like he was at peace with performing a sacred duty for his emperor. It was as if his completion of that duty was in a way also honoring his own death.

"When I thought about it later, I understood that his assigned role was not too different from an American GI's selfless devotion to his country. Racing up a beach on most of the fortified islands was in a way a suicide mission, too, with a soldier sacrificing his life so that his homeland would remain free.

"In the moments after the plane hit, I couldn't hear anything, but I could see, and what was visible through the flames, black smoke, and airplane parts was frightening."

Dad stopped talking again, as if he had suddenly remembered that we were all there listening.

"Kids, I don't think you'll want to hear what happened next . . . It was gruesome, and I still have nightmares about it once in a while."

Nightmares? Dad? The idea was shocking to me. I considered that he might be joking or at least exaggerating, but his expression was grim.

"C'mon, Dad," said Jeff. "We can handle it."

Kacie piped in, "Yeah, Dad, we're old enough now."

Dad looked hard at us, nodded, and continued his story.

"Squirrelly's head had been completely severed from his body. His eyes were staring up at me. Blood was squirting out of his arteries and splashing on the deck. His mouth was open, as if beseeching me to help him by reattaching his head to the rest of his body. I wanted to cradle his head or do something to try to help him, but to be honest, I was afraid of the headless torso of a person who I had just been talking with a few moments earlier."

Mom exclaimed, "Jackie, you never told me about this. I'm hearing it for the first time. It must have been dreadful. I don't know how you could endure it."

Dad shrugged as if there was no response that would make sense to her.

"I moved aside pieces of the kamikaze plane searching for the other crewmembers," he continued. "I couldn't find Bobby, who had been in the gunner's chair at the time of the crash. Either he was jettisoned overboard by the impact, or his body had simply disintegrated. I looked for Swanson's remains, too, but I couldn't find any part of him either. It would be a hell of a thing to have to tell his parents: 'Your son died in an enemy attack on our ship, but we couldn't find his body.' He had just turned nineteen and was fairly new on our ship.

"I was really concerned about Bobby. For some reason I sensed that he was still alive and kept frantically sorting through the wreckage. I came across a large part of the aircraft that was on fire.

"Riley, who was also unscathed, rushed off to get a fire extinguisher. Meanwhile, the acrid smoke off the fire was awful. It burned my eyes so badly that for a while I couldn't see. When Riley returned with the extinguisher, he knocked down the flames. We looked underneath everything but still no Bobby. I was so frustrated that I kicked off part of one of the wings.

Pointing to the piece of metal that had led to this tale, Dad said sadly, "Liz, that's the piece right there.

"The breeze was freshening, and it was turning out to be a nice day. But it was not nice for us. Riley and I found another dead body. It wasn't Bobby.

"The Jap pilot was sitting up in the partial remains of the cockpit. His flight suit was covered with blood, and he was still wearing his goggles. I could tell he was still alive, and I ordered Riley to bring a medic and stretcher bearers. But before he could rush off, the pilot's head flopped over and he was dead. I figured he must have died from his severe blood loss. It was eerie to be so close to these dead bodies."

Dad paused, and from the distant look in his eyes, he seemed to be fighting off his memories. I even thought he was going to break down. If he cried, I was sure it would jump-start all of us. Then he slowly—and it seemed reluctantly—began talking again.

"I was shaken, but I had to continue my search for our crew. As I did so, I thought about the dead guy in the cockpit. He was the enemy who had killed a number of our crewmembers. My dead crewmen had been my friends. Why should I care about this kid? Or should I? When we brought his body down, the medic and I searched through his pockets. I found a photo of him sitting with a pretty woman and two small children . . . his family. I again almost lost it. I wondered why he wanted to kill himself when he had such a beautiful family. I realized that there are things in this world I just don't understand.

"Now my search for Bobby intensified. I ripped aside a panel that was blocking part of the deck. That area had been heavily burnt by the fire, and the panel was still hot to touch. We moved the panel, and there was Bobby lying on the other side. His body looked hideous, blackened with burns. One side of his face had melted away. I got on my knees and felt his neck for a pulse. There was one, but it was weak. I put my ear to his mouth and more sensed than heard or felt his breath. Bobby was alive but going fast. He moved a hand and grasped one of mine. He opened his eyes, and I swear I saw him smile.

"'Bobby, can you hear me?' Having a conversation was impossible, because one of his ears had melted off and the other was not functioning due to the blast. My hearing was also temporarily shot.

"Despite the futility of communicating with him, I pleaded, 'Bobby, hang in there! Help is on the way.'

"I again checked his face for any sign of life. I only detected a nearly imperceptible shake of his head. What was he trying to tell me? I guessed that he preferred not to have any medical treatment. He didn't want to live in that condition. The pain must have been intolerable. He figured his body would be scarred for life. I was sure he didn't believe in plastic surgery and wouldn't want endless rounds of it. I knew Bobby well enough to be certain that he just wanted us to let him go. I thought that he considered war and death as nearly equivalent."

My sister interrupted, "What's that word mean, Dad?"

"The same or equal to," answered my brother with undisguised irritation.

"Anyway," Dad continued, "Bobby didn't care that he died. Maybe he got a glimpse of heaven or hell. Who knows? Whatever he was thinking, though, I felt I had a duty to try to save him. I couldn't just leave him to die in his own blood and melted skin. 'Medic, medic!' I shouted.

"Riley ran over to check how Bobby was doing. I yelled at him, 'Bobby's still alive! Go get a medic, pronto!' He took off across the deck at double-time. I turned to Bobby and said again: 'Hang in there, Bobby. Help is on the way. It'll be here soon.'

"The color of his eyes turned from a deathly dullness to a sparkle that was the color of the sea on a bright day. He let out a gasp, closed his eyes, and was gone.

"I was sick that I couldn't save him. I felt that wasn't asking for too much. 'I guess it was Bobby's time to go,' I said out loud to no one in particular.

"I couldn't hear the medic's steps behind me or when he shouted, 'Out of my way!' Rather than arguing with him that it was too late, I simply walked away. As Bobby would say, his timing was perfect.

"There was still the possibility that the bombers and kamikazes would return, and someone had to man the big gun, so I ordered Riley to get into the chair while I fed ammo into the chamber. I could see seamen sweeping Squirrelly's body parts off the deck and into a large, black plastic bag. I felt nauseous, and then I saw

Bobby's body being carried out on a stretcher. *Those are the ravages of war*, I reflected.

"Then, someone shouted at me to report to the bridge right now. I could barely understand him, but I was thankful that my hearing was returning.

"I figured that the captain was going to lower the boom at me. Deaths of his crewmembers never sat well with him. I didn't know him well, but guys had informed me that in a one-on-one meeting, he could be very ornery. What skipper wasn't?

"There was a mixture of soot and blood all over me. I silently ordered myself not to talk back or go on the defense. Once I reached the bridge, I announced myself: 'Jack Bailey, crew chief, reporting for duty, SIR.'

"The Captain said, 'We still have a battle to fight even though our ship is heavily damaged. It's still afloat, and, therefore, it can still fight.'

"'YES, SIR.'

"'I'll get right to the point. I'll be recommending that you and your entire crew be awarded the Navy Cross for extraordinary bravery under severe battle conditions.'

"I tried not to show any emotions even though they were mixed between a heavy sadness at the death of some of my crew and appreciation of the captain's recommendation.

"The captain continued, "Because of the courage shown by you and your men, our vessel was rescued from certain destruction and sinking. Hundreds of lives were saved.'

"'Thank you, sir.'

"'No, thank you, Bailey. Dismissed.'

"I saluted crisply and turned to leave.

"Over my shoulder he stated, 'Jack, keep up the good work.'

"I detoured to my bunk below. My mood was in mourning for my fallen crewmates. I would have given up all the promised accolades for the lives of Bobby, Swanson, and Squirrelly.

"Anyway, that's the story of how I got that so-called piece of junk."

He glanced at Mom, and she looked more sympathetic to him.

I inspected the metal like it was an idol from a lost civilization before asking, "What exactly is it?"

"Oh, I thought I explained." He lowered his voice as if he were revealing an intimate secret. "I'm holding a piece of the plane that smashed into our gun mount—the one that killed Bobby, Swanson, and Squirrelly."

I was silent, reverent in my contemplation of the events that occurred so many years before.

My brother, always the practical one, asked, "Dad, that's quite a story, but whatever happened to your Navy Cross? You've never shown it to us."

Dad peered at Jeff like he had posed a mystery to solve.

Finally, Dad explained, "After the war, I was shipped home to New Jersey. I drove to Bobby's house and spent some time with his mother. Somehow the paperwork for Bobby's medal never went through. There are lots of bureaucratic mix-ups like that in wartime. So, I dedicated my Navy Cross to Bobby and presented it to her. He was the real hero that day."

For the first time during Dad's remembrance of the battle for Okinawa, I detected moisture in his blue eyes.

A Fresh Start

I woke up one day in 1994 and realized that I was living a life I hated. After decades of going with the flow and taking things as they came, I was a thirty-one-year-old woman, still single, working a dead-end job, and not quite getting by. My name is Dana Collins, and this is the story of how I escaped and began to create a new me.

I couldn't fathom how fast I had become so old. I could still remember myself—a spoiled, only child and a relentless teenager—running around the small agricultural town of Scott's Valley with fuzzy dreams of someday attending college. I imagined the wonder of obtaining a higher degree, but I had no clue as to what subjects I'd need to study or how long it would all take. My true goal was to become rich after college by writing popular novels. Fat chance!

I applied to many four-year colleges, but I received so many rejection letters that I could have papered our living room walls with them. Maybe it was my C- high school grade point average or my 850 total SAT scores. Joining academia seemed like an impossible dream.

In the end, I attended Valley Community College directly over the mountains in San Jose. I blame my unspectacular first year at Valley CC solely on my own laziness. Truthfully, my brief stab at higher education was doomed in its infancy because I lacked the brainpower and ability to concentrate. Both my parents died that year of lung cancer, leaving me little in the way of money or assets to begin life in the "real world."

After washing out of community college, I moved a bit north to Santa Clara, in the heart of what everyone called "Silicon Valley." I chose this location to begin my career because it seemed like everything was more exciting there. I had no clue what "silicon" meant, but I imagined I had a chance for a career and riches in this fast-paced, growing area.

When I shopped for an apartment, I discovered the high rents and wondered if I should have stayed in Scott's Valley growing apples like my parents had—barely eking out a living on a small, rented farm—or just left California altogether. But I finally secured a one-bedroom apartment in a low-rent district.

Next came my job search. I went through a series of unremarkable temp jobs, but by the time I was twenty-five, I had landed a permanent position at DelRay Computer, the largest computer company in Silicon Valley. Not as a computer engineer—I wasn't qualified for that job. They had an opening for an unskilled worker on one of the assembly lines. At least DelRay Computer was paying me a fair hourly wage plus benefits. I figured it was a perfect stepping stone to my rewarding and lucrative career in a still-unknown field.

At DelRay, I was assigned to insert tiny parts into slightly larger parts. It wasn't difficult, even for me, but the work was tedious, and I was bored to tears. Excuse the pun, but my job was as exciting as watching apples grow, which is the kind of boredom I had left Scott's Valley to avoid. Standing up for eight hours a day wasn't easy on my back or my feet, but I was young, and I muddled through.

I even made a few friends who did much the same work as me. At noon on weekdays, we got together at DelRay's giant cafeteria for lunch. The free food was delicious and plentiful, and so was the gossip.

A couple of times a week, the same friends and I congregated at a local watering hole called "The Crab Apple." We complained incessantly about our jobs and laughed up a storm.

Some of my coworkers wanted to move on to secretary or some other desk job.

Sheila asked me after a few drinks one night: "Do you plan to stay on the assembly line or are you going to apply to move up in the company?"

"Gee, Sheila, I haven't thought about it much," I told her honestly. "I'm not happy where I am, but I'm too nervous to apply for a position that I don't have the skills for. What about you?"

"I've already applied for a secretary position. I have good office skills and I get along well with people. I might as well put them to work. Don't you think, Dana?"

Alice was the snottiest member of our group. Before I had a chance to respond to Sheila, she cut in. "Gosh, Dana," she said sarcastically, "I cannot believe you're happy with the mindless job we do. It is soo . . . boring!"

I felt like I was being attacked. My usual reflex was to go on the defensive, but this time I decided to counterattack. I said sharply: "As I said, I've got no secretarial skills, but I used to cocktail waitress where I came from, so I plan to put in an application for that job."

I looked directly at Alice and asserted, "I, too, have people skills."

Andrea was listening to our conversation. She cut in abruptly. "What little ol' town did you come from, Dana?"

I ignored the question, not because I was ashamed of Scott's Valley but because I just didn't want to get into that subject.

Apparently, Alice had been mulling over what I said about applying to be a cocktail waitress. "Dana, you're barking up the wrong tree," she said snidely. "Those jobs are immediately snapped up by experienced waitresses who they don't have to train. They don't offer them to a girl whose only experience is working in some Podunk bar in East Wazoo, Arizona."

The girls all laughed at that one.

I knew my face was red and that it'd be best to beat a hasty retreat, so I said cavalierly: "Gotta go. Date with Charlie. Tata, girls."

Despite the critical abuse from my friends, this was a relatively happy period of my life. In addition to socializing with my work friends, I had acquired a boyfriend . . . sort of. His name was Charlie Blackwell, and he, too, worked for DelRay.

I met Charlie in the cafeteria at work. He was in line right behind me one day, and I caught him checking me out, but neither of us said anything. After we got our trays, he tapped me on the shoulder and boldly laid some pick-up lines on me, which quickly made me wary of him. Then he sat down at my table without even asking me.

Trying to be polite without encouraging him, I asked him: "What's your job?"

"Computer programmer," he said, which I knew was way above my pay grade. He asked me out anyway, and that started our relationship.

Tension soon developed between Charlie and me. He constantly boasted that his job was superior to mine, and it didn't take me long to figure out that Charlie's personality was condescending in other aspects of life too. His erratic streak also drove me crazy. I wondered more than once whether he had a mental disorder, but I never mentioned my concern to him for fear that he'd blow up at me.

We were an on/off couple and sometime lovers for six years without any progress in our relationship. During that period, even though I've been called good-looking, I didn't hook up with any other guys. I was faithful to that crumbum.

It's not that I had any moral qualms about cheating, and I certainly didn't have any notions of romantic love with Charlie. He bullied me, made me pay for most of our dates, and generally treated me like dogshit. But I remained available to him, mainly due to my laziness.

Charlie, on the other hand, ticked me off because he often dipped into the large pool of single—and sometimes married—women at DelRay. He did this while we were supposedly a couple. It was frustrating as hell, but eventually I somewhat got used to it.

When Charlie grew tired of his flings, he always came back to me whether I wanted him back or not. He facetiously referred to me as his "old standby" or "squeeze." Despite my laziness, I don't know why I stayed with him so long.

One afternoon Charlie and I were trying to figure out what to do. I said, "Let's go to Funby's Arcade. We've never been there before."

Charlie responded in his usual cynical way. "Funby's. That place is for kids."

"That's exactly why I want to go there," I pressed. "Loosen up some. Get out of our rut. I'm going whether you're going or not."

"Well, I'm not going. It's a complete waste of time." He scanned the newspaper for the Arts and Entertainment section, poked a page and exclaimed, "Hey Dana, there's a good movie playing at the Bijou at two o'clock."

I asked unenthusiastically: "Oh yeah. What's playing?"

"*Defense of a Kingdom*. I've wanted to see it for a long time. What do you say?"

"Sounds boring."

"Don't be such a spoilsport, Dana-O."

"Don't call me that!"

"Ooh, touchy! I'll tell you what. Let's compromise. We'll go to Funby's if you'll agree that we go to the movie afterward."

"Deal."

The most fun I had with Charlie was the afternoon we spent at Funby's. Its centerpiece was a giant chess board with human-sized pieces. Another couple was using the attraction when we arrived. I watched them with envy because they appeared to be having so much fun. They helped each other move the heavy pieces, and after each move, they flagrantly hugged and kissed. They laughed frequently, something I had not done for a long time.

We watched this show for a while, but Charlie was impatient. He had a hyper personality, so he got bored quickly.

"Let's go, Dana."

"No, I want to watch." I was happy to wait until the other couple finished and thought maybe Charlie and I could play the game next.

"We're going! C'mon."

We left to see the movie across town.

The film turned out to be ponderous and dull, a depiction of ancient armies fighting with swords and spears. Charlie loved it, but I wanted to leave halfway through. Guess what? We stayed until the bitter end. Charlie bribed me with some buttered popcorn, which I had to pay for anyway.

Throughout my time working at DelRay, I had lived by myself in a cramped one-bedroom apartment that I could barely afford and never liked much. I considered a roommate but hesitated. I thought I'd have to give up my bedroom to a stranger and sleep on the sofa. Either that or snuggle in the bed with her, and I wasn't into that type of hanky-panky.

I kept hoping that Charlie would ask me to move into his larger apartment. I should have known by then that this idle thinking was nothing more than a false hope and a waste of time. He seemed to be content to share his place with two long-haired, dedicated pot-smokers. They were unsuccessful musicians who constantly played their guitars in the living room.

After six years on the job, I hardly ever got together with any of my old friends. They were all married, and some had children. They had their separate lives, and I was rarely invited into them.

One Friday evening after a couple of drinks, I decided to call Alice at her home. Her four year-old picked up the phone: "Who can I say is talkin'?"

"This is Dana from work. Can I talk with your mammie?"

". . . Mammie, it's Ana from 'erk."

Alice was hovering nearby because she immediately came on.

". . . Danaaaa." She stretched out my name like I was a long-lost relative. "So nice of you to call. But isn't this something we could handle at work? I've got two screaming kids here, and Larry's at his regular Friday night poker game."

That answered my question. "No problem. I just called to see if we could get the girls together—you know, have a few drinks and yuk it up like the old days. But it sounds like you're too busy tonight."

"Oh, for sure. Sorry. Maybe some other night," she said doubtfully. "But it's good to hear from you outside of work. Take care, Dana." Click.

The only relative I had in the Bay Area was my Great-Aunt Edna, who never married. Before she retired, Edna also worked in a factory and lived in a small, shabby downtown apartment. Her senior complex was on a congested, noisy street in a risky neighborhood. She had few friends, no hobbies, and seemingly no interest in anything.

I visited Aunt Edna once a month. Each month we sat in the same chairs and snacked on the same things—tea and biscuits—and talked about the same subjects. But I still looked forward to these visits because she was at least company for me.

She would ask, "How do you like your new job?" (She always asked this, even when I had been working at DelRay for years.)

"I love it!' (I hated it.)

"What do you do at Hew . . . I always forget that name."

"Hewlett-Packard. No, I work at DelRay Computer. I have a very important job. It's essential for the company."

"Any boyfriends?"

"Oh yes. A wonderful man named Charles."

"Do you think he'll ask you to get married?"

"I'm sure he will. He's very loyal to me." (I lied.) "We'll let you know. Don't worry about that."

As she got older, the first thing she always said when she opened the door was: "I hope you're not here to borrow money."

"No Auntie. It's Dana . . . you know, your niece. We get together every month."

"Oh."

She died the year I turned thirty.

When Edna died, I sank into depression. I envisioned the same fate for myself: working to the bone until age sixty-five and living out my days on Social Security in a lonely apartment in a questionable area of Oakland with no friends and nothing to do. I knew it was morbid to view my future through a prism named Edna Smith and to foresee my forlorn death in such a lonely place, but I seemed to be headed in that direction.

After fighting off those gloomy thoughts, I focused on my present life, and I perceived that I had already fallen into the same regrettable patterns and austere lifestyle that trapped Edna for her retirement years.

I thought, *My job is barely enabling me to stay afloat until I retire or die. I'm not getting ahead. I'm actually slowly falling behind in that my wages are not keeping up with the rate of inflation in the Bay Area.*

I had to consider getting a second job, maybe at a fast-food joint. A real boyfriend would have helped me financially, but Charlie was unusually stingy, and I sensed there weren't any new boyfriends for me on the horizon.

One day, I heard a rumor in the community laundry room that the landlord planned to raise our rents substantially. That was it. I knew it was time to find a roommate to share the cost of rent and utilities. Rita soon moved in, and I regretted my decision right away. She took the bedroom; I got the sofa. I was quiet; Rita was into alcohol, drugs, and raucous men.

At night, and whenever I had a day off, I sat around my apartment watching the tube or trying to read a magazine. It was a numbing existence.

I did use some of my free time to contemplate all aspects of my life, and I arrived at some simple conclusions: *I hate my job because it is so boring, monotonous, and fails to present any challenges. There are no prospects for future advancement. It is the ultimate dead-end.*

I am not into the giant corporate rah-rah mentality, its college campus cheerleader atmosphere, and its pathetic efforts to create togetherness among its employees. It seems that those juvenile efforts have the opposite effect, at least for me.

The company blew everyone apart. My old girlfriends at the company are amenable to their jobs and the company's hypocrisy. They refuse to acknowledge that DelRay's attempts to bond everyone are superficial. As Alice demonstrated in that brief telephone conversation, I am an awkward burden to my former friends. They have been able to hook chumps to marry them and lately some are pregnant. Big deal!

Then there is my sometimes boyfriend, who always takes me for granted, belittles me, and makes me pay for everything. He is never satisfied with me because I work at a low-level job. He regularly two-times and three-times me, and I put up with it because I am such a lonely wimp.

In truth, I really hated Charlie. I was sick of him and sick of myself for staying in such a pathetic relationship. I knew I needed to end it and stay away from him. He was toxic to me.

Six years after I started working for DelRay, the corporation that owned my apartment building notified me that it was raising my rent again by 25 percent. That was the final straw in my decision to find an escape from my private hell.

That night, I walked to my local park, which was empty, and screamed repeatedly as I slowly rotated 360 degrees: "I'm fed up and I'm not gonna take it anymore!" I had seen someone do this in an old movie, so I figured I'd try it. I kept saying those words until I believed what I was saying.

That was when I made a vital decision. The next morning, I quit my job without advance notice and was out of the building before lunchtime.

I rented a small storage unit and transferred my essential stuff into it, leaving the rest for my party-girl roommate, who was so high on drugs most of the time that it was unlikely she'd even notice I was gone. I delivered my key to the resident manager and informed her that I had turned my apartment over to my roommate. She looked like she wanted to object—the lease was in my name—but I turned and walked away without a second thought or regret.

I didn't tell anyone about my plans or destination. I didn't want to take any baggage along with me. Besides, who would I have told?

Then I got in my car and drove to the nearest REI. With the help of a knowledgeable salesman, I used what would have been my next month's rent money to purchase everything he suggested I'd need, including a lightweight tent and sleeping bag, shorts, a velour sweatshirt for cold nights, a small propane burner, a battery-charged lantern, a Swiss army knife, and an assortment of packaged food that he said would last six months.

After loading up my ancient Toyota, I gunned the engine and headed east for the hills, taking the fastest route to the Sierra Nevada Mountains.

I turned onto the road that led to the main entrance to Yosemite National Park and spent forty-five minutes meditating at the railing and taking in the view of the majesty of this phenomenal place.

The lush, green valley with the silver ribbon of the Merced River bisecting it was a sharp contrast to the soaring walls of gray granite in the background. They surrounded the valley and were inspirational. They were also so rugged that they produced fear that I would soon have to overcome.

The granite massif they call Half Dome appeared to display a giant face, like the man in the moon. He was staring at me, challenging me: "Go ahead; you're only a girl . . . and by yourself . . . you have no clue what you're in for."

The tourist pamphlet I picked up at the park entrance stated that the immense walls of rock were carved by glaciers during one of the ice ages. Ice slicing through rock seemed illogical, but I reflected, "Who am I to question a park ranger's guidebook?"

I followed a winding tree-lined road to the top of the park, where a confluence of two fast-running streams created an exciting wilderness environment. There, I spied a small dirt parking lot with only five cars. I assumed this lot was for backpackers, so I parked and unloaded my gear.

I asked myself, *Where is everyone?* Then I answered my own question: *It doesn't matter. This is my dream adventure, and I'm gonna do it on my own.*

On a lark, when I was sure no one could hear me, I yelled to my car: "See you when I get hungry! Onward to the John Muir Trail or bust!"

My backpack was heavy and seemed to crush me like a pile driver right into the ground. Despite the unfamiliar weight, I picked up my pace and pranced along the access trail. I reflected, *My pack is heavy, but my spirit is light.*

My trail soon intersected with the main trail. I was unsure which way to go—south or north. Trusting my intuition and my compass, I took the main trail to the left. I was southward bound and, according to my map, in the direction of mighty Mt. Whitney, the highest mountain in the lower forty-eight.

It was the first time I had used a compass, but I figured it out easily. "Good choice." I soon learned that talking to oneself is a staple of solo backpacking.

"Ah, company." A chipmunk greeted me from a nearby branch with an assortment of critter chatter.

I replied, "Hey lil' fella, how ya doin'?"

I kicked up some dust, did a dance, and felt happier than when I was a little girl playing outdoors with my friends—which was the happiest memory I could muster from my life to date.

For the first thirty-one years of my life, I could only guess what freedom felt like, but somehow I now knew. I was enthralled among all this splendor.

I kept my head up and my eyes searching, curious what was waiting for me in the unknown. "Hello, Dana," I said in a loud, clear voice. "Happy to finally meet the new you."